Please Wait For Me

Emma Pathy

Copyright © 2026 by Meraki Creations LLC

All rights reserved.

No part of this book may be reproduced in any form or by any electronic or mechanical means, including information storage and retrieval systems, without written permission from the author, except for the use of brief quotations in a book review.

Characters and events portrayed in this book are fictitious or are used fictitiously. Any similarity to real persons, living or dead, is purely coincidental and not intended by the author.

All brand names and product names used intros book are trademarks, registered trademarks, or trade names of their respective holders. Author is not associated with any product or vendor in this book.

Published by Meraki Creations LLC

Cover Design by Love Lee Creative

Editing by Deliciously Dark Editing

 Formatted with Vellum

Author's Note

Dear Reader,

This book is the third book in the Please Me series. If you have not already read Book 1 (Please Don't) and Book 2 (Please Stay), I would encourage you to stop and read those first so you have all the context for Book 3 (Please Wait).

This book takes place after the Epilogue of Book 2 (Please Stay) where the friend group is all at Evie's family cabin for the 4th of July. It is a few months later and the friend group is headed back to their home town for a wedding. During this book, you will learn about Evie and Liam's origin story.

The book is different from the previous two book in the fact that it is written in dual timelines. The first timeline is the present day, at the wedding. And the additional time line is flashback to high school and college when Evie and Liam's love story took place.

This book contains explicit sexual descriptions and recreational drug use. Please proceed with that in mind.

*Dedicated to
My husband, who fought for what
he wanted and never gave up,
no matter how many times
I broke his heart.
I love you.*

Playlist

Chapter One

EVIE

Even after all these years, it never gets any easier. I moved away from here seven years ago, and every trip back to my hometown since then feels the same. I get this pit in my stomach as I see the sign two exits from town, announcing our impending arrival. My anxiety spikes, and my mind starts racing with the list of public places I don't allow myself to go to, out of fear of running into someone I don't want to see.

When Liam and I come back to spend holidays with our families, we typically go straight to our parents' houses and then straight home. In college, I was actually able to convince my parents to do several holiday vacations so I could avoid coming here altogether. Occasionally, we venture into town to get groceries or to grab a drink at a local bar with Lou and B Blake. When we do, we always run into people we know. That's what happens in small towns like St. Francis. There's no escaping your past when you're here.

Only once has running into someone unexpectedly

turned out to be a positive experience. That was the time when we ran into Bear at the ice cream shop last summer. It led to him moving in with us, which eventually led to him dating Liam's younger sister, Iris. That is a relationship that has greatly improved all of our lives. I couldn't have hand-picked anyone better for my sister-in-law or my husband's best friend. It was a win, win, win, win.

I look through my review mirror and smile. Now that's another relationship that I support with my whole heart. Sam and Lou are snuggled up in the back seat. Lou is asleep on Sam's shoulder, and his hand rests gently on her leg. Lou and I weren't close friends until our senior year of high school, but I now consider her to be a good friend of mine. About a year ago, she started dating Sam. He's been an exceptional addition to the group, and we've gotten to know him quite well over the last year of their relationship.

This is the first time Sam is coming back to our hometown for a wedding. Sam's generally a quiet guy, but I can tell he's excited to get a better picture of what life in our small town is like. Of course, we've told him some stories, and he's been here for a couple of holidays, but Sam grew up in the suburbs, so small-town life is a foreign concept to him. He has quite the entertaining night ahead of him, with our whole friend group coming back for this wedding. In the other car, Bear is driving Iris, B, and Sofia, B's new roommate.

When Iris went back to school, halfway through the spring semester to finish out her final months of college, B was left without a roommate since Lou had moved in with Sam after Christmas. I can't exactly remember how they know each other, but Fia moved in shortly after Iris moved out. From what I know about her, she seems cool. Liam is pretty sure she and B have been hooking up, and though I'm dying for the tea, it's none of my business. I'm pretty sure Fia grew up in the heart of the city, so I'm interested to see what she thinks of all this as well.

Despite my anxiety, this should be a pretty fun wedding. The whole gang was invited, so in the worst-case scenario, we all just hang out with each other and avoid the judgment of the other small-minded guests. To them, we're all just a bunch of wildlings who choose to live in the city, surrounding ourselves with drugs and sin. And they're right, we absolutely do that. We just don't think we're going to burn in hell forever for doing it, and that's where the disconnect is.

All of us, except Sam and Fia, went to the same private high school. It's called St. Francis, after the name of our tiny town. I graduated with Lou and Liam; Bear was a year older, B was a year younger, and Iris was three years younger than us. Despite the few years that separate us, we all had a relatively similar small-town experience. We grew up surrounded by adults who used fear-mongering in an attempt to get us to behave and grow up to be just like them. Now, I'm not saying they're all bad. There are several devout Christians whom I love dearly and think the world of, and my religious upbringing taught me a lot of things. I just didn't take the information they gave me and come to the same conclusions as most of my peers did.

That's why coming back is so hard for me. I can't help but notice the looks of judgment from people who think they know what my lifestyle is like. They have this image in their mind of how someone like me thinks and acts on a daily basis, but most of the time, their assumptions are grossly wrong. I'm sick of trying to convince people who don't understand me that I'm completely content with my life and that I'm not lost or going through a phase.

After leaving our small town behind, Liam and I continue to be just as kind and generous to all as we were before. We still welcome people into our home with love and hospitality. We just don't follow the same set of religious ideologies we used to. And in addition, we treat *all* people with the respect a human being deserves, regardless of whether their beliefs, sexual orientation, pronouns, or political views match ours.

"You okay, babe?" Liam places his hand on my thigh. It's warm and comforting.

He knows that driving into town always gets me in my head, swirling around with my thoughts. "Yeah, I'm good." I look over at him and melt at the sweet expression on his face. He's so cute when he worries. Those green eyes always see right into me. I run my hand through his auburn hair, down to his sun-kissed cheek that's sprinkled with light freckles from the summer sun.

"I know you're nervous about him being there." He gives my thigh a little squeeze.

That's the other thing. Part of my anxiety about being back here has to do with my fear of running into one person in particular. My ex, Alex. The high school classmates who are getting married tonight are also friends with my ex, so I'm sure he'll be there. We didn't end things on good terms, so I dread events where we might run into each other. Luckily, Liam is an amazing support for me and always manages to calm my nerves and remind me of what is, and isn't, important in my life.

I don't need to say anything in response to Liam. We both know he speaks the truth. I give him a little smile in hopes to reassure him that I'm going to be okay, because deep down I know I will be.

I pull off the highway and make my way into town,

toward my parents' house. We decided that all eight of us would stay at my childhood home together instead of everyone staying at their own homes. That way, we can all get ready and go to the wedding together. Plus, my parents have a big enough house that will easily fit all of us.

I pull into the driveway, and Bear's SUV pulls in next to us shortly after.

I walk through the front door that was left unlocked for us and set the dogs down. Bert and Ernie love it here because my parents spoil them like they're their grandchildren. Speaking of which, here comes my mother, greeting the dogs before she greets any of the humans standing in her entryway.

"Hi, babies!" Ernie hops on his back paws until she picks him up.

"Hey, Mom." I greet her with a hug, squishing Ernie between us.

"I have all your rooms set up. I'm so excited you're all here!"

"Where's Dad?"

"He's out back making sure the hot tub is all ready to go."

I told them not to fuss over us, that we'd just be staying the night here and heading back tomorrow morning. But I knew my mother wouldn't be able to help herself. She's the ultimate host, thriving off the gratitude of others.

I show everyone to their rooms, and we all take a moment to unpack our things and change. The wedding ceremony starts in three hours, plenty of time to get ready and stress. Plenty of time for me to get in my own head and practice my responses to the questions I know we're going to get asked. I can hear them now...

"How can you stand all that traffic? I would go insane if

I had to deal with that every day." That's what podcasts and audiobooks are for. You get used to it.

"Wow, you two are still together?" Yep. Been married for three years.

"How do you handle all the crime there? Aren't you scared?" It's not as bad as the news likes to make it seem.

And now that I'm pregnant, the questions are going to multiply. They just don't get it. To be fair, neither did I before I moved away from St. Francis. I always felt like I needed to get out, but it wasn't until I actually experienced more of the world that I realized just how much I needed it.

Chapter Two

LIAM

We're just about finished getting ready for the wedding when I glance over at Evie. She looks like a snack in her new dress. The way it hugs her curves and her baby bump makes it difficult to tear my eyes away. As she tries to zip up her makeup bag for the third time, the seam rips. She throws the bag down on the bed and lets out a little growl as brushes and tubes of god knows what go rolling off the mattress and onto the floor.

I can tell she's stressed, regardless of the lies she tells me. She's trying to act like running into her ex isn't going to bother her, but I know it will. Evie and I have always had very open communication about her feelings toward her ex, so I know it took her a long time to get over him. It even lasted a few months after we officially started dating. It doesn't make me jealous at all. I understand that she loves me and that I'm the one for her. We both know that. But that doesn't mean she's not allowed to still be affected by her past. I think it's completely normal for the memory of your first real love to linger.

I walk up behind her and slip my arms around her waist. I brush her long, dark hair off her shoulder and kiss her tanned skin. My hands are pressed against her baby bump as I start to sway back and forth. She's about six months along now, so she had to buy a new dress for the occasion. The satin material is cool and soft under my touch as I run my hand over her stomach and further down, between her legs.

"Liam..."

I'm sure she was about to complain about us being late, but my other hand on her swollen breast took the words right out of her mouth. I kiss my wife's neck, up her jaw, to her soft cheeks.

I whisper in her ear, "Lie down on the bed."

"We're going to be—"

"This won't take long, trust me."

She cranes her neck so she can look back at me with questioning eyes.

"Lay. Down." My voice is a little more forceful this time, the way she likes it.

A smirk tugs at the corner of her mouth, and she does as she's told. She turns to face me before sitting down and stretching out on the bed.

I get down on one knee. My dress pants are tight around my thighs in this position, but I don't care. I take her ankles that are hanging off the edge of the bed and kiss them. Later tonight, I'm sure they'll be swollen from the heels she is dead set on wearing, so I know one of my tasks before bed will be to rub them for her. And I'll gladly do that for my beautiful Evie, my wife, my goddess. The woman growing our baby like a goddamn saint. I never thought Evie being pregnant would be such a turn on, but fuck me. Something about knowing I did that to her, that we chose to take that next step in our marriage, just does something to me.

I kiss my way up one of her thighs, and she bends her knees to rest her feet on the bed. I use both hands to spread her legs wider apart, giving me more room to sink in between them. I tug her closer to the edge, closer to my face. I grab the straps of her thong and pull them over her thick hips and down her legs. Before diving in, I look up to make sure that I'm getting my intended response. I see Evie lying back, arms above her head, eyes closed.

"Good girl. Now just relax." All I want is for her to be as stress-free as possible going into tonight. I know that she'll have a good time if she allows herself to let loose. Usually, a glass or two of chardonnay will do that, but with Baby McAllister cooking in there, my alternative fix is to make her come.

I bunch up her dress above her bump, trying not to wrinkle it too much. I lick up her center and pause at the top, focusing on that little bundle of nerves. Evie moans, and I feel her hands start to weave into my hair, tugging gently. After five-plus years together, I know exactly what she likes and how to make her come hard. Unfortunately, we didn't bring any of her favorite toys with us, so we're going manual this time.

I slip two fingers into her slick slit and curl my fingers up, applying pressure on her front wall. I move my tongue across her folds until her legs start to shake. I take my other hand and use my fingers to apply pressure on either side of her clit, moving them in small circles. She's close, I can feel it. Her arousal is leaking down my hand and all over the sheets.

I'll wash them later, so my poor mother-in-law doesn't have to.

I suck her clit between my lips and move my tongue across it. Evie screams out, but muffles her own cries with her pillow. I feel her clenching around my fingers, legs squeezing on either side of my head. There's nothing more satisfying than being pinned to the woman I love as she comes all over me.

She slowly releases me, and I slide my fingers out of her. I rub them across her inner thighs, soothing her as she comes down from her orgasm. I can feel my hard cock in my pants, dying to be let out, to have a taste of what my hands and mouth just experienced. But we seriously don't have time for that, so it'll have to wait.

I stand up and reach a hand out to her, helping her sit up. Before standing, she looks up at me as she sits on the edge of the bed. "Thank you. I needed that."

I lean down and kiss her, careful not to smudge her makeup. "I know. I love you."

"I love you, too."

After making ourselves presentable again, we head downstairs to where everyone is waiting for us.

"Sorry, guys, I couldn't find my shoes." It's a lame excuse, but it's the only one I could think of on the spot.

B sees right through it. "You seriously think any of us is going to believe that?"

Bear looks at us with a knowing smirk on his face. "Yeah, a few of us have lived with you guys, remember? We know you can't go 24 hours without—"

"Alright! Who's ready to go? Next person to give us shit is getting left behind." Evie jingles the keys in the air as she walks to the front door.

Everyone eagerly follows behind, and Bear digs his keys out of his pocket, handing them to me. Evie is one of our sober drivers tonight, for obvious reasons. I offered to be the other one in solidarity with my wife. Bear originally offered, but we all said no to that. Poor Bear has to deal with his ex-wife, Olivia, prancing around all night. The worst part is that she's newly single, so who knows what kind of shit she's going to pull. At the last wedding we went to, we found Olivia grinding up on a sleaze bag. That's when she was still dating the guy she cheated on Bear with. So all bets are off tonight.

———

EVIE

We walk into the hotel ballroom and look around for an empty table that will fit all eight of us. It appears as though the big round tables have exactly eight chairs around them, so we migrate over to one of those. We came here right from the ceremony to ensure we were all seated together.

"Wait, there's no assigned seating?"

B turns to Fia and explains, "Nope, it's the wild Midwest out here. Every man for themself."

"That seems more complicated than just making a seating chart."

I chime in, "It is." At the look on Fia's face, I feel the need to explain. "Every wedding in this town is pretty much exactly the same. The ceremonies are always at the same church. The receptions are always in this hotel ballroom or the other, more budget-friendly venue across town. God, don't even get me started on that place. They all use the same caterer, the same florist, etc. If you've been to one wedding here, you've been to them all."

"Did you and Liam get married here?"

"No," Liam and I say in unison. I look over to Bear, who has his arm around Iris's waist. "Bear didn't either. But pretty much everyone else we went to high school with has had a similar wedding to this one."

"And that doesn't bother them...?"

I shrug. "It's definitely easier to just get married in your hometown, where all your family and friends are, rather than making people travel. But it was important to Liam and me that the people at our wedding were the people who truly wanted to be there. You'll see tonight that there will be plenty of wedding crashers who show up to the dance uninvited. No one really cares, though; it's just part of the culture here. Everyone's done it."

"Shit. It really is the wild west out here."

"Wild *Midwest*," B corrects her.

We all claim our seats around the table with our jackets and purses before heading over to the bar. There's already a line, but luckily, no one that I'm actively trying to avoid is standing in it. I scan the room for the tenth time since being here. Despite Liam's best efforts to calm my nerves earlier, I still have a pit in my stomach. And no, I'm not talking about the little papaya I'm growing in there.

Liam orders me a ginger ale and a Coke for himself. This whole pregnancy, Liam has been really good about not making me feel left out. He's cut back on his social drinking and edible consumption, typically staying sober with me. Actually, our whole friend group has been pretty great about it. Being the first of our friends to have a baby made me nervous. I was worried I was going to feel isolated and grow distant from them. But everyone has been so supportive and is incredibly excited to meet Baby McAllister.

Most of our high school classmates who will be here tonight already have one or two children, so I'm sure I'm going to get plenty of unsolicited parenting advice. But I'm actually excited to have something in common with them again, since we've led such different lives after graduating high school. Though if one more person asks me when we're moving back here (because, of course, we wouldn't want to raise children in the city), I'm going to lose my goddamn mind.

Chapter Three

LIAM

We get all but ten minutes of peace at our table before I spot him. Luckily, Evie hasn't noticed yet. She's deep in a conversation with an old classmate of ours about what life is like in the city and answering questions about why we're not moving back to St. Francis once the baby is born.

Our classmate spots him shortly after I do and takes their leave, promising to come chat with us after dinner. I switch my attention from him to my wife, so I don't notice that he's headed straight toward me until I feel a hand on my shoulder.

"Hey," he pauses as if he forgot my name for a second, "Liam." His voice is loud, which usually comes with confidence, but I can hear a slight wobble in his voice. He's nervous.

I turn to see Evie's ex standing behind me with a woman, who I'm assuming is his girlfriend, next to him. As I turn, I shrug his hand off my shoulder. "Hey, Alex." I keep my tone pleasant, but it's definitely void of any enthusiasm.

Why the hell is he approaching me of all people? When

I was looking around earlier, I didn't notice anyone from his inner circle here, but there has to be someone else here that he's more comfortable approaching than me. We're not friends. I mean, we had classes together in high school and hung out occasionally at parties, but Alex always had his core group of friends, and I wasn't in it.

I transferred to St. Francis my freshman year, after my mom remarried. I came after everyone had already established their friend groups. Most of our class had gone to school together since elementary school, which didn't leave much room for me to insert myself.

Our class was divided into two major groups. As cliché as it sounds, it was essentially the athletes and the non-athletes. Of course, there were some athletes in the non-athlete group and some non-athletes who were friends with the athletes. But for the most part, that's how things were separated. Then, within those two groups, people broke off into even smaller cliques. I was, unfortunately, not part of any group. I was friends with people on both sides, but not close enough with anyone to be considered a part of either group.

A quick assessment in my head leads me to believe that no one from his close friend group is here, so as strange as it may seem, I think I *am* his best chance at not looking like a loser to his new girlfriend. Fine, I'll play along.

Clearly not fazed by my cold greeting, he asks, "Can we pull up a couple of chairs?"

I look around at our already full table and then over to my wife. Knowing Evie and the look on her face, this pains her, but she would rather be the bigger person than make anyone feel left out. Even if that someone shattered her heart into a million pieces and never looked back.

"Yeah, sure," Evie says before I get the chance to.

Without even acknowledging Evie's presence, Alex and his girlfriend steal two chairs from a nearby table that is only half filled by a group of older people. Alex wedges their chairs between Iris and me, so I scoot mine closer to Evie.

I take a moment to check in with her. "Are you okay with this? I can ask them to leave at any time."

"No, I'm fine. That poor girl looks nervous. It would be rude to kick them out, so I can deal with him for her sake."

I look over at Alex's girl, who now sits between Alex and me. She does look pretty anxious. I would too if my boyfriend sat us at a table of strangers and didn't even bother to introduce me. Alex placed her between him and me, seating himself next to Iris. Safe choice, given that Iris wouldn't hurt a fly. Bear, on the other hand, looks like he wants to reach over Iris and punch Alex in the face. He knows all too well how much Alex affected the start of my relationship with Evie and the amount of pain that situation caused me. He was my best friend even then.

I turn and introduce myself to the stranger sitting next to me. "Hi, I'm Liam, and this is my wife Evie."

She looks relieved that someone is finally breaking the awkward silence. "Hi, I'm Hallie." She reaches for my hand and shakes it. "Did you guys go to high school with Alex?"

Oh shit. That asshole didn't brief her at all. She likely doesn't know that everyone at this table hates her boyfriend's guts.

While my shock sets in, Evie leans across me to shake Hallie's hand. "Yeah, we did. And so did Lou, B, Bear, and Iris." She goes around the table and points everyone out, introducing them. "And this is Sam, Lou's boyfriend, and Sofia, B's roommate."

Everyone waves at Hallie as they're introduced. B

chimes in from across the table, "There will be a pop quiz later."

"Ignore her," I say, giving B a quick eye roll, which only makes her smile. B is the queen of pushing buttons. She's been a thorn in my side ever since becoming best friends with my younger sister years ago, but I love her like a sister.

———

EVIE

Alex and Hallie sit at our table for the rest of the cocktail hour. Alex attempts to make small talk with the others, but Liam and I are the only ones engaging in conversation with them. Well, Alex refuses to even acknowledge my presence, so he mostly talks to Liam. But I take the time to get to know Hallie, and she's actually really nice. We have a lot in common and even discovered we have some mutual friends from college.

I know Alex well enough that I can tell he's getting uncomfortable with how much his girlfriend and I are hitting it off. His little side glances and his twiddling thumbs give him away. It's just a reminder that I know him more than I care to admit. But I brush it off because I actually don't give a shit if he's bothered by me being the bigger person right now. This poor girl still has no clue who Liam and I are to Alex. As far as she knows, we were all friends in high school. She's completely oblivious to our turbulent past, and for her sake, I'll keep it that way. I clearly meant nothing to him if he didn't bother mentioning me to her ahead of time. That's just one more reason why Alex and I would have never worked out. He doesn't consider other people's feelings the way I do. At all.

The emcee gets on the mic and announces that dinner

is about to start, asking everyone to return to their tables. I notice Alex glance back at the half-empty table a little ways away, then whisper something to Hallie. A minute later, they're standing up, and Alex is dragging his chair away.

Hallie hesitates beside Liam before following Alex. "We're going to head over to that table for dinner, so it's not so crowded. It was nice to meet you guys."

Everyone mumbles a farewell, and she turns to follow Alex.

There's a moment of silence at the table, but once they're out of earshot, B erupts. "The audacity! Oh my god, why the hell did he come up to you? That was weird, right!?" B's question is directed at Liam, but everyone is listening in, likely also curious as to why Alex chose to approach our table. I know why, though. He'd rather pretend to be our friend than let his girlfriend think everyone hates him.

"I mean, look around. Do you see anyone else whom he'd be more comfortable approaching?" Liam gestures to the rest of the packed ballroom.

I guess none of his friends could be bothered to show up. Or they weren't invited. Who knows and who cares.

Sam leans across Lou to ask me, "That was your ex-boyfriend?"

I nod. "Unfortunately, yes."

"He could barely look at you."

"I know." I hate how small my voice sounds. I hate that despite my best efforts, he still has this effect on me.

Lou puts a hand on my arm that's resting on my bump. "They didn't end on good terms," she explains to Sam.

Lou and I got close during my senior year after my childhood friends ostracized me and my breakup with Alex.

That was my all-time low. She was there to witness Alex's sudden indifference toward me and to see how much I pined after him for far too long. That's how she knows, but to be fair, everyone knew, even our teachers. Because that's what happens in small towns like St. Francis. Everyone knows everyone's business. Boundaries do not exist here.

I can tell Sam is hesitant to ask, but his curiosity gets the best of him. "You don't have to talk about it if you don't want to, but what happened between you two? Was it a long relationship?"

"We dated for three years in high school. And I don't mind. Lord knows it's been long enough." Yet here I am, struggling to soothe the sting that irritates the very depths of my heart.

I didn't realize everyone was listening to us, but I'm made aware when Fia asks from across the table, "Wait. You dated that guy for three years? I thought you dated Liam in high school?"

"Liam and I never officially dated in high school. That's... a very long story."

"I mean, we've got all night, don't we?" Fia looks around at our table of friends. "Unless everyone's heard this story a million times already, and I'm the only clueless one."

"I don't think Sam knows the story," Lou says.

"And actually, I don't really know the whole story either," B adds.

I guess she wouldn't know, would she? It's not like her best friend was dying to tell her about the time her older brother fell in love with someone who wanted nothing to do with him.

"I mean, if you guys want us to bore you with our story, we can," I say hesitantly.

When a chorus of encouragement sounds around the table, Liam looks at me with a smirk on his face. "Do you want to start, or should I?"

Chapter Four

Seven years earlier, Senior Year of High School

EVIE

Do you ever look around and feel like everybody's looking at you? Like they know something about you that you don't know yet. That's how I've felt since lunch today. Everyone's been acting so strange toward me. I know that probably sounds conceited, but I can't shake the feeling and it's making my stomach churn.

The parking lot is only half full since most of the students left at the end of the school day. The only cars left are those that belong to people involved in extracurricular activities. I just finished up volleyball practice, and a lot of the football players are hanging around outside, still in their practice pads. I wave to a group of my guy friends, but they don't wave back. The only thing I get is a few half-assed nods.

Okay, something is seriously not right.

I check my phone for the first time since the end of the school day and find a text from Alex. He sent it just before practice, but I'm only seeing it now.

ALEX

Can we grab dinner after practice?

My heart flutters like it always does when I see a text from him. Maybe Alex will know why everyone is being weird. I didn't see him outside with the other players, so I text him back and wait for him.

EVIE

Sure! I'm waiting by your car.

ALEX

Okay. I'll be out soon. Just talking to Coach.

I lean up against his car and scroll on my phone while I wait.

"Hey. Sorry that took so long."

I look up from my phone and see him walking toward me. He looks exhausted. "That's okay. You have a hard practice today?"

"Not too bad."

He gets closer, and I can see his hair is wet. "Is this sweat or shower water?"

"I showered."

After confirming he's not going to smell like stinky football pads, I give him a hug. I breathe in, loving the familiar scent of his body wash.

"What did Coach want to talk to you about?"

"What?"

I walk around to the passenger side of his car and get in. "You said you were talking to Coach after practice."

"Oh yeah. Ummm, nothing really. Just wanted to ask him a question about the game this Friday."

I buckle my seat belt, and he starts driving toward our favorite restaurant. And by favorite, I mean the most tolerable one out of the four restaurants in town. It's the one we always go to together or with our friends.

"Did you notice people were acting weird today?"

"Huh?"

"It's probably just me, but I felt like people were being really weird."

"Weird how?"

"I don't know. Like, I waved at the guys on my way out of the gym, and they didn't wave back."

He's silent for a moment before responding. "They're probably just tired from practice."

"But this afternoon too. I felt like people weren't as chatty with me in class as they normally are. And when I was at my locker, I felt like people kept staring at me. Ohmygod! Did I have something on the back of my jeans?" I start digging in my gym bag to check my pants.

"No, you didn't."

My hands slow, and I start stuffing my clothes back into my gym bag. "Is everything okay?"

"What do you mean?"

"I don't know. You just seem off..." I turn in my seat to look at him better.

He just shrugs. God, I feel like I'm losing my damn mind.

"You don't think it's about what happened this summer, do you?"

He looks at me like I'm crazy. "No." He shakes his head, little drops of water flying off the ends of his shaggy brown hair. "The guys don't care about that."

This summer, Alex and I finally had sex. After years of being pressured and doing just about everything *but* having sex, I finally gave in. Overall, I don't regret it, but it hurts that I lost friends over it.

Going to a Catholic school makes those things more complicated. You think people get slut shamed in public school for having sex? Now add in the fact that you're taught from a young age that you'll burn in the fires of hell for eternity if you give in to those physical temptations. When my "friends" that I've known since kindergarten found out that I finally slept with Alex, they completely disowned me. It was devastating to say the least. After not eating or sleeping well for weeks, my mom finally stepped in and got me the help I needed. I had to start taking antide-pressants and going to therapy twice a week. It's helped, but nothing can fully heal the pain of that loss. The rejection from people who know me better than anyone else—except Alex, of course.

Alex was there with me through it all, and so were his guy friends. I don't know how I would have survived without them. Since the girls stopped talking to me, I've mostly been hanging out with Alex and his friends. I'd consider them my friends, too, of course. In such a small school, you sort of become friends with everyone, or so I thought. I just can't figure out why they were being so weird toward me today.

"You're right. I'm probably just overthinking it."

We pull into the parking lot of the restaurant, and as I start to get out, Alex stops me. His hand on my arm feels familiar but strange all at the same time. When I look over my shoulder, waiting for him to say something, I note the changes in his face. The crease between his eyebrows. The way his lower lip is clenched between his teeth. He looks uncomfortable, pained even.

"Alex...?"

I settle back in my seat and face him, shutting my door. He can't even look me in the eyes.

"Alex, talk to me." I reach out to put my hands on his arm, needing to feel closer to him right now. He seems so distant.

He tenses under my touch.

"I think we should break up."

———

It's been over an hour since Alex said those dreaded words to me, and I still can't accept what's happening. At some point, Alex started driving around because my crying was "embarrassing him" and he didn't want anyone in the parking lot to see us.

I can't stop crying, and my hands won't stop shaking. I don't get it. There's been nothing wrong in our relationship, other than typical growing pains. We're happy.

"Three years, Alex." I can barely get the words out through my sobs. "How could you throw this away after three years?"

"Evie, please stop crying. I can't do this much longer. We've been going in circles for an hour." He reaches over and puts a hand on my shoulder, gently rubbing.

It brings me a bit of comfort, but the thought of never having access to his comfort again just shreds my heart into even tinier pieces.

"Because you won't give me a straight answer." I've

never been more confused in my short life. He's comforting me, but in the same breath, he's breaking my heart, and I don't even know why. What happened? What went wrong? "What did I do?"

"Nothing, Evie, I told you. I just don't want this anymore."

"It doesn't make any sense." I bury my face in my hands, using the already damp sleeves of my sweatshirt to soak up my tears. We drive over a bump, and for the first time in a while, I look out the window. "What are you doing?"

Alex's car rolls up next to mine in the school parking lot. "Dropping you off." When my only response is sobs, he continues, "You should go home."

"And do what?"

"I don't know, call your friends... Just don't be alone, okay."

"I don't have any friends left!" For the first time during this conversation, I raise my voice at him. "All my remaining friends are *your* friends, and I'm guessing based on their lovely greeting after practice that they're staying loyal to you."

"I don't know what you want from me."

"I want the truth! I want to know what I did wrong so we can work this out. We've always been able to work through our issues."

"We're not gonna be able to work through this one, Evie."

"You've got your mind made up then." I can't decide if it's a question or a statement.

He's quiet for a moment, staring through the windshield. "Yeah. I do."

The hesitation kills me. I almost wish he had answered with more confidence; that way, there wouldn't be any room for doubt. I take a deep breath before reaching for the door handle. Time moves in slow motion as I step out of the car. With every moment that passes, my hope that he'll stop me dwindles. As I walk around the front of his car, toward my own, I hear his door click open, and my heart stops. I'm frozen in place as he walks over to me, staring at my feet. I force my mind to go blank, not allowing any room for hope.

He silently wraps me in a hug. I keep my arms tucked into my chest and lean my cheek against the soft fabric of his sweatshirt. This doesn't feel real. My tears stream down my cheek, soaking into cotton. And all too soon, he's releasing me. This can't be it. That can't be the last time we hug, the last time we touch. I'll give him some time; he'll eventually come to his senses. Right?

Chapter Five

LIAM

God, she's even beautiful after she cries. You know how most people get red, puffy eyes and their faces get all blotchy? Not Evelyn Bordeaux. Somehow, crying makes her eyes bright and even more blue than normal. She takes up her usual seat next to me, opens her textbook, and starts taking notes again.

I lean across the aisle. "Everything okay?" I keep my voice low so our classmates won't overhear.

She glances up from her notebook. "Yeah, totally."

Not wanting to press the matter, I give her a soft smile and nod. If she's not ready to talk about it, I won't force her. Evie and I have never been close, but over the last few years we've had several Advanced Placement classes together. Unfortunately, her ex, Alex, is usually in those classes with us. I can't imagine having to spend four hours of my day in classes with an ex who won't even acknowledge my existence. Since the day he broke her heart two weeks ago, he's become a completely different person.

Alex wasn't the kindest person in our grade to begin

with; that title goes to Evie, hands down. But he at least wasn't an outright asshole, like he's being now. The event that triggered her tears today was painful to watch. Right now, we're in our fifth-period study hall. Most of the time we study, but occasionally some of us hang out and talk. Our "supervisor," Mr. Ellington, is extremely chill and basically lets us do what we want. Perks of being seniors, I guess. Evie was telling me a story about this time when she and her former friends were trying to get eggs to balance upright—clearly some silly trend they saw on the internet. I'm not sure how we got on that topic, but I could listen to any story she tells, no matter how strange.

At one point, she looked over to Alex and asked him a question about that night, trying to recall specific details. The guy completely ignored her. And not the kind of ignoring where he pretends he didn't hear her. No, the guy literally stared at her with a blank face and didn't say a word. Eventually, she realized she wasn't going to get an answer out of him and continued on with her story. But when she finished, she went to the bathroom and just returned, clearly having cried in there for the last ten minutes.

I can't stand seeing anyone hurt like that, let alone someone as kind and friendly as Evie. Wanting to lift her spirits, I make a bold move. "Hey, what are you doing after school?"

She tries to hide her sniffle. "I have practice."

"Right. What about after that?"

"Doing homework, I guess."

"Great. Would you wanna study for our AP Chem test together?"

"Ummm, sure?" She's rightfully confused since we've never studied together outside of school before.

"Great. I'll pick you up after practice."

Only because I'm paying close attention to him do I notice Alex's head cock slightly at my invitation. He's pretending to be reading his textbook, but I can tell he's trying to listen. Good. Eventually, he'll realize that letting a girl like Evie go was the biggest mistake of his life. But by the time he realizes that, she won't be available anymore, if I have anything to do with it. A few guys have already started swooping in and making their interest in her known. As far as I know, she hasn't taken any steps forward with those guys, but I worry that my window of opportunity is slowly closing. I won't miss out on my shot with her again.

Three years ago, before Evie and Alex started dating, I almost got up the courage to ask her out. Back then, I was still the new kid and didn't have many friends. Once I realized that Evie's bubbly personality wasn't a facade, I was hooked. Unfortunately, I let her slip through my fingers and right into Alex's arms. I've been patiently waiting, respecting their relationship since then. I wasn't in their inner circle of friends, so I had to get my time with her in class and at school events. Not ideal, but I'm not a home wrecker. I never *wanted* them to break up. I just wanted to be around her, even if it was just as a friend. Evie has this way of making whoever she's talking to feel like the most special person in the room. At first, I thought it was because she liked me, but once she got snatched up by Alex, I realized that's just who she is at her core. And that's what I love...yikes!...*like* most about her.

"What did you get for number six on the practice test?"

Evie leans over to check my work. "That's exactly what I got."

I take advantage of the closeness and inhale the sweet smell of her shampoo. It smells fruity and fresh. Her hair was wet when I picked her up, so I'm guessing she showered in the locker room after practice. She leans away, but the scent still lingers. I wish there were an excuse for me to sit next to her instead of across the table, but I don't want to be weird.

I take another sip of my coffee and make a fool of myself by choking on it. I pound on my chest and try not to make a scene as I attempt to clear my lungs.

"You okay?"

I nod, not able to get out any words. She watches me carefully until I finally recover. I can feel my cheeks turning red, not from the choking but purely from embarrassment.

"Here." She slides her glass of water over to me.

I take a sip and slide it back. "Thanks."

I manage to get another half hour of studying done without any more incidents. We finished our practice exam and are wrapping things up, but I don't want to leave her just yet.

"Wanna go get slushies at the truck stop?"

She gives me a look that I can't place. Can she tell that I'm just trying to buy more time with her? Does that make her uncomfortable?

"I already had a coffee, and I try to limit my sugar intake during the season."

"Come on, one slushie isn't going to hurt. Plus, I'm pretty sure you ordered a sugar-free coffee."

She cracks a smile. Got her. "Fine. I'll go."

Yes!

We pack up our stuff and head out to my car. As we walk down the sidewalk, leaves crunch under our feet, filling the silence until she speaks. "Do you have any siblings?"

"I have a little sister, Iris. She's a freshman."

"The cutie with the bright red curly hair?"

"Yeah, that's her."

"I should've known."

"Come on. My hair isn't *that* red."

"No, but the freckles give it away."

I subconsciously touch my face, hoping that my summer freckles are starting to fade.

"I like them."

She says it in such an endearing way that I actually believe her. "I've always hated them."

"Why?"

Not knowing how to explain what seems obvious to me, I just shrug.

"They make you unique. I wish I had a defining feature like that. I have such a basic look that I get mistaken for someone somebody knows all the time."

"I don't think you're basic looking."

She opens the car door and throws her bag in the back before settling into the passenger seat. Then she completely changes the subject. "You know, I'm not used to being the passenger. I'm usually the one who drives around when I'm with friends."

I click my seatbelt and start the car. "Why's that?"

"It's embarrassing, but I get car sick pretty easily. So it's just easier for me to drive rather than risk getting sick. Plus, I like being the one in control."

"That doesn't really seem like you. Needing to be in control, I mean."

"Oh yeah, I'm a closeted control freak."

I chuckle at her attempt at a self-deprecating joke. I find it ridiculous that this girl barely has a single flaw, so she has to make them up. "Asking for things occasionally doesn't qualify you as a control freak, Evie. You're probably the least demanding person I know."

"Well then, you must not know me very well. Alex used to always tell me—" She cuts herself off mid-sentence, hurting her own feelings at the mention of Alex.

"If he was dumb enough to let you go, he's not as smart as everyone thinks he is."

"You don't have to say that just to make me feel better."

"I'm not. Evie, you're a catch. You're smart, athletic, and one of the kindest people I know."

She rolls her eyes and shakes her head, clearly not believing a word I say. She nervously plays with the ends of her hair, refusing to look over at me. How does she not realize these things about herself? Or is she just too humble to admit it out loud?

"I'd date you."

She stops playing with her hair and freezes. Shit. Why did I say it like that? There are a million other ways I could have phrased it that would have landed better.

"I mean. If you want, I'd like to take you out sometime. On a date."

I pull into the parking lot of the truck stop and park the car.

"Liam..." She finally looks up at me. "I'm sorry, but I *just* got out of a relationship two weeks ago. I think it's a little too soon for me to be thinking about dates."

"Yeah, of course. Sorry."

"Don't apologize. I'm just not ready."

"I understand." I give her a smile to reassure her that I really am okay. Of course, I would have liked her to say yes, but at least now she knows I'm interested. "What are you doing for Halloween?"

A crease forms between her eyebrows. "Liam, I don't think I'll be ready by then either..."

"I figured. But there's this farm party someone in the grade below us is throwing. I heard about it from Louisa Blake. Would you want to go with me? Not as a date. Just as friends."

My heart races as she thinks about it.

"It's not really your typical crowd of people, but I think you'd have fun."

She chuckles, but not the funny kind, the uncomfortable kind."My crowd? I don't have a 'crowd' anymore."

I noticed that the mutual friends she shared with Alex haven't been as chatty with her as they usually are. "Maybe this is the perfect opportunity to get closer to some other people in the class. I don't really have a friend group either. I've never really had one. I just kind of float between the groups and occasionally get invited to things.

"I thought you were really close with the hockey guys?"

"During the season, yeah. But my best friend, Bear, graduated last year. And since then, I haven't really had a friend I'm super close to."

She reaches over and grabs my hand, her face finally showing signs of the girl I know is in there. "Sounds like two lonely islands just found a friend."

I look down at our connected hands and wonder if she can feel it too, or if it's just me. There's electricity firing between us. I can pretend to be just friends with her for as long as she needs me to. But the moment she opens it, I'm wedging my foot in that door and squeezing my way through. "So you'll go to the Halloween party with me?"

"Sure."

"Not as enthusiastic as I was hoping you'd be, but we'll

work on that." I wink at her, and she graces me with that addicting laugh.

Chapter Six

EVIE

When I was getting ready at home earlier tonight, I was so nervous that I was about ready to throw up. Being around a bunch of people I don't know isn't my problem. It's the fear of running into people I *do* know. I don't want people seeing me with Liam and getting the wrong idea. I can't let it get back to Alex that I might be seeing someone else already. In my nightmares, Alex would hear that and then take that as his sign to start hooking up with other girls. Or worse, he might not think I'm available, and what if he wants to get back together? I don't want to risk losing him for good over some dumb rumor.

So far, I don't see any of Alex's friends as we walk through a packed hallway that opens up into the kitchen. "Whose house is this?"

I feel Liam's hand barely brush the small of my back as he guides me through the crowd. "Not sure, actually. Some kid who goes to public school."

"I'm assuming by the amount of underage drinking going on here that their parents aren't home?"

Some random girl standing next to us by the keg butts into our conversation to answer my question. "No one who lives here is home."

My shoulders tense. "The kid who lives here is home, right?"

"Nope. Their whole family is gone on vacation this weekend."

"What?! How did people get in here?"

"The idiot leaves his bedroom window open for when he sneaks out at night. One of his buddies knew that and broke in. He just slipped right through the window and unlocked the front door."

My heart starts racing, and panic creeps in. The girl goes back to her conversation with her friends, leaving Liam and me alone. "Ohmygod, Liam! You didn't tell me we were breaking and entering!"

"I swear I didn't know." The shocked look on his face makes me think he's telling the truth. "If you're uncomfortable, we can leave."

A memory of Alex calling me a buzz kill for wanting to leave a party early flashes in my mind, making my whole body tense. "No, we can stay."

"You sure? I really don't mind leaving if that's what you wanna do."

"I'm sure. But we're out of here at the first whisper of cops, okay?"

"Deal," he says without hesitation.

A drunk kid dressed as a zombie stumbles up to the keg and attempts to fill his partially crushed plastic cup, which I'm pretty sure is going to spring a leak as soon as he successfully gets any beer in the cup. When he notices us staring, he asks, "What are you guys supposed to be?"

I look down at my pumpkin costume, thinking it's pretty

obvious. Then I realize that he thinks Liam and I are a couple and can't figure out what a pumpkin and a prisoner have to do with each other. It could look like Liam is trying to be a pumpkin, too, in his orange jumpsuit. But with the way the jumpsuit is rolled down to his waist, exposing his fitted white t-shirt underneath, and the handcuffs attached to his wrist, it's pretty obvious what he is, too.

"I'm a pumpkin thief."

I choke on a laugh and look up at Liam. It rolled off his tongue so effortlessly. Has he been thinking about that all night?

"Really?" The drunk kid scrunches his face.

"Yep. When I see one I like, I just can't keep away." He steps behind me and wraps his arms around my waist. He's smooth, I'll give him that. He's been good all night at keeping things platonic. This is the first time he's actually touched me, and I don't hate it. Liam is 6'3", so he can see clear over my head, and his arms wrap around me with ease. My butt is currently against his upper thigh, and I may or may not be pressing back into him, just a smidge.

"Cool." The guy goes back to filling his cup, or at least attempting to.

Liam lets go and steps around me, grabbing the guy's cup from him. "Hey man, you know what? I heard there's a special drink in the kitchen. Let me run and grab one for you. Stay right here with my girl." He takes the guy's cup and runs off, glancing back at me to make sure I'm okay. I give him a reassuring nod.

His girl?

A minute later, Liam returns with a new cup filled to the brim with a clear liquid. "Here you go, man. Made special, just for you."

"Ohhhhh thaaaaank you." The idiot enthusiastically

takes a few gulps of his new drink. "What is it? It doesn't taste like anything."

"It's this super expensive type of vodka that tastes just like water."

"Sweet! Thanks, man." The drunk guy fist bumps Liam and stumbles off, back where he came from.

For a moment, I was concerned that Liam was getting that guy more alcohol, so I'm pleasantly surprised by his creativity.

"Learned that one from Bear Michaels."

"Oh yeah? Did he use it on you?"

"He did, actually." Those adorable cheeks of his turn pink, and I can't help but giggle.

"We've all been there," I say reassuringly.

"Come on, let's go see what's happening in the basement. That's always where the real fun is." He reaches out as if to take my hand, but I place both hands around my cup and take a sip.

He puts his hand back down by his side and starts walking away. I follow close behind, trying not to lose him in the crowd of strangers, slightly regretting not taking his hand. I'm sure he was just offering to be nice, but I don't want him to get the wrong idea. I follow him down a set of stairs to an unfinished basement.

Liam was right, the basement is a whole different atmosphere. Where upstairs is all booze, music, and dancing, the basement has a massive couch full of people smoking. The music down here is still loud, but the vibes are more relaxed, and there seem to be several different games going on.

Liam leans in so I can hear him better. His hand that was holding mine is now around me, gently holding my shoulder. "Are you okay being down here with the weed?"

I nod. "Yeah, it's fine."

"Have you ever smoked before?"

"Once, but I don't think it did anything. Have you?"

"You probably just inhaled incorrectly. And yeah, I actually prefer it to alcohol."

Out of the limited things I know about Liam McAllister, that was not one of them. I pretty much know what everyone in my class has tried, but Liam is somewhat of a mystery. I've been thinking more about what he said the other day, about him not belonging to a friend group. When I think about it, I see what he means, but I never noticed it before. I just always assumed he was a part of the group that wasn't mine. He would occasionally show up to parties my friends threw, but we rarely interacted outside of school until now. I'm not sure why.

"You wanna play?"

I follow his line of sight to find he's referring to the game of spin the bottle happening on the floor in front of the couch.

"Oh god, I haven't played that game since I was in middle school."

"I would hope not, since you've had a boyfriend for pretty much all of high school."

"Exactly." I swallow, thinking about how mad Alex would be—correction, *would have been*—if he found out I played spin the bottle. "Alex is definitely not the type of guy who likes to share his belongings."

"And you? Do you like to share?" His smirk tells me exactly what he means by that.

"Liam McAllister!" I playfully swat him on the shoulder. "You're going to have to get me way more drunk if you expect me to answer questions like that."

"Come on, don't friends talk about those sorts of things?"

He squeezes my shoulder, and it reminds me that he still has his arm around me.

"Some do, I guess." I stare into his green eyes, scanning for any reason why I shouldn't trust him. Finding none, I decide to trust him. "I've only had sex with Alex. But I've definitely thought about it and didn't hate the idea."

"Yeah, I heard that..."

Tension takes over my whole body. "Heard what?"

"That Alex was your first."

My shoulders sag with relief, but my heart sinks. It makes sense that he would know. With a graduating class size of only 50 people, it's pretty easy to know everyone's personal business. And it's not like Alex taking my virginity was some huge secret. But the idea of people who aren't my friends talking about me like that makes me uneasy.

Sensing the shift in my mood, Liam uses his arm that's draped behind my back to gently shake me. "Let's not talk about him, yeah?" I nod. "So, are we gonna play?"

I take a deep breath before I make a decision I might regret. "Fuck it. Let's play. But I either need a hit or a shot before we start."

"That can be arranged. Come with me." Again, he doesn't bother trying to grab my hand this time, likely trying to save himself some embarrassment.

We approach a group of guys I recognize who are our age but go to public school. I'm not sure how he knows them, but they seem to know Liam.

"Hey, man! How are you?"

"Doing good. You getting ready for the season to start?"

Hockey. That's how they know each other. Our private school is too small to fill an entire hockey team, so we've always co-oped with the public school. Alex doesn't play hockey, so I never really went to any of the games, except for when they won the state tournament last year. That was an exciting time, and pretty much everyone went to cheer on our small town schools.

"Counting down the days."

"Same." He puts his hand on my back and pulls me forward from where I was slightly hiding behind him. "This is Evie. She goes to St. Francis with me."

A chorus of hellos is tossed my way, and I wave awkwardly. "Hi."

Liam's hand leaves my back, and I realize I kind of miss it. It felt like a bit of a security blanket in this unknown environment. "Do you know where we could find some safe liquor for shots?"

"Of course." One of the guys digs in a dirty backpack that's sitting by his feet and pulls out a huge bottle of rum. "This is my personal bottle, so I promise you it's safe." He cracks it open and takes a swig of it to prove his promise.

Satisfied, Liam takes the bottle from him and takes a pull before handing it to me. I can feel my organs cringing before the bottle even touches my lips. But I'm set on letting loose tonight and having fun, so I'm not about to let this dude's poor taste in liquor stop me. I tip the bottle back, take two big pulls, and try to suppress my gag reflex.

"Damn girl. You're having fun tonight."

I hand him back his bottle with a smile. "Thanks."

"Anytime." He looks at Liam. "She your new girlfriend?"

"Just a friend." He says it very matter-of-factly. If the words are painful for him to say, you can't hear it in his voice.

"Mmhmmm, sure. Better keep her close, someone might try to snatch her from you," the guy says with a sly grin. Then he winks at me. Fucking *winks* at me.

I should be offended by him objectifying me, but I'm a sucker for a compliment, so I keep my mouth shut.

"You think I don't think about that all day, every day?"

Okay, now I know I must be blushing. Fuck, am I so attention starved that I'm getting worked up by these subtle compliments? Yeah, I think I am. And apparently, that rum is kicking in fast because words start slipping out of my mouth before I can stop them. "We're headed over to play spin the bottle if you want to join."

The guy, whose name I still don't know, grins like the Cheshire Cat. And I'm the mouse. "You said she's just a friend, McAllister?" He doesn't break eye contact with me while he addresses Liam.

"That's what I said," Liam says through gritted teeth.

"This is going to be fun." The guy stands up and follows us over to the other side of the room, where the game is still going on.

Who am I, and what have I done with Evie Bordeaux? I don't do this. I don't tease and taunt men with empty promises and play them against their friends. If Liam asked me to leave right now, I would. But he doesn't. I'm having a hard time reading him. Like he's conflicted between giving me my space to be my own person and attaching the other end of his handcuffs to my wrist and never letting me out of his sight. It sounds evil, even in my head, but it's kind of hot. I've never seen him like this before, whatever *this* is.

———

LIAM

At least she's not thinking about Alex. I know when she's thinking about him because her bright eyes go foggy and her expression goes blank. Every time, it's like she's being sucked into the void he left in her heart. I can't stand seeing her like that. I'm hoping this game will help keep any memories of him at bay, at least for a little while. I also secretly hope that the bottle will set us up for a kiss that I've been too chicken to initiate up to this point.

The open spots in the circle left us separated by two people. She's currently squished between a girl dressed as a sexy bunny and a guy dressed as a pepper shaker. I hope for his sake that his salt isn't the jealous type. As we were walking up, he was just returning to his seat after crawling across the circle to kiss a girl dressed as a fairy. I can even see some of her glitter stuck to his cheek.

"Alright! Newcomers, the rules are simple. You have to be open to kissing any person in this circle that the bottle lands on, regardless of gender. So if you're not down for that, get out of the damn circle. We won't deal with time wasters around here. Got it? Good. You can spin next, lovely." He hands me the empty vodka bottle and winks at me.

I hesitantly take it from him, suddenly getting extremely nervous. Am I actually okay with kissing anyone around this circle? I do a quick scan for friends, exes, and anyone else who would be a hard pass. Seeing none and being moderately satisfied with the quality of people around me, I lean forward and place the bottle on the carpet in the middle of the circle. My fingers lightly grip the cool glass of the bottle as I wind up and spin it.

It spins wildly at first, then it starts to slow to an anxiety-provoking speed for longer than physics should allow. It passes by Evie more times than I can count, and each time the feeling in my gut telling me I shouldn't be doing this gets stronger.

The bottle finally comes to a halt, and I follow where it's pointing with my eyes. From this angle, it's hard to tell exactly who it's pointing to, so I look between the two people I think it might be, waiting for one of them to inform the rest of us of who it's actually pointing to. My heart races as they talk amongst themselves and both glance my way. Fuck, this is making me so anxious. Why did I do this?

I look to the other side of the circle, where Evie is, and give her a look, letting her know I'm panicking. I don't want her to think that this is easy for me. But Evie appears completely unbothered by this. She's actually...wait...is she laughing at me? What the fuck? My face must give my thoughts away because she immediately covers her mouth, stifling her laughter. All I can do is roll my eyes at her and look back to the two girls who were deciding my fate when I last saw them. To my surprise, they're still debating.

The guy next to me leans over. "I guess the bottle is pointing directly between them, so they're doing a tiebreaker.

Sure as shit, the girls are fucking playing rock, paper, scissors. Kill me now. I look down at the carpet for a moment, and the winner is chosen. I didn't see if the winner or the loser is the one crawling toward me, but at this point, I'm so sick of all the attention being on me that I'm just glad it's almost over. I lean forward, into the circle, to meet her halfway. All my anxiety didn't allow me to notice how pretty she is. Now being face-to-face with her, I can see that her lips look soft, her eyes are a beautiful caramel brown, and her smile is gorgeous. When we're close enough, she sits up on her knees and reaches her hands out to pull my face into hers. Our lips touch, and I can feel her smile against my mouth. We kiss for a moment before the circle starts clapping, breaking us apart. I shift back into my spot without a glance over at Evie. No matter how she's feeling right now, I don't think I want to know.

The bottle gets passed to the person next to me, and a few more people take their turn. Both Evie and I are spared until it's her turn to spin. When she leans forward to grab the bottle, her costume hangs down, revealing her cleavage. Fuck, I want that bottle to land on me so bad. She gives it a big spin and sits back to watch her fate unfold. I see a giddy little smile peak out just as the bottle slows to a stop.

Fuck me.

The bottle landed on the same girl that I kissed. This, obviously, is not what I was hoping for, but getting to watch her make out with a cute girl that I just kissed is making me hot all of a sudden. The girls look at each other and nod, mutually agreeing to the kiss. They both giggle as they crawl across the circle toward each other. Everyone around us is now watching. I wonder if Evie's aware that all eyes are on her. They meet each other in the center and situate themselves up on their knees. They whisper back and forth, but I'm too far away to hear what they're saying.

Evie glances over at me so quickly that I almost question if it even happened. Next thing I know, she's wrapping her hands around this girl's face and pulling her in. The girls make out hot and heavy, definitely putting on a show. Everyone hoots and hollers, while all I can do is stare with my jaw on the floor. I'm so fucking hard under my bright orange jumpsuit, I'm thankful I'm sitting down so no one can see.

"Evie? Are you a lesbian now?"

———

EVIE

I rip myself away from the girl I'm kissing and spin

toward where the voice came from. A voice I know all too well.

Layne. Alex's best friend.

He's standing there with more of my old guy friends, just staring and giggling to themselves. I get a pit in my stomach, and the only place I want to be right now is buried six feet underground. Seriously, can someone kill me *right fucking now?*

I look around frantically, but don't see who I'm looking for.

"Alex ain't here, honey. And thank god he's not, because he would have a cow if he saw what I just saw."

Several people in the circle start booing Layne and telling him to fuck off. Suddenly, I realize I'm still in the middle of the circle, but now I'm alone. The other girl must have left as soon as our not-so-little kiss ended. The goal of that hot and heavy make-out session was to tease Liam and his friend. I never imagined it would get back to Alex.

I scramble to my feet and walk toward Layne and the guys. Before I reach them, I feel someone behind me, their hand gently resting on my lower back. "Are you okay?" Liam's voice is full of genuine concern. I should feel comforted that he's here with me right now, but I don't. All I can think about is Alex and what he's doing right now.

"Hey, Layne. Hey guys." Everyone grumbles a half-assed hello, clearly not thrilled to find me here.

Layne at least has the decency to fake being nice and gives me a side hug. "So, you're hanging out with Liam and kissing girls now? Who are you?"

He's teasing, but his words sink in like poison.

"We were just playing the game." I point toward the bottle spinning on the floor. The gaps we left in the circle have already been filled, and the game has moved on without us. "Who do you guys know here?"

"No one really, just heard about the party and decided to come check it out."

Alex and his friends were always in the know when it came to the best parties, so, of course, they heard about this one. My main question still remains unanswered. "Where's Alex?"

"He's not coming out tonight."

"But he loves Halloween."

One of the guys snickers behind Layne, and my stomach drops.

"Oh...I get it."

"If it makes you feel better, I don't think it's anything serious. Just a little rebound."

"Please stop." I put my hands up to stop him from tearing my heart out any further. "I don't wanna know." I throw my hands down to my side, embarrassed that I put them up in the first place, as if I needed to physically stop Layne from speaking.

Layne almost looks sorry for me. I've known the guy since kindergarten, and I've never seen him feel sorry for anyone. The one and only person Layne loves, other than himself, is his momma. To be fair, that woman is a saint. But not once in all those years has Layne ever attempted to spare my feelings like he is now by holding his tongue.

"Alright, well, we're gonna head upstairs. Have fun on your date. Holler for me if you're about to kiss any more girls, I'd love to watch." He winks at me before turning on his heels and following the rest of the guys up the stairs.

I just stand there, staring after them. A few months ago, those were my friends. If Alex hadn't dumped me, I'd probably be here with them tonight, and Alex, of course. God, Alex...

I startle and turn, frightened by the sudden hand on my shoulder. "Sorry, I forgot you were standing there."

"You wanna get out of here?" Liam's eyes look the same as Layne's just did. Except with Liam, I want to lean into his touch and take shelter in his arms. With Liam, I don't feel like the dunce standing in the corner by myself. With him, I don't feel alone. And I definitely don't want to be alone tonight.

"Yeah, but I don't wanna go home just yet."

"Anywhere in particular you want to go?"

I shake my head. "Anywhere I won't run into anyone else we know."

Liam winces, and I start to worry that I'm hurting his feelings. It's not that I don't want to be seen with him. I just don't want it to get back to Alex that I was with Liam... which is basically the same thing as not wanting to be seen with him. Fuck, am I an asshole?

"Let's go." He takes my hand and leads me up the stairs, and we dip out the side door before Alex's friends can see.

Chapter Seven

EVIE

"I'm sorry, Liam." My head hangs down, and I stare at the floor of his car, unable to see the hurt in his eyes any longer.

"Sorry for what?" His hands on the wheel are turning white from how hard he's gripping it.

"I don't want you to think that I don't want to be seen with you."

"I wasn't thinking that."

"Good." I take a deep breath, calming my racing heart that hasn't slowed since I heard Layne's voice. "I really appreciate you, and I'd hate for you to think I don't want to be around you."

"But you don't want to date me."

"Is that what you're mad about?"

"Mad?" He glances over at me. His eyebrows are scrunched together, creating a wrinkle between them. "Evie, I'm not mad at you."

"Then why have you had a death grip on the steering wheel the whole drive?"

His hands instantly loosen their hold on the steering wheel. "I'm just...It's not you."

"Then what's bothering you?"

"I just hate the way they make you feel."

"Who?"

"Alex, Layne, all those guys. You care so much about what they think when they clearly don't give a shit about you."

I'm taken aback by his harsh but true words. "I know I shouldn't...but I can't..."

"You don't have to explain anything to me. I'm not upset by your reaction. I'm just upset that they hold so much power and don't even bat an eye when they toy with your emotions like that." Now his hand is on my thigh, comforting me. His touch is warm and gentle.

"I'll be fine, Liam. It's all just so raw still. I'm not ready to move on. I can't."

"I understand."

"Where are we?" We've pulled into the driveway of a house I don't recognize.

"My house. Just wait here a second, I'll be right back."

"Okay." I'm so confused. Why are we at his house? And how come I've never seen Liam's house before? I know where most of my classmates live, so the feeling of being in an unfamiliar place in my own town is strange.

A couple of minutes later, a young girl with bright red curls dressed as a rag doll steps out of the front door and waves. I smile and wave back. I've never actually met Iris, but from what I've heard, she's a total sweetheart.

Liam walks out directly behind her, carrying blankets and a full backpack. He gently shoves Iris back in the house and shuts the door behind her. When he gets to the car, he throws all his stuff in his trunk and hops back in the car.

"What's all that for?"

"You said you didn't want to go home yet, so I had an idea."

I look at him skeptically, but I can't hide my smile. "This is not a date, Liam."

"I know," he says, but the look on his face says otherwise.

"We're just two friends hanging out on Halloween."

"I know. Now will you just relax and play along?"

"Okay." I sit with my arms crossed over my chest for a minute before asking, "How long till we get there?"

He laughs, likely annoyed by the fact that I can't just trust him. "Five more minutes."

———

LIAM

I know I told her to relax, but I didn't ask for silence. The quiet is allowing my thoughts to run wild, and my nerves are about to get the best of me. I missed my turn because I was too busy looking out of the corner of my eye, trying to read her expression. This girl does not know how to chill.

I've always known that about Evie, though. She's always been wound a little tighter than most. It's gotten her a lot of success in sports and academics, but it makes her care too much about what people think, and she never allows herself to relinquish control and let others do things for her. Last year, I was working on a group project with her in physics, and she pretty much did the entire thing by herself. The rest of us offered to help, but now that I know her a little more, I know she prefers to be in charge.

We finally arrive at our destination, and the confusion on her face is exactly what I'd hoped for.

"What are we doing in an empty dirt lot?"

"Relaxing." That's the only hint I give her as I get out of the car and start to set things up. I pop down the back seats and spread out the blankets. I go back to the front, turn on some chill instrumental music, and open the moonroof. I thought about lying outside, but the air is a little too chilly for that, so I opted to do it from inside the car to keep warm.

The whole time I'm setting up, I feel her gaze as she patiently watches me.

"Come on." I motion for her to follow me into the back seat, which is now laid out flat like a bed, extending into the trunk space of my SUV.

She does as I ask and silently crawls into the back. I think she gets it now as she lies down on her back and stares up at the stars. I lay down next to her, careful not to get too close, and rest my hands behind my head.

We lay there next to each other in silence and stare up at the stars.

"Thanks for this."

I turn my head to look at her. She's lying on her back staring out the moonroof. Her blue eyes sparkle in the light, her face slightly illuminated by the almost full moon that's out tonight. I fight the urge to roll onto my side and stare at her. Instead, I force myself to look up again, at the second-best view.

"My dad used to take me stargazing all the time."

"Really? That's cute. Did Iris go too?"

"Yeah, but she was really young, so she didn't sit still very long."

She laughs, and something inside me starts to turn molten. After seeing how upset she was when we left the party, I was worried I wouldn't hear that laugh again for the rest of the night.

"You don't talk about him very much..."

"No..." And I don't really like to.

When she doesn't ask a follow-up question, I chance a glance over at her. I immediately regret my decision because I know, with the way she's looking at me right now, I'd tell her anything she wants to know. But it's not a question that comes out of those beautiful lips. Nothing does. She simply stares back at me with sadness in her eyes. Whether it's sadness for her or for me, I don't know.

She shocks me by scooting a little closer, so now her arm brushes up against my costume, barely making contact with my side. Her stare has migrated back to the sky above us, so I drag mine that way too, letting the silence continue.

It's not an awkward silence, but a peaceful one. One that has my eyelids feeling heavy.

I pry my eyes open and blink to clear them. Shit, did I fall asleep? I look over and find Evie sleeping too, curled up on her side and facing me. I reach into my side pocket for my phone to check the time. We're approaching midnight, which means I was asleep for almost an hour.

Sleep is a hard thing for me to come by—always has been. Well, not always. Mostly since my dad passed. At the ripe age of twelve, my world came crashing down, and the weight of the world has been on my shoulders ever since. The constant worrying about my mother and Iris doesn't leave much room for sleep. Something about lying here with Evie allowed me to finally take a breath. Something about her eases my mind.

I gently shake her until she's looking up at me with sleepy eyes.

"Hey, sleeping beauty. Do you have a curfew?"

Her eyes widen, and she sits up. "Shit!"

"What time do you need to be home?"

She squints at the time on my dashboard and relaxes a bit. "Midnight. Thank god. I about had a heart attack."

"I tried to wake you as gently as I could." Instead of sitting the rest of the way up like I expect her to, she settles back into me. Not as close as before, but I'll take it.

"Don't worry, I panic awake all the time. My body doesn't know any other way."

I look down at her, fighting the urge to put my arm over her again. "That sounds stressful."

"It can be. But honestly, this is some of the best sleep I've gotten in weeks."

Same. But instead of saying that out loud, I simply laugh to myself.

"I'm serious. I haven't been sleeping well lately, for obvious reasons."

"So why now? You think your body said enough and finally gave out on you?"

She props herself up on her elbow and looks down at me. "I think you just make me feel safe and comfortable."

My smile falls, despite this news making me feel really good. Not knowing how to respond to that, I just tuck a piece of her hair behind her ear.

"Sorry, I know that sounds really dumb."

"No, it doesn't. I'm just sad that you don't feel safe and comfortable all the time."

"I don't know, it's just my anxiety gets the best of me a lot. And with my past friendships blowing up and now with Alex, I have some serious trust issues."

"Very understandable."

"My parents are extremely supportive, and they always mean well, but sometimes they can be overbearing. Since

I'm an only child, they pour all their time and energy into me. It adds a lot of pressure to my life, and they don't even realize they're doing it."

If only she knew how lucky she was to have all that time and attention on her from people she loves. I'd kill for my mom to pay half as much attention to me, instead of letting her depression take over every aspect of her life.

"And it's crazy, but I feel like you would never *intentionally* hurt me. You're too sweet. I don't know, that's probably super ignorant to say, I just feel it."

"I won't. I couldn't."

I fight the urge to pull her in and finally learn what her lips feel like on mine. I can't do that, I can't mess this up. I'll take things at her pace, even if it kills me.

"I should get home." Her voice is almost a whisper, as if she's denying reality, like I wish we could.

I nod and close my eyes, waiting for her to sit up before I do something I'll regret. Tonight ended perfectly, and that's how I want her to remember it.

Chapter Eight

EVIE

Juggling my coffee, my backpack, and these posters is a lot harder than I anticipated, but somehow I manage to make it to the senior hallway without dropping any of them. I set my coffee and the rolled-up posters down on the ground and unlock my locker. Once my books are in place and swapped out for the ones I need for my morning classes, I close the door and head to another wing of the school. I love being here early in the morning before everyone arrives. It makes me feel important, special even. As I roam the halls, looking for available space to hang the new physics club posters, the only people I pass are a few early-bird teachers and the janitor.

I turn the corner and walk through a hallway that I don't spend much time in. This wing is mostly filled with art classrooms, the band and choir room, and other fine arts related classes. Not having been gifted with any of those talents, I scarcely find myself down here. But I'm sure there are plenty of artsy kids who may also be interested in the physics club, so I look for a spot to hang my last poster.

As I fold up the tape and stick it to the back of the poster, I find myself humming along to a familiar song. You know when a random song just pops in your head out of nowhere, and you can't help but sing it? That happens to me a lot, but this time it's different. I pause what I'm doing and listen closer to the silence of the halls. But that's the thing, they're not silent. Quiet piano music emanates from a room at the end of the hallway. If there were even a few voices in the hallway, you wouldn't be able to hear them.

Since I'm alone, I let my curiosity get the best of me. I quickly press the taped poster onto the wall and grab my backpack off the floor. I wander down the hall, following the sound of the piano. It leads me to a shut metal door. I try the handle, and to my surprise, it opens. It's probably against school rules to have the doors locked with students in here, for good reason. Or wait, maybe it's the choir teacher practicing. I should turn around, but of course I don't.

That door only led to another hallway with more doors. The sound of the piano is louder from in here, and I follow the noise until I find the right door. This one isn't shut, but left open just a crack. Against my better judgment, I put my face up to the crack and peek in. I'm dying to see who in our school plays the piano this well.

"Liam?!"

The piano abruptly stops, and a full head of auburn hair whips around, revealing those green eyes. "Evie? Why are you standing outside the door like a creeper?" His words aren't judgmental, they're curious. A little amused, if anything.

Embarrassed, I push open the door and step in. "I didn't know you could play the piano."

"Eh, just a little for fun."

"That didn't sound like just a little."

"I used to play a lot more when I was a kid, but when we moved here, we didn't have room for the piano in Frank's house."

"So you just play in the band then?"

He laughs. "There isn't a piano in the school band."

"Oh, duh." I run my hand through my hair.

"The choir director lets me come in the morning to play for a bit. I mostly just do it when I need to sort out my thoughts."

"That's really nice of him. Is he here?" I peek out the still-open door and look down the hallway. I swear there wasn't anyone out there when I walked in, but I was also so mesmerized by Liam's playing that I could have just missed him.

"He's probably in the teacher's lounge or something. He usually goes there after he lets me in."

I stand there for a minute, just staring at him. The more time I spend with Liam, the more layers I peel back. Last week, I learned that Liam does pottery. Not only has he taken a class at the school, but he also does it in his off-season at a pottery studio in a nearby town. The only reason I found out is because we were driving around when he got a text from the studio manager letting him know that a bunch of his pieces had just been taken out of the kiln. I'm pretty sure that's the right word. Regardless, he drove us there to pick up his stuff. He tried to hide it from me in a box full of bubble wrap, but I beat him in rock-paper-scissors, so he had to let me peek at one of the pieces. I picked the biggest-looking one, and he unwrapped it. It was the most beautiful handmade thing I've ever seen. Liam, being Liam, got embarrassed and didn't want to talk about it.

Apparently, not many people know that side of him. Now here we are again, a couple of weeks later, and I'm uncovering something new about him yet again. "How have you kept this a secret for so long?"

"I just don't tell anyone."

"But why not? You're talented, Liam. Are you going to audition for the school's end-of-year talent showcase?" The look on his face is saying no. "Oh, please, Liam. You have to! It's your last year. Tons of seniors come out of the woodwork with hidden talents at that concert."

He runs his hand over the back of his neck and shakes his head. "I don't know..."

"Please..." I lean forward onto the piano and give him the biggest puppy dog eyes I can manage. "For me?"

He huffs, leaning into me. "And what do I get out of it?"

I'm suddenly aware of how close we are, and I can feel my blood pumping through my body with every beat of my heart. "A standing ovation."

He grins, and I stand up, pulling back from him. I've been trying my best not to lead Liam on, but I can't help occasionally leaning in to the pull of attraction between us. There's only so much a girl can do to resist the urge for companionship. And after being in a relationship for so long, I'm afraid I forgot how to be on my own.

"Is there anything else about you that I don't know?"

"Not that I can think of. Is there anything about you that I don't know?"

"Unfortunately, what you see is what you get. An anxious, people-pleasing, try-hard with newfound trust issues." I frame my face with my hands and bat my eyelashes at him.

"Yeah, you're right, you are pretty boring."

I scoff. "Am not!" I playfully swat the back of his head. "How rude. I'd like you to know that I do break the rules sometimes."

"Oh yeah? Like when?"

I pause for a moment, thinking. Then, I remember something. I stand there, second-guessing whether or not to let him in on the biggest secret in the school.

"Are you about done here?"

Liam checks his phone resting on the piano and nods. "Yeah, I was just about finished."

"Good. Come with me. I want to show you something."

"Where are we going?"

He follows me out of the music room and down the still-empty hallway. "More students and teachers should be arriving soon, so we'll have to make this fast."

"Evie, where are you taking me?"

I grab his hand and pull him down another hallway, this one darker than the last. We stop at a set of giant metal doors that lead to the back of the auditorium. Oh god, this is so stupid. "Before we go any further, I need you to promise me you won't tell a soul about this."

"Of course."

I stare at him and wait.

"I promise, I won't tell anyone."

Satisfied with his pledge of fealty, I turn and open one of the doors. It's pitch black in the auditorium and eerily silent. I turn on my phone flashlight and shut the door behind Liam. Adrenaline courses through my veins. I can't believe we're doing this.

"Can't we just turn the lights on?"

"No." My voice echoes off the brick walls, and I cringe. I lower my voice. "Whisper."

"Sorry," he whispers back.

He follows me up the side stairs and onto the stage.

"Is this your way of trying to convince me to do the talent show?"

I quietly giggle to myself. "No. But if it's working, then yes."

"This might be a good time to tell you I'm a little afraid of the dark."

"Quit being a big baby. We're almost there."

"Almost where?"

"Have you ever heard of the whale?

"The what?"

"The *whale*."

"The movie about the overweight man and his—"

"No, not the movie." I roll my eyes, even though he can't see it. "The whale is a place, here in the school. It's a top-secret hiding spot that only a few people know about."

"You're joking, right?"

"Do I look like someone who would drag you into a dark auditorium for a joke?"

He shrugs.

I kneel down on the stage. "No, I'm not. Now get down here and help me."

Liam crouches down next to me, and I direct him to the small ring that's embedded in the wood floor. "I'll hold the light, you pull this up."

"Seriously?"

"Liam. We're running out of time."

"Okay, okay!" He does as he's told and yanks the trap door open.

It's a small opening. I look Liam up and down, all 6 feet 3 inches of him. I didn't quite think this through.

"I'm not sure I'm gonna fit down there."

"I was just thinking the same thing. I'll go down first."

I slide through the opening, down into the space under the stage. A few seconds later, I see Liam's legs dangling through the opening. He slides in slowly, the opening getting tight around his thick thighs and hockey butt, which I'm definitely *not* checking out. But he manages to get through, surprising both of us.

"Now you just can't give me a boner, or I'm definitely not getting out of here."

My laugh reverberates through the mostly empty space under the stage.

Liam takes a moment to look around. "Damn, Evie. This is cool."

"Right!"

He takes in the doodles on the walls, the blankets neatly folded in the corner, and the Nintendo 64 attached to an old box screen TV. "A mini fridge? Are you living down here?"

"No, silly. We just come down here to hang out sometimes during free period."

"Who's we? I thought you said no one knew about this place?"

"Only a few people per class are allowed to know about it. It's been used for years, probably since they built this stage. I came down here with Alex and Layne."

"I'll bet Bear knows about it."

"Yeah, probably, he was pretty popular."

He gives me a strange look. "So you think you're popular?"

"No, that's not what I meant!"

Liam covers his mouth with a fist to laugh at me. "I'm just kidding, Evie." He playfully pats my shoulder as I continue to glare at him. "Everyone knows you're popular."

"Ohmygod, I am not! Quit saying that."

He shields himself from my arms that are aiming for any part of his body they can make contact with. He manages to grab my wrists, his hands strong but gentle.

"What's so bad about that? Don't people want to be called popular?"

I stop trying to attack him, and he releases my wrists. I settle back into a seated position on the rug. "Well, when all your friends abandon you, you start to feel anything but popular."

His face softens, and his eyes get big. "Ev—"

"One day, you have all these friends that you've had since kindergarten, and you think you'll be best friends for the rest of your lives and raise your babies together after marrying your high school sweetheart. But then those friends find out you're a sinful *whore*, so they excommunicate you from the friend group. Then you become close friends with your boyfriend's friends, but they all ditch you after he dumps your ass unexpectedly, leaving you *completely alone*. And then, when all the other people in your class that you at least thought you were friendly with start feeling comfortable talking shit about your old friends around you, you start to realize that people thinking you're 'popular' really just means they think you're an asshole who thinks everyone likes you. So now you're a friendless loser who used to be popular, aka hated by everyone not considered popular, and now you have no friends except for one guy who likes you but you don't like him like that but you like the attention he gives you and he's really nice so you hang around him an— " I take in a large breath, realizing that I hadn't done so in several minutes. A knot forms in my throat, and I start to sob, my face already soaked with tears.

"Whoa, Evie, breathe." Liam crawls over to me and places a hand on each of my shoulders. "Breathe."

I suck in a deep, slow breath, and when I let it out, my lungs are shaky. Tears continue streaming down my face, and it feels like they may never stop. Liam wraps his arms around me, and I bury my face in his chest. I let out a few sobs, and he holds me tighter. The muscles in my body relax, letting every ounce of me hang completely in his arms.

A bell rings off in the distance. Not just any bell, the warning bell for the start of the school day.

"Fuck."

That bell means we have five minutes to make it to our first period class on time. I wipe my face, and we scramble out of the whale as fast as we can, latching it shut behind us. Luckily, I brought my backpack with all my books in it. Liam starts to head down the hall toward our lockers. "You don't have time to go back!"

"I don't have my books!"

"We have all the same morning classes, you idiot, you can borrow mine. Come on!"

We run down the hallway as far as we can before transitioning into a speed walk so we don't get stopped by a teacher. We round the corner and bust through the door of our first period classroom just as the tardy bell goes off. We're doubled over, hands on our knees, laughing.

Liam is the first to stand up. "Well, that was thrilling."

I right myself and lean into him. At this point, the laughing is less because this is funny and more so from the anxiety. "I'm so sorry."

"Worth it."

We start making our way back to our seats, and I notice a few people in particular staring at us. Two are girls who used to be my friends, and then there's Alex. He's not looking now, but the moment I looked his way, his head shot down, suddenly very interested in his book cover. I know he saw us. And I'm honestly not sure how I feel about it.

Chapter Nine

EVIE

"Liam, I'm starting to think you're losing on purpose."

"I am not, I'm just distracted, that's all."

"Yeah, sure..."

I watch Liam stripping off his shirt out of the corner of my eye. "I'm inclined to agree with everyone else. I think you're just looking for an excuse to strip in front of us girls."

He leans over the center console, and I can feel the heat coming off him. "Evie, if I *were* doing this on purpose, it would only be for you."

The two girls in the back seat overhear him, easily since we're in a car, and start booing him. We all laugh and continue the conversation we were having prior to Liam losing the game for the fifth time.

Earlier tonight, Liam and I were texting when he convinced me to hang out with him and some of his public school friends. Well, one hockey friend of his and that guy's two girl friends. The five of us have been driving around for over an hour now, and Liam has already managed to lose most of his clothing.

In a small town where there's not much to do, we teenagers have to find creative ways to entertain ourselves. For some kids, it's parties. For others, it's all-night gaming sessions. But one thing most teens in our town have in common is that everyone finds themselves driving around with friends. There usually isn't a set place we're going. We just drive, talk, and listen to music. And occasionally, we play car games made up by some dumb teenagers long ago that somehow everyone knows.

'Foreplay' is the name of the game we're playing now. The rules are simple. When you see a car with a headlight out, you slam your hand against the ceiling of the car. The last person to do so loses and has to remove an article of clothing as their punishment.

Typically, someone's curfew comes up before anyone is even remotely close to being naked, but here we are driving around at 10:00pm with Liam nearly naked in my passenger seat, and three strangers in the back. Though I've never played this game with Liam before, I swear to god he's doing it on purpose. There's no way he's this bad at the game.

Someone in the back seat smacks the ceiling, and two other hands follow shortly after. I throw my hand up last. Well, not last. Liam is last, again.

"I'm going to kill you!" I glare over at Liam.

"Ooops. Looks like it's just my underwear left."

"Good, that means you lose." My hands grip the steering wheel so tight my knuckles turn white.

A girl from the back seat chimes in. "No way! He's gotta take them off. *Then* he loses."

The other girl has my back. "Gross, no. He loses now and puts his clothes back on."

Last to chime in is Liam's teammate. "Oh, he definitely needs to be naked."

Liam looks at me with a devilish grin. "What'll it be, driver? What are the house rules?"

I stare straight ahead at the road and try not to glance over at his naked torso covered in lean muscle. Say no, Evie! Tell the man to put his clothes back on! "Well, I'm clearly outvoted three to two." What the fuck did I just say!?

"Alright. Naked it is."

The girl who sided with me lets out a little squeal as Liam slips his underwear down to his ankles, and I throw my right hand up to shield my eyes.

The confidence of this man! Jesus Christ... I'm guessing he's not at all ashamed of what's on full display at the moment. And I hate this, but it kind of makes me curious. Damnit! Don't look, Evie!

We stop at a red light, and I lower my hand, glancing over at Liam's face. I make a point to stare only at his eyes and not an inch lower. "Okay, you lose, now put your damn clothes back on."

The idiot has the most obnoxious grin on his face right now, and I want to smack it off of him...then pin him against the window and...

NO! Fuck, fuck, fuck. Evie, get your shit together!

I look straight again and notice the light is already green. I keep driving, ignoring the hot naked guy to my right. The next light turns yellow as I approach, but I am not about to sit at another red light while Liam still has his pants off, so I gun it.

Seconds later, I see red and blue lights flashing in my rear-view mirror. "Shit!"

Everyone starts to panic and frantically throws their clothes back on. I pull over as slowly as possible, buying them a little more time to get dressed. I only lost once and had to take my sweater off, so I'm still fully clothed in my tank top and leggings, but everyone else has at least two items of clothing to put back on. Liam, obviously, has the most left to do. He manages to get at least his base layer on before the officer taps on my window.

"Hello, Officer," I say as I roll it down.

"What are you kids up to tonight?"

"Just driving around." I'm shaking, but I'm not sure why. We haven't been drinking or smoking tonight, but I'm not sure if being naked in a car at night is illegal or not. Ohmygod, is it illegal? Did he even see it?

"Do you know why I pulled you over?"

I wrack my brain thinking of everything that happened in the last two minutes. "Ummmm, probably the yellow light I just ran."

"It was red when you crossed the intersection."

"I'm so sorry, sir, I thought I could make it."

The officer shines his light in the faces of the people in the back. "You kids been drinking tonight?"

"No, sir." It's the truth, but for some reason, my voice is shaky like I'm lying.

"I'm gonna have to ask you all to step out of the car."

"All of us?"

"Yes. Leave your coats where they are."

"Okay."

We all slowly crawl out of the vehicle. As we huddle together on the snowy sidewalk, shivering from the cold, the officer opens the doors and checks through the car, shaking out our jackets. Thoroughly. Again, there's nothing for him to find, so I don't know why I'm so nervous. I guess my heart is still racing from Liam being naked in my car.

"Alright, you guys can get back in."

The officer waits for us to get back in and gives me a final piece of advice before leaving. "Next time you're getting pulled over, try not to panic like you're hiding something."

"Yes, sir. Sorry."

He must have seen the shadows of everyone frantically putting their clothes back on and thought we were hiding something.

As soon as my window is fully rolled up and the officer is clear of the vehicle, everyone in the car bursts into laughter.

The people in the back start a chain of anxious word vomit, while Liam and I just look at each other and shake our heads.

"Holy shit, my heart has never beat so fast in my life!"

"I totally thought we were busted!"

"Guys, I'm pretty sure I shit my pants!"

"At least you were wearing pants!"

The chaos settles down as I start driving again. As terrifying and thrilling as that was, I can't get Liam's naked body out of my mind. Who knew all it would take was one stupid car game to have me leaning into the sliver of something I feel for him. Despite all my efforts to push him away, he keeps coming back. I think he's asked me out six times already, yet he won't give up.

My fear is that he's eventually going to wear me down. But I can't let that happen. I made a promise to myself that I would go to college single. In the weeks following my breakup with Alex, I did a lot of self-reflection. There are things I want to experience in college, and I don't need anyone holding me back. Plus, Liam and I aren't planning on going to the same college, and I really don't feel like doing long distance with a new boyfriend. It just wouldn't make any sense. That's not what I need, despite how good it feels to be desired by him. I just need to stay focused and have fun the rest of the year, then I'm free. As long as I don't give in to him, everything will be fine.

Everything will be fine, Evie.

Chapter Ten

LIAM

It's only Wednesday, but this week has been hell so far. Our teachers have been piling on the homework, and hockey practices have been brutal. Coach found out that some of the guys from the public school pulled a prank on one of their teachers, and he's been punishing the whole team for it. He's been making us do bag skates every day, and I don't see it stopping any time soon. I need something to look forward to this weekend. So I text the one person I want to see, the one person who always makes me happy when I'm around her.

LIAM

Want to hang out this weekend?

EVIE

Sorry, I can't. I have a volunteer thing.

LIAM

All weekend?

EVIE

Actually, yes.

LIAM

If you don't want to see my ugly mug, you can just say that.

EVIE

No, that's not it. I seriously have somewhere to be.

LIAM

Alright, I believe you. Can I come?

EVIE

Not sure it's really your thing.

LIAM

Was it Alex's thing?

EVIE

No, he would have hated it.

LIAM

Then I think I'll love it.

EVIE

You don't even know what it is yet.

LIAM

Doesn't matter. I'll be there if you'll be there.

What's the address? And when should I be there?

EVIE

Let me talk to my supervisor to see if there are any open spots left.

LIAM

What kind of volunteer gig turns down volunteers?

EVIE

The kind that is super organized and requires beds.

LIAM

Beds? Are we staying the night there?

EVIE

Yep!

My supervisor said she has a spot for you if you want it. Feel free to say no. It's a big commitment.

LIAM

I don't have practice this weekend, so I should be fine. Sign me up!

EVIE

Alright. But remember...I warned you.

THE ADDRESS EVIE gave me is for an old school in a neighboring town. The school got shut down a few years ago because enrollment was too low. Those kids were combined with a school in another town over. Apparently, they still make use of the building, which is a good idea given that there's nothing wrong with it. Hell, our small, private school is a bigger dump than this place.

I WALK through the front doors with my overnight bag and down the hallway until I find someone. "Excuse me, do you know where the kitchen is? I'm supposed to be meeting someone there."

"It's down this hallway and then to the left. Follow the smell of the chocolate chip cookies."

"Thanks."

I walk in the direction she pointed, and about halfway down the hall, I start to smell the cookies. I turn left, and I know I'm going the right way when I hear Evie's laugh echoing down the hallway. I go through a door labeled 'Staff Entrance' and find her wearing an apron covered in flour.

"Liam! You actually came!" She pulls the apron off over her head and sets it on the counter. She jogs over and gives me a hug.

"I said I was coming, didn't I?"

"Liam, I want you to meet the other staff members. This is Bonnie, Shirley, and Dan. Everyone, this is my classmate Liam. "

Everyone waves, and I say hello. Luckily, everyone is wearing name tags, so I don't have to memorize any names. "Do I get a name tag?"

"Of course. Guys, I'll be right back. I'm going to show Liam his bed and get him situated."

She seems so happy. I've always known she's bubbly and outgoing, but since Alex broke up with her, I haven't seen that sparkle. Here, wherever we are, she seems like herself again. I'm already glad I came, and I don't even know what I've gotten myself into. I see several adults milling about the hall-ways. Some are carrying boxes, others are hanging signs up on the classroom doors. "So what exactly is it we're doing here?"

"Welcome to camp!" She spreads her arms wide as if

pointing out that we're in a school is going to answer my questions.

"Camp?"

"This is Camp ReCreation. It's a fun getaway weekend camp for children and adults with developmental disabilities."

I feel my mouth fall open, and I slow my walking pace.

She stops abruptly and turns to face me. "Is that okay? Oh god, I knew I should have told you what you signed up for. It's totally okay if you're not comfortable. You don't have to work directly with the campers if you don't want to. There are plenty of other roles-"

"Evie, stop." I cover her mouth, that's moving a million miles an hour, with my hand. "I'm not sure what face you thought I made just there, but I'm not scared. I just didn't know something like this existed." I lower my hand, her mouth still hangs open, stuck mid-sentence. "I think it's really cool." She gives me a skeptical look, her body rigid. "I promise, I'm actually excited."

"Really?"

"Yeah."

"Okay. If you change your mind or you get overwhelmed, promise me you'll let me know?"

"I promise."

She shows me the classroom where the male volunteers are sleeping. There are several cots spread out across the room. Evie picks out one for me that's near the heater because she said it can get a little chilly at night.

"How many times have you done this?"

She shrugs as she pulls the sheet over the corner of my cot. "I honestly don't know. I lost track. But my first time was about three years ago."

"I didn't know you did this."

"I don't really talk about it much at school."

"Why?"

She looks at me with sad eyes, then she looks around the room to make sure no one can hear. "Honestly. I kind of like having this place to myself. I didn't want all the girls who were looking to boost their college resumes to volunteer for the wrong reasons. The people who work here do it because they love it, and that's what makes it so special."

"I think that's a perfectly sound reason." I help her finish making the cot and throw my bag on top. "Wait. So why invite *me* then if you wanted to keep this place for yourself?"

A smile grows on her face, stretching her lips wide. "I had a feeling you'd be really good at it. And I think some of the campers would really benefit from someone like you being here."

"Thanks, I hope I'm good at it." I pause, registering what she said. "What do you mean by '*someone like me?*'"

"We don't get a lot of male volunteers. There's a dispro-portionate number of male campers to male volunteers. And someone young, artistic, musically talented, and athletic like you...they're going to have so much fun with you."

"What's that look?"

"I hope you brought some comfortable shoes you can run in."

"I'm not sure what that means, but now I'm a little scared." She laughs and starts walking out of the room, and I follow. "I packed everything on the list you sent me. Do I really need a swimsuit in the middle of winter? It doesn't seem like there'd be a functioning pool here."

She only laughs harder and continues walking back toward the kitchen. I chase after her.

"Evie...why did I bring a swimsuit?"

"The campers will be here in an hour, so we'd better hurry up. Lots to do!"

"Evie..."

———

EVIE

I walk through the doors of the gymnasium and just about drop my tray of cookies on the floor when I spot Liam playing the piano with one of the campers. Or should I say, Liam is trying to teach her how to play the piano, and she's slamming on the keys. The sound makes my ears ring, but the smile on both of their faces makes the nails-on-a-chalkboard feeling melt away.

There are campers spread out all across the gym at the various stations we have set up. When I left here thirty minutes ago to bake more cookies, Liam was at the art table, finger painting. I can't decide what has my heart fluttering more, the finger painting or the piano lessons.

All of it is just confirmation that I made the right choice bringing him here. He is so good with the campers.

I meant it when I told him that I keep this place to myself. The campers here are so special to me, and I couldn't fathom the thought of someone coming here and having a bad attitude, spoiling even an ounce of fun for the campers. Working with adults and children with special needs is not for everyone, though I strongly believe that *everyone* could learn something from these campers. I know I've become a better version of myself since I started volunteering here.

Liam is always so patient and kind—qualities that I've always admired about him. Now seeing him thrive at a place I hold near and dear to my heart, everything makes sense. Liam is the type of guy I *should* want. The fact that I never brought Alex here was a red flag I let my love for him overshadow.

I walk over to the table of snacks and set my tray of cookies down next to the cups of milk. When I glance back up at Liam, he's looking at me with a huge grin on his face. The grin is quickly replaced with shock when the camper sitting on the piano bench with him grabs his head and starts peppering his cheek with kisses. Laughter erupts from deep inside me before I can stop it. I shouldn't be laughing at him getting assaulted like that, but those things happen around here, especially when you're a fan favorite like Liam quickly became.

I jog over there to rescue him, but by the time I get to them, he seems to have the situation under control.

"You two look like you're having fun here."

"We are," the camper nods vigorously as she continues to make heart eyes at Liam.

"Mind if I steal Liam from you for a second?"

She looks at me with a sour face, probably hoping I'll leave. When I don't move, she unwillingly concedes, "Okay."

"He'll be at the craft table next if you want to wait for him over there."

She bolts off the piano bench quicker than I thought possible and runs over to the craft table to claim a seat.

"Bet you didn't think you'd be getting that much action this weekend, did ya?"

He laughs as he uses his shirt to discreetly wipe his cheek. "From you, maybe, but not the campers."

I suck in a breath, taken aback by his comment. I've definitely thought about kissing Liam. In fact, several times I've come close to caving. But I haven't let myself go there.

"Can you teach me something?"

"Sure." He pats the seat next to him that's not vacant. "Have a seat."

I slide onto the bench next to him, our thighs pressing against each other. My skin tingles, and I try talking myself into pulling away, but I can't.

"What do you want to learn?"

———

LIAM

Out of all the things I guessed we'd be doing this weekend, getting water balloons thrown at me by grown adults with developmental disabilities was not one of them. I guess they do this outside in the summer, but during the winter months, the campers still beg for it, so someone got creative and suggested the pool. I was right that there isn't a functioning pool here, but I never imagined that we'd be playing water balloon dodgeball inside of an empty one.

The pool is shallow, only six feet deep throughout, but the pool deck surrounding us is blocked off for safety reasons. We all entered using a ladder, most of the campers needing assistance. The campers who aren't playing are watching from a safe distance on the pool deck, sectioned off with ropes and carefully watched by the volunteers. The inside of the pool is divided in half by an old pool lane divider, or whatever those things are called, to create the perfect water balloon dodgeball setup.

This round is campers versus buddies—that's what they call the volunteers. Sadly, we buddies are getting our asses kicked.

I didn't understand the purpose of the swimsuits until someone broke out a couple of hoses and started raining water down on us from the pool deck. It did add some drama to the whole thing, which was fun. Watching Evie run around in her little one-piece swimsuit and short shorts, soaking wet and throwing water balloons, is very distracting. She's so damn cute, especially when she's this happy.

Watching her with the campers this weekend has opened my eyes to just how kind and selfless Evie is. I knew she was before, but seeing how much these campers love her and how much she loves them back melts my heart. I'm learning so many new things about her. Like how when she's really hungry, and she finally gets food, her shoulders dance. It's so adorable, and she doesn't even notice she's doing it. Or how she never says no to anyone. If someone needs something done, all they have to do is ask Evie, and they can consider it crossed off their list. Regardless of how busy she is, she always gets it done. I made a note to be mindful of this in the future. Just because she says she can do everything doesn't mean it's not hard on her.

I'm so glad she invited me here, and I hope she asks me to come back. I've really bonded with some of the campers, and it makes me sad to think that I'd never get to see them again. One of Evie's favorite campers is named Bert. This morning, Evie made me play piano for everyone while they ate breakfast, and later Bert came up to me and asked if I wanted to hear him play an instrument. I enthusiastically told him yes, excited to see what he was going to show me. He then proceeded to plug one nostril with his thumb and flick the other nostril while making twangy banjo noises with his mouth. I tried so hard to not laugh. Luckily, it didn't last long, and I applauded as he took a bow.

I told Evie about it later, and she told me about a time

when he offered to play a song for her. That time, I guess he just started slapping his butt cheeks like a set of drums. Evie told me that he's trying to make people laugh and that it's okay that I cracked up at his nose song.

I stare at Evie as she throws a water balloon just to the left of a camper. I've seen this girl throw a ball in gym class; she was definitely trying to miss. Someone on the camper team takes advantage of my distraction and smacks me square in the jaw with a balloon. It explodes on my face, and I gasp, shocked by the cold water. When I turn to see who threw it, two other campers are pointing at Bert as he rolls on the ground laughing.

"Oh, you're gonna get it next round, Bert. You'd better watch your back." I wait till he looks at me before I point two fingers at my eyes, then shoot them back at him. He grins and responds to my gesture by twiddling his fingers under his chin.

Chapter Eleven

LIAM

The last time I was here, Evie's mom told me not to bother knocking anymore and to just come in when I get here. But that feels wrong, so I knock gently before opening the door.

"Evie?"

She comes bouncing around the corner dressed in sweatpants and a sweatshirt. We've gotten to the point in our friendship where we both stopped trying to impress each other, and honestly, it's refreshing. Plus, Evie is one of those girls who would look beautiful in a paper sack, so doing herself up for my sake is just a waste of time.

"Happy Birthday!" She walks up and wraps her arms around my neck, having to stand on her tiptoes to reach. Her same familiar smell is mixed with something new.

"Happy Birthday to you too." I kiss the top of her head, something I started doing recently. She hasn't put a stop to it, so I'm going to keep doing it until she tells me not to. "Did you get a new perfume?"

"Yeah, my mom got it for me as a birthday gift." She

sniffs her wrist, then puts it up to my nose to smell. "Do you like it?"

I inhale the floral scent. "Yeah, it's nice. Just different, I'll have to get used to it."

She lifts one brow and cocks her hip. "What? Do you have my smell memorized so you can track me easily?"

"Well, of course, that's what every professional stalker commits to memory first."

"I thought I saw someone outside my window last night." She narrows her eyes at me, but her smile stays in place.

"I can neither confirm nor deny my whereabouts at that hour."

She snorts and starts leading the way to the basement, where we usually go to hang out. Evie has the coolest basement of any of my friends. Her dad is a successful business owner, and her mom is an engineer, so they're very "comfortable," as Evie likes to say.

Comfortable is not the word I would use to describe a family of three who live in a two-story house with a movie theater in the basement and also own a second home on a lake. As much as Evie likes to call it a lake cabin, I've seen pictures, and it is definitely a *house* that happens to be on a lake. Most people would kill for that to be their only home.

I didn't actually know how rich Evie's family was until we started hanging out. Of course, I knew they had money, but pretty much everyone at our private school does, so that wasn't a shock. But Evie doesn't go around bragging about her multiple homes and all their amenities like some kids do, so I never knew she was *rich, rich.*

Being Evie's friend definitely comes with perks. I'd be lying if I said I wasn't excited to get invited to her cabin this summer, if everything goes as planned. I wouldn't dare say that to her, though. I know she's sensitive about her wealth and thinks friends in the past just used her for the entertainment she could offer them.

That's not why I hang out with Evie. No, this girl has me wrapped around her damn finger, and we haven't even kissed yet. Something about her just sucks me in, and I can't let her go, no matter how many times she rejects me. I'm addicted to her. I know we would be great together as a couple, I'm just waiting for her to see it too. But until she comes to her senses, I'll be here, waiting.

As we make ourselves comfy on the couch in front of the screen, I ask, "What movie do you want to watch tonight?"

She hands me the remote. "It's your birthday, you choose."

I hand it right back to her. "It's *your* birthday too, so you also get a say."

She looks at me with her fake annoyed face. "Technically, my birthday is next week. Yours is today, so you pick." The remote somehow makes it back into my lap.

"Bu—"

She puts her finger up to my lips. "No! No arguing with me. It's my birthday next week, so you have to be nice to me."

My lips spread into a smile, her finger still pressed against them. Then I open my mouth and bite the tip of her finger. She squeals and pulls her finger out of the loose hold my teeth had on it.

I laugh as she sucks on her finger, as if it actually hurts. "You're stubborn. You know that, right?"

"I like to think of it as me knowing what I want and making sure everyone else knows it too."

"*Do* you know what you want, though?" I tease.

"Oh, you just shush and pick a movie!" She playfully punches me in the arm.

"You know it's not nice to beat people up on their birthday," I say as I rub the spot where she hit me.

She leans over and lifts up the short sleeve of my shirt and gently kisses it. The feel of her lips on my skin starts a fire that spreads down my arm.

"All better."

She pushes me down so I'm lying flat on the couch and wiggles her way between me and the back cushion. I lift my arm up and around her, pulling her into my side, and she snuggles right in. This is what we do now. We hang out, watch movies, and cuddle. You know, typical things that "friends" do.

I've been busy the past couple of months with hockey, so we haven't been spending as much time together as we did at the beginning of the year. But every second of free time we have is spent together, whether we're studying, hanging out, or watching a movie. Evie has also come to all of my home games so far. I definitely play better when she's in the stands, wearing my jersey.

I click through the options and finally decide on a romantic comedy. They're not my favorite, but I know Evie loves them. And when Evie's happy, I'm happy. Plus, she gets a little extra cuddly when we watch them.

I tried picking a scary movie one time, hoping she would bury her face into me the whole time, but that backfired. She got so scared she jumped at every little sound, and later that night, I had to stay on the phone with her until she fell asleep. Needless to say, I haven't picked one since.

The movie plays, and we lie there, tangled up in each other. A steamy scene plays where the main characters finally hook up after an hour of building sexual tension.

I can feel a shift in the way Evie's touching me. Her hand, that's splayed out on my chest, slowly curls up into a fist, her nails lightly scratching across my shirt. She's more tense than usual. I watch her instead of the show for the next couple of minutes. For the first time in a while, I'm anxious around Evie.

"Hey, is everything okay?"

Her head pops up, her eyes misty. I didn't notice her phone in her hand, tucked into her chest, until now. Her messages are open, but I look at her face instead, not wanting to be nosy.

"Evie, what's wrong?"

She sits up. My body takes up most of the couch, so she straddles my thighs. I lift up onto my elbows so I can see her better.

"Seriously, Evie, you're starting to worry me."

"It's nothing." She shakes her head and tucks her phone into the pocket of her sweatshirt.

I sit up further. Since I'm not super flexible, I have to bend my knees to sit all the way up. The bending of my legs slides her off my thighs, so she's now straddling my waist. Her chest is inches from mine, her forehead just about resting on my shoulder. I lift her chin with my knuckle until we're eye to eye.

"Talk to me. Please."

Her blinks release a few tears she was trying to hold back. I wipe them with my thumb, waiting for her to respond.

"It's Alex."

Well, that's definitely not what I wanted to hear. "What about Alex?"

"You know how I've been texting him recently, asking him to talk?"

"Mmhmmm. Even though I told you it was a bad idea."

She can't even look at me right now. "Well, he finally texted me back."

I don't even know what the douche said yet, and I'm already seeing red. Whatever he said hurt her, and that makes me want to hurt *him*.

"He agreed to talk."

"Okay...I thought that's what you wanted. Why is it making you upset?"

"He's being really stubborn."

I keep my mouth shut, not wanting to say anything I'll regret.

"He said if I want to talk, it has to happen tonight."

"That motherfucker." I didn't mean to say it out loud, but it slipped.

She bursts into tears, and I immediately regret my lack of self-control. I wrap my arms around her and hold her close. She goes full koala, wrapping both her arms and legs around me.

———

EVIE

"I'm so sorry."

He responds by rubbing his hand up and down my back. I know he doesn't want me to go, but he's not the type to stop me from doing something I've been waiting on for months.

I know it's selfish to abandon Liam for Alex, especially on his birthday, but I need closure. It's been eating me inside, not knowing what went wrong. I can't get over it until he talks to me. The silent treatment he's been giving me for the past four months has been nothing shy of torture.

To be so close to him in all of our shared classes and not talk has killed me. I still cry myself to sleep at least three nights a week, usually with Liam on the other end of the phone calming me down.

I've always been a people pleaser. It's the only child in me, for sure. I learned that in therapy. I realized that growing up, if I got in a fight with a friend, they could just choose not to invite me over anymore, leaving me lonely at home by myself. This forced me to become accommodating, avoiding conflict at all costs. I can't stand it if I think someone is upset with me. I will literally do everything in my power to resolve the problem.

Things with Alex are no different. If anything, it's worse. To have someone who knew the most deep and intimate parts of me be able to drop me out of the blue doesn't compute in my brain. He broke something in me that day. And I can't keep going on living like this, not knowing if he hates me and not knowing why. I can get over the fact that he doesn't want to love me anymore. But I can't get over the idea of him not even *liking* me.

I eventually collect myself and unwrap my limbs from around Liam.

"You're really sure you want to do this?"

I nod. "I'm sure. If I thought I could stomach turning him down, I would. But I just—"

"It's okay, you don't have to justify it to me."

"But I feel like I do," I say through my tears. "It's your birthday."

"I know. And so does he." I look at him with a question in my eyes. "You think Alex didn't choose today on purpose? You think that after four months of going out of his way to ghost you, he just so happened to change his mind tonight? He's dumb, Evie, but not *that* dumb."

Realization hits me. "Ohmygod...you're right. He must have overheard us talking about our weekend plans in class."

"Probably."

I let out a sigh of frustration that sounds more like a battle cry. "I hate him!" I slump over, resting my head back on Liam's shoulder.

"No, you don't. You still love him. Or else you wouldn't be doing this."

No. "No, I don't."

"Yes, you do." He embraces me again. "And that's okay, Evie. He was your first love, and he broke your heart. Most people in your shoes would crave closure. And I want you to have that. I think if we ever want things between us to work out, you need to do this."

"Thank you." I whisper it into the warm skin of his neck and seal in my words with a kiss.

"What time is he coming to pick you up?"

I sit up and unlock my phone. His last message taunts me.

ALEX

We both know you're going to say yes. I'll pick you up at 10.

"In a half hour."

"That should be enough time."

I look him in the eyes for the first time since this dreadful conversation started. "For what?"

He lifts me off his lap, and I swing my leg over him so I'm standing next to the couch. He gets up and grabs my hand, leading me toward the stairs.

"We're taking a quick trip to my house."

"Your house?"

"Mhmm. Unless you'd rather wait here for me."

"Actually, would that be okay? I need to wash the tears off my face and change."

He leans in and presses his lips to my forehead. "Put on something that will make him regret every decision he's made since October." With that said, he releases my hand and jogs up the stairs, leaving me to clean myself up.

———

Twenty minutes later, Liam walks down the stairs holding a large container.

"What is that?"

He sets the container outside the door before stepping into my room. He looks me up and down, eyes wide.

"Fuck, Evie. I said you should make him regret his choices, not kill the damn fool."

Despite the crippling anxiety I'm feeling, I laugh. "That good, huh?" I do a full spin for him, showing off the best revenge outfit I could put together in ten minutes. I went for my most exposing top that makes my tits look amazing and denim that hugs my ass just right. I rarely say this to myself, but I look hot.

"Uhhh, yeah. Maybe too good? Please don't let him fuck you. He's going to want to after getting a good look at you in that, but he doesn't deserve it."

"Ohmygod! I'm not going to fuck him!"

"Good."

I can tell he's mostly joking, but a part of him is afraid. I can see it in the way his smile doesn't quite reach his eyes. If I sit and think about it too long, I'll start to feel awful and potentially change my mind. I can't let my compassion for

Liam get in the way of what I need right now. He'll understand, at least he claims he does.

"What's in the hallway?"

"Is he almost here?"

I quickly check my phone even though I just finished reading the text five times before Liam walked in. "Yeah, he left Layne's house a little bit ago; he should be here in a few minutes."

Liam walks back out into the hallway and grabs what I see now is a cat carrier.

"Merlin?"

Liam chuckles to himself. "Yep."

Liam pulls the cat out of its carrier and holds him. I walk over and scratch the top of his head. I can't help but talk to him in a baby voice. "Hey buddy, I missed you. Last time I was over, you were hiding. Next time, come say hello, okay?"

Merlin is the first cat I've ever met that I actually liked. I wouldn't say I used to be afraid of cats, but they definitely didn't like me. Liam claims it's because they can sense my fear and hesitation. The first time I met Merlin, he hopped right up on my lap and curled up in a ball. It was love at first snuggle.

"I figured if Alex is determined to ruin our night, then we can ruin his right back."

I give Liam a questioning look, not following his logic.

"He's allergic to cats, right?"

My eyes go wide. "Liam! That's awful."

"I'm not saying you take him with you, I'm just saying it wouldn't be the worst idea to rub him all over your clothes. Make Alex's eyes itch a little, that's all."

"You are evil."

"But you kinda wanna do it, don't you?"

"Oh, I absolutely do."

Chapter Twelve

EVIE

Everything I've wanted to say to Alex over the last four months swirls through my head as I slide into his passenger seat and shut the door. A tornado of emotions is tearing its way through my body.

"So, you wanted to talk?" He puts the car in gear and starts driving down the block.

I take him in. He looks different. Not just his new haircut or new clothes, but his essence. There's something about him that isn't familiar, and it's an eerie feeling. It's jarring, going from having known someone so intimately, knowing every line on their face, the nuances in their expressions, and their hidden meanings, to not even recognizing that person.

"Alex, those are literally the first words you've said to me since you ended things back in October."

Silence.

"You even sent your mom to answer the door when I came with a box of your things."

More silence.

"Alex! We have four classes together every single day, and you can't even be bothered to say hi."

"Hi."

My blood is starting to boil. He never acted like this when we dated. I don't even know what to say. Everything I wanted to say to him deserves a response, an answer. If he's going to be closed off like this the entire time, then there's no point to this. Then I just ruined Liam's birthday for nothing.

"I hear you kissed a girl."

My body tenses, and I start fidgeting with my fingernails in my lap. "What are you talking about?"

"Layne said he saw you kissing a girl on Halloween."

So they do talk about me... Goddamn, Evie! Why is that what matters to you? "Why did you agree to talk to me tonight if you're just going to be an ass?"

"Because you won't shut up about it, and I just want it to stop."

"You want what to stop? Me caring about you? Me trying to salvage any sliver of friendship that might still be here?"

"There's no chance of us being friends, you know that."

"Alex, we were friends long before we were boyfriend and girlfriend. We've known each other since the first grade. There's so much history between us. How can you be okay throwing this all away without a second glance back? I just don't get it."

"I told you, Evie, it just wasn't what I wanted anymore."

"But *why* isn't it what you wanted anymore? What changed?"

"I did."

"Clearly."

He can't even look at me right now. For a moment, I

swear I see a flash of something familiar behind his eyes. I slow my heart rate down with my breathing before speaking again, this time quieter and calmer.

"It just happened so suddenly. Was there a slow progression that I missed? Was I not paying close enough attention to notice you drifting away from me?"

"Probably."

Probably? That's still not an answer! Does he know and won't tell me, or is he just that dense?

I hear something shift behind me, so I glance over my shoulder. All that's back there is his backpack and gym bag on the back seat. My attention gets drawn back to Alex when he sniffles. He does it again, but this time he rubs the back of his hand across the tip of his nose.

I purse my lips together to hide my smirk. Liam is going to die when I tell him it worked. Alex isn't deathly allergic to cats; his eyes and nose just get a little itchy. We're not that close, but the heat blowing through the vents must have kicked up enough of Merlin's dander to have an effect on him.

I hear a noise come from behind me again, and it sounds like a laugh. While Alex is distracted by his allergies, I peek behind me, but again, there's nothing. I take note of the position of his backpack, perched up on the cup holder that folds down from the backrest.

"Alex, can you please take me home?"

Without a response, he makes a U-turn and starts heading back toward my house.

Trying my best to hide my smile, I do something my mother definitely wouldn't approve of. "How's your little issue going?"

"What?"

I can tell by the way his right eye barely twitches that he knows exactly what I'm talking about.

―――

LIAM

Right after Evie left, I ran Merlin home, then quickly came back to her house to wait for her. She told me that it wouldn't take too long and that she wanted me to be here when she got back so she could spend the rest of my birthday evening with me. So here I am, sitting on the couch finishing the movie we started. Right now, it's the part of the movie where they show a sappy montage of the happy couple in love. It's Evie's favorite part of romantic comedies.

Off in the distance, I hear the front door open, then slam shut, followed by speedy footsteps racing down the stairs. I barely have time to sit up before she's pouncing on me. I slam back into the couch, now lying flat on my back with a beautiful girl on top of me.

"Whoa, hi. How did it go?"

I can't read her expression because her face is buried in my neck at the moment, but I think I feel her nod.

She sits herself up, and we're right where we left off, with Evie straddling me. Now that I can see her face, relief washes over me. She's not crying, and she doesn't seem upset. But wait. If she's not upset, then that means things went well. Was he nice to her? Did they get back together?

"Evie, wha―"

"Ohmygod, Liam, you won't believe what happened!"

"He died from anaphylactic shock?"

She rolls her eyes. "No."

She readjusts her legs, causing her to grind her hips into me. I press my hips back into the couch, but it's useless.

"First off, Alex was a complete dick the entire time. Like completely shut off, didn't give me a single reasonable response, and guess what!"

"What?"

"At one point, I swore I heard a laugh come from the back seat. But no one was back there. I checked several times. So I thought that maybe he had a phone back there that was on speaker so his dumb ass friends could listen in on our conversation."

"Was there?"

"No. Worse."

"Worse than his friends listening in? That's pretty fucked up."

"Well, it was worse than having a phone back there."

I look at her, questioning.

"His friends were in the mother-fucking *trunk*."

"Huh?"

"They were hiding in the trunk and listening through the peephole."

"Peep hole?"

"Keep up." She playfully smacks my chest. "You know, the little opening that older cars sometimes have, where you can pull down the cup holders from the middle seat, and behind it, there's a little access hole you can open that leads to the trunk?"

"Yeah, yeah." I nod. "How did you know for sure they were back there?"

"It started with Alex acting strange. I could tell he wasn't himself. I know to you it looks like he's been that way for a while now, but I know Alex. If we were alone, I'd like to think that he would have been slightly reasonable."

Of course she's still giving him the benefit of the doubt.

"Anyway, I was really suspicious when I started hearing

laughter. Then, one of the times I looked back, he turned a corner, and his backpack that was blocking the opening to the trunk shifted. I could see that it was open. I didn't see people through it, but after that, I heard someone curse, and then I saw a not-so-sneaky hand reach out and readjust the backpack to block the hole again."

"You've got to be fucking kidding me."

"I wish I were."

"So what did you say? Did you call them out?"

"God no. You know I'm not that confrontational."

I give her a look. A look that questions her statement, since we both know that I'm the victim of her confrontation all the time.

"It's different with you. With normal people, I hate confrontation, and you know it."

"I know, I'm just teasing." I give her thighs a light squeeze. "But seriously, you had to have done something. You ran in here like a kid who found out they *actually* got a pony for Christmas."

"I didn't call them out. But I did start spilling all of Alex's secrets, faking genuine concern. He played each one off like he had no idea what I was talking about, but the laughs coming from the trunk started to get louder. So, regardless of whether they believe him or me, I know there's going to be some awkward conversations amongst that friend group over the next few days. And that is enough to make me feel like I *actually* got a pony for Christmas."

I can see the joy and amusement in her eyes. I was worried about her. As much as I didn't want to see her get hurt, I couldn't stop her. She's always wondered how that conversation would go. I hate the idea of her being deceived by people she thought were her friends, and I'm sure when the amusement settles, she'll feel it. She'll feel the betrayal and the pain of not getting answers. But for now, I'm going to embrace this optimism that's oozing out of her and be here with her.

Her face sours slightly. "I'm sorry I ruined your birthday."

"You didn't ruin my birthday."

"But it would have been a lot better had Alex not interfered."

"It's possible." It definitely would have.

"I had an idea of how I could make it up to you." She splays her palms on my chest and runs them down my stomach. Her eyes never leave mine, but her touch is thorough. Mapping out every muscle, every line, by touch alone.

"Oh yeah?" There's a fire blazing in my core, heating my whole body. I'm sure my cheeks are red, but I don't care.

"Mhmm." She lowers her chest towards mine, bringing her lips close to my ear. "But I'm kind of scared."

My hands trail up her back and down her sides, resting on her hips. "Why are you scared?"

"I'm afraid to cross the line."

I turn and let my lips graze her cheek. A cheek I've kissed dozens of times by now, but never like this, never with so much promise behind it. "You know we've both been tiptoeing on that line for a while."

Her chest shakes with a laugh, likely from nerves. I'm nervous too. I have no idea where she's going with this, and she's the one driving the bus. Any ounce Evie gives me, I'll take. I can feel her heart beating through her chest, against mine.

"Evie..."

"Yeah?"

"I don't want you to do anything just because you feel bad about leaving."

She backs up enough so I can see her face hovering above mine. "I'm honestly not sure what the driving force is behind this decision, but I know I want to. There's no question about that."

I wrestle with the confession for a moment. She's being honest with me, which I appreciate. But do I really want her like this if it's triggered by something Alex did to her?

Her mouth parts, and she leans down, pressing her lips to mine. They're warm and soft, if a little hesitant. I move my lips against hers slowly, careful not to startle her. Weaving her fingers into my hair, she takes my head in her hands and deepens our kiss.

Fuck Alex and fuck what he did to Evie tonight. But if it led to this, to Evie finally giving into this physical chemistry she's been pretending doesn't exist, then so be it. We move so perfectly together, so in sync. Just like I knew we would. I know she and I are meant to be, even if she doesn't see it yet. The way we talk, the way we argue, the way we fit so perfectly together... She has to see it too. There's no way she doesn't.

Chapter Thirteen

EVIE

The room is filled with the clacking sound of keyboards as everyone types their essays, or at least pretends to write them. We're supposed to be writing about who we want to become when we go off to college. I finished mine yesterday, which allows me to dick around on the computer in class today, while everyone else works on finishing theirs up.

I always used to wonder why Mr. Johnson gave us designated class time to work on our assignments, rather than just assigning them as homework. Then one day, I went to the bathroom and overheard him flirting with the art teacher in the teacher's lounge. It all made a lot more sense after that. If he doesn't have to be present to teach us, then he can have more time to hit on her. I don't blame him, she's a 10/10 but *way* out of his league.

This old computer lab always smells like something's burning. It's probably these dinosaur computers working overtime to stay alive. You would think a private school would have enough money to buy us all laptops, but apparently, when your enrollment is only 200 kids, that's not in the budget. So here we are, stuck back in the early 2000s, working on outdated desktop computers in a dingy computer lab.

I check my email again, waiting to see if I heard anything from the colleges I applied to. In total, I applied to seven, but there are really only two that I'm debating between. The other five are just back-ups and reach schools, just for fun.

Nothing.

"Have you decided where you're going yet?" Liam slides into the chair next to me and wiggles the mouse to turn his computer on.

"Where were you?" Liam wasn't in class when it first started, and he wasn't in last period either.

"The dentist." He smiles at me as if his teeth are ever anything but perfect. Except for one tooth in the front that's slightly chipped, I believe from a hockey incident. He hates it, but I think it's cute. It makes him look unique, if the auburn hair and freckles didn't do that already.

"No, I haven't decided. I'm still debating between my top two, if I get in."

He chuckles. "Quit acting like there's a world in which you don't get in."

I shift my eyes over to him, keeping my head facing the computer.

"I'm serious. Stop stressing about it. You're the smartest person in our class."

With my eyes back on the screen in front of me, I reply, "A class of 50 people. I'm competing against kids who are at the top of their class at huge, prestigious high schools."

His hand is now on top of my hand that rests on the mouse. "You'll get in."

I stare down at our hands until he pulls his back. Liam

and I aren't as affectionate at school as we have been in private recently. In an attempt to uncomplicate things, I put hard lines in place, PDA at school being one of them. Liam likes to push those boundaries to get a rise out of me. But the genuine care I felt just there with his hand over mine made my body relax, and for a moment, the stress that was coursing through my body halted.

What the hell am I thinking? I shake my head and blink hard, removing those thoughts from my mind. Trying to shift to a more light-hearted tone, I open a tab on my computer and start typing.

"What are you doing now?"

I click a few links until I'm on the page I'm looking for. I open another tab and make a similar set of searches. "Trying to decide which school I'd want to go to if I did happen to get into both."

"And how are sports rosters supposed to help you with that decision?"

I select this year's men's basketball roster and start scrolling through the pictures. "I'm trying to see which school has hotter guys."

I can feel Liam's body tense next to me, and I can't help but giggle to myself.

"Can you grab my notebook out of my bag?"

He bends over and slowly pulls out my notebook, trying to play it cool. He sets it in front of me, and I grab a colorful pen out of my pencil pouch. "Thanks." I make two lists, one for each school, and start marking tallies under the first one as I continue to scroll. "What do we think of him?" I ask Liam, pointing to a guy on the screen. "Do we think he's worth a tally?"

I glance over at Liam's and catch the corner of his mouth slightly turned up.

"Something funny?" I ask.

He just smiles and shakes his head at me. "You're cruel, you know that?"

I widen my eyes and play dumb. "Whatever do you mean?"

His hand clamps down on my thigh, and I squeal, trying to pry it off. "I'm sorry, I'm sorry, I'm sorry," I rush out.

He releases me, but now I find myself leaning over into his chest. I sit up and look around to see if anyone is looking at us. A few eyes glance this way, but for the most part, people are fixated on their own screens, trying to finish up their essays or doing their own pointless scrolling. When my eyes meet Liam's, I realize that while I've been looking around, worrying about everyone else, he's been looking at me.

He looks at me with those hungry eyes that I've gotten to know well over the past few weeks. "What?"

"What are you doing after school?"

I narrow my eyes at him. "Nothing. Why?" I know why.

"I don't have hockey practice until seven. Do you wanna come over before?"

I take my time responding. I don't want him to think I'm too eager to be alone with him again. "Yeah, I could swing by. Can I bring my homework?"

He blinks, but his eyes stay closed a moment longer than normal. "Yeah. Bring your stupid homework." He's holding back a smile, and so am I. We both know the odds of us actually doing homework are slim. But I'm not going to let him win that easily.

———

LIAM

I'm sitting on my basement couch when I hear a gentle knock at the front door. I jump up to answer it, knowing no one else will. Iris is at the Blake sisters' house, Frank's still at work, and my mom... Well, she doesn't ever have a reason to be answering the door. No one comes to visit her. And she never bothers to check who we have over.

Ever since my dad died, my mom hasn't been the same. She's been a shell of herself. She used to be so involved in mine and Iris's lives. Now, she mostly keeps to herself. She doesn't ask about our friends or really anything about our lives outside of, "Are you passing your classes?" and "What time is your game?" I don't blame her, though. Losing my dad was the hardest thing our family has ever been through. And Mom took it the hardest of us all. My mom and dad were best friends; they did everything together. Of course she wouldn't be the same person without him.

If she hears me answering the door, she'll probably just assume it's one of the hockey guys, and I'm perfectly fine with her thinking that. She's met Evie in passing, and she doesn't have a problem with her being over here. But the one time my mom asked about us, she was confused that we're just friends, and I'm tired of trying to explain it. Especially when I don't understand it myself.

I answer the door and see a smiling Evie. God, I love her smile. "Hey, you."

I eye her backpack that's slung over one shoulder. She catches my glance, and her smile turns into a devilish grin. "Ready to get some homework done?"

My eyes involuntarily roll. "Get in here." I grab the smooth fabric of her puffy, winter coat and pull her inside.

I shut the door behind her and lock it. When I turn around, she's already kicked off her boots and is headed down the stairs. I follow her and watch as she slings her backpack onto the floor near the couch and starts to unzip her coat. I walk up behind her and grab the shoulders of her jacket, pulling it down her arms. I toss the coat in the direction of the recliner, not bothering to check if it made it or if it fell to the ground. Right now, I can't take my eyes off of her as she gets snuggled in, sitting sideways with her feet up on the couch.

Ever since English class today, I haven't been able to get her out of my head. I wanted to smash that computer when she started scrolling through the men's team rosters, taking a tally of how many hot guys she saw. I know she was just doing that to get a rise out of me, and unfortunately, it worked. She knows where I want her to go to school. Of her top schools, one is six hours from where I plan to go, and the other is only three. I selfishly want her to be closer to me, but I'd drive 6 hours every weekend for her, if that's what she truly wanted.

She watches me as I walk past her and stand in front of my spot on the couch. I don't sit down just yet.

"What?" Her eyes narrow, questioning my odd behavior.

I put one knee on the couch, so I'm half-kneeling, half-standing. "Which school won?"

"Wha—"

"Which school had more hot guys on their sports rosters?"

She bites on her lower lip, trying not to let her mouth slip into the smile I know she's concealing.

"Evie...I'd like to know where I'm switching my enrollment to."

Her mouth drops open, shocked by my threat. "You wouldn't."

"No. I wouldn't," I say, showing my bluff. "You know I've had my heart set on the U of M since I was a kid." That's where my dad went. "But I do wanna know the results of your diligent research."

"Why are you standing there like that?" She completely ignores my question.

"So I can do this." Before she can even change her expression, I grab her by the ankles and yank them across the couch toward me.

She cries out, similarly to how she did earlier today when I was grabbing her thigh. Except this time, there's no pleading, no glancing around to see if anyone is watching us. No shame in enjoying the closeness. As I lean over her, she stares up at me with her lips parted, eyes eager. Her legs are spread, one on either side of me. I brace one hand by her head and the other takes one of her legs behind the knee and wraps it around my waist. Her other leg follows suit.

"Liam..." Her voice is nothing more than a whisper.

Before she can get out another word, I silence her with my mouth. My lips melt into hers, and she kisses me back. I lower my body for more contact, being careful not to put too much of my weight on her. I can feel her heart beating in her chest against mine as she runs her fingers through my hair.

I feel myself start to lose control, as I often do around Evie. My lips pull away from hers, and I stare down at her, brushing my knuckles across her flushed cheeks.

"What's wrong?" Her eyebrows scrunch together, and I hate the look on her face right now. "Did I do something wrong?"

I can't help but laugh a little, which leaves her with an even more confused look on her face. "No, Evie. You're perfect. I just..." I take a deep breath. "I need to slow down, or I'm not going to be able to stop."

Realization spreads across her face. "Oh." She bites her bottom lip and, damn, I want to bite it for her. "I'm sorry."

"You seriously don't need to apologize for *my* lack of self-control when I'm around you."

That makes her smile, which, in turn, makes me smile. I steal one more kiss before reluctantly sitting up. It's taking all my willpower not to pin her down and show her how her body deserves to be treated. Someday, Evie. Someday.

———

"I can't believe I never noticed this one!" Evie picks up a picture frame that's hidden behind a larger frame, exactly where I left it. She just came back from the bathroom and took it upon herself to browse through the collection of pictures on top of my mom's bookshelf. "You were such a cute baby." Her voice transitions to baby talk, making me laugh. "Oh my goodness. Look at little toddler Liam."

She holds the picture up to me, even though I could tell you the details of that picture with my eyes closed. It's me on my dad's shoulders at a Gopher hockey game when I was four. After my dad died, I used to sleep with it under my pillow until my mom found it. I was so embarrassed that I put it back and never wanted to look at it again. When we moved here, I was hoping it wouldn't make it back on the bookshelf, but it did. So I hid it behind the others, not wanting to have it staring at me every time I sit on this couch.

"Yeah, I was pretty adorable."

"But not as cute as Iris." She sets down the picture of my dad and me and picks up a different one of Iris. "These red curls are to die for! If my babies looked like this, I would leave permanent lip imprints on their cheeks from kissing them so damn much."

"I know a way you could increase your odds of having a little carrot top baby." My cheeks hurt as my smirk takes over my face. My cheeks always get sore from smiling when I spend time with Evie.

Her eyebrows lift. "Oh, you'd like that, wouldn't you?"

"I would."

She shakes her head and sets the picture back down, skimming across the others. "Did your dad have red hair?"

I shouldn't be taken aback by her comment, but I suddenly find myself staring at the back of her head, not answering, the amusement on my face now gone.

"He's wearing a hat in this picture, so I can't tell. Your mom has brown hair. Well, I guess she could dye—"

"Yeah, he did."

She turns around to face me. She must hear the change in my voice. "I'm sorry...I didn't mean to pry."

"It's okay." I blink, and a tear that I didn't even know was there runs down my cheek. I quickly wipe it away, but I know it's useless. She saw it.

She reacts in the most Evie way possible. She hurls herself across the space between us and lands on the cushion facing me in a kneeling position. "Liam..." She wipes away another tear that's falling.

I just sit here as she holds my face in her palms, gently stroking my cheeks. Her eyes are gentle and warm, calming me.

"You never talk about it. I should have known not to bring him up."

I place my hands over hers. "I miss him."

"I'm sure you do." She pulls me into her and kisses my

forehead. "And if you ever want to talk about him, I'm here to listen. Okay?"

I nod, and she releases my face. I've never had someone offer to let me talk about him. I've just been shoving down these feelings for years, trying to be strong for my mom and Iris. They needed me to step up and be there for them. I was only twelve, but I took on a role that was well beyond my years. There's never been anyone that I wanted to talk about all this with, not even my best friend, Bear. But with Evie, I feel different. She makes me feel vulnerable and...and cared for. It's a new feeling for me. One I didn't know I needed.

Another tear falls from my eye. But this time it's not from sadness over the loss of someone I love. It's from the relief I feel knowing there's finally someone in my life who makes *me* feel safe and not just the other way around.

Chapter Fourteen

EVIE

My body is shaking with excitement, or I guess it could be from spending two hours in a cold ice rink. Our boys' hockey team is going to state. Again! After losing some key seniors, we didn't think we'd win sectionals again this year. Last year, we made it all the way to the end and won the state championship. Who knows if we'll be able to do it again, but just getting there is exciting.

My car has been running for a while, outside the rink, as I wait for Liam. Before the game, we decided, win or lose, we were going to hang out. Now our hangout will be a celebration, which is always more fun than a pity party.

LIAM

Almost done. Be out soon.

EVIE

No rush! I'm in the back corner of the parking lot.

LIAM

Would you mind if we hung out with some of the guys?

EVIE

Of course!

I mean, of course they can come, not of course I mind. Because I don't mind.

LIAM

Cool. It'll just be Jax and Jace.

EVIE

Sounds good.

AFTER ATTENDING Liam's first game this season, I learned that the guy who was hitting on me at the Halloween party's name is Jaxon. Everyone on the team just calls him Jax. We've hung out a few times in groups with some of Jax's friends from the public school. They're nice, but I'm not sure I totally fit in with them.

After Jax found out that Liam was seriously pursuing me, he cut down on the flirting a little. I think he mostly does it to get a rise out of Liam, which I also find funny. Jax is a stellar defenseman who gets in a lot of fights, making him very entertaining to watch.

At the start of the season, I didn't know much about hockey, and I still don't. But Liam has slowly been teaching me. I could watch him skate all day. He just looks so happy out there. But not as happy as he looks when he's creating art. Sometimes I force Liam to play the piano for me, just so I can listen and watch him. There's something so serene about the way he plays. My house has a baby grand piano in the sitting room, so he'll play, and I'll lie on the sofa. I try my best not to fall asleep, but I usually do. And then I wake up with my head on Liam's lap. Usually, he's playing with my hair, which makes me melt.

Since our first kiss on Liam's birthday, things have been up and down. I go through phases where I can't get enough of him, but then something flips, and I remember that this isn't what I want. I'm always brutally honest with him about how I'm feeling as my moods change, whether he wants to hear it or not. After not getting any answers from Alex, I feel that it's very important Liam knows where I stand at all times.

He doesn't get why I won't just date him since that's how we act, and it's what everyone thinks anyway. I explain to him over and over again that I don't want a boyfriend before I go off to college. I need a clean slate, a fresh start. I was dating someone for most of high school, so I need a change.

At least that's the advice my parents are giving me. Don't get me wrong, they love Liam, but they worry that I'm going to get stuck in our small town bubble and I won't go out and experience the world. They said the same things when I was dating Alex, but we were so deep into our relationship that I think my parents had accepted that he was what I wanted for my future.

I told my mom about Liam asking me out shortly after my breakup with Alex, and she encouraged me to take my time. My parents are smart people who love me, and I trust them. So I'm going to stick to what my gut is telling me and go to college single.

I know I'm leading Liam on, but I can't stay away from him. We're like magnets. It just feels so good to be wanted again, and I crave the affection. I miss always having someone there to make me feel loved and support me when

I need it. At this point, he's my best friend. We've learned so much about each other and grown so close, I can't imagine my life without him. So as long as we can maintain the balance of friends who make out sometimes, everything will be fine.

But that's much easier said than done.

A knock on my window startles me out of my thoughts. There's an exchange between the guys outside my car, but I don't quite catch everything they're saying. Jace and Jax walk away, toward their cars, and Liam hops into my passenger seat.

"Are they not coming with us anymore?"

"They're meeting us there. Someone's throwing a party to celebrate, and most of the team is going. Is that okay if we go? We can just go for a bit and then hang out after if you don't want to be there."

"I don't mind at all! We have to celebrate, and if the team is getting together, I want you to be there. Congrats by the way! You played really well." I lean over the center console and give him a hug. His hair is wet from his shower, and I notice that it's dripping onto the collar of his suit jacket. "Do you wanna change before we go?"

"I packed some extra clothes in my bag for when we were going to hang out. If it's okay, we can just go to your place so you can change, and I'll get ready there."

"Works for me."

———

LIAM

The party is a lot more chill than I was expecting, which is a nice relief. After a couple of hours of screaming fans, pictures with the team and parents, I'm ready for some peace and quiet. And it appears that my teammates would agree.

Several of the guys brought their girlfriends, some of whom Evie had met and sat with at the games. Though she has made it very clear to everyone that she's not my girlfriend, they still talk about her like she is. On our drive over here, she even got added to a group chat of all the girlfriends. Apparently, they're planning some stuff for the state tournament that I'm not allowed to know about.

Though I love what she's wearing now, I was sad to see Evie change out of my jersey. Every time I catch a glimpse of her in the stands wearing it, I can't help but smile. I've learned not to look *during* the games the hard way. I was distracted by her for less than a second and got absolutely railed into the boards a few games ago, so now I just wave during warmups and then find her after.

I'm head over heels for this girl, but I'd be lying if I said she didn't drive me nuts at times. This cat-and-mouse game we're playing got old a while ago. And I can't figure out what she needs from me for her to commit. She says her heart is set on going to college single. But why go out and search for something that's already right in front of you? I don't get it, but I'm not giving up. I'm stubborn like that. When I know what I want, I won't let it go until I have it. Like when I was twelve, and I was set on memorizing Clair de Lune. I didn't leave my piano bench until I did it. I was there for six hours.

"Whatcha thinkin' about?"

I tap the tip of her nose with my finger. "You. Always you."

She shakes her head and rolls her eyes at me like she thinks I'm lying. She should know by now that she consumes my every thought, every spare second of my day.

Even surrounded by all these people, she holds all my attention. I'd give anything for that type of longing to be reciprocated.

"Liam! Evie! Come sit with us." Jax waves us over to the living room, where a smaller group is sitting around on the couch and chairs.

Evie follows me over there. All that's left for seating is a small chair next to the couch.

"You can sit in the chair." She grabs me by the shoulder and guides me into the chair. "I'll sit on the floor in front of you." She does just that. Situating herself between my legs, she leans back on the chair.

I lean forward, feeling bad that she's sitting on the ground. "You sure you don't want the chair. I don't mind sitting on the ground."

She turns around with the cutest sassy look on her face. "Don't be ridiculous. I'm not the one who played a hockey game tonight, so I'll be the one on the floor."

Jax must overhear us and decides to butt in. "Come on, Liam, you really gonna make your girlfriend sit on the floor?"

"For the thousandth time, I'm not his girlfriend," Evie snaps at Jax.

She's just teasing him, but the words sting. Everyone here is well aware that we're not dating, but having her verbally confirm it enhances the invisible divide between us.

"You guys are basically dating, though."

"No, we're not."

"Come on, you guys are clearly hooking up."

I step in, trying to end this ridiculous argument. "Jax, are you seriously that drunk already?"

"Maybe." He snorts and takes another sip of his beer.

Just as I start praying that Evie won't respond, she does. "Actually, we're not hooking up. Like I said, we're just friends."

While she's not entirely telling the truth, we haven't done anything more than make out since we first kissed on my birthday. But she clearly doesn't even want people to know about that.

"Damn! My bad. Guess I made a wrong assumption." Jax downs the rest of his drink, then cracks a fresh beer that's sitting on the end table next to him. "But you at least want to, right? I know Liam sure does. He can't keep his damn hands off you." Jax gestures to my hands that are lightly massaging Evie's shoulders.

"What does it matter to you anyway?" I can't tell if Evie is annoyed by Jax's prying or if she finds it amusing. I'm here on standby in case things really start to escalate, but I'm pretty sure Evie can handle Jax's teasing all on her own.

"I'm just looking out for my boy."

"Oh, is that what they call being nosy these days?"

The group around us laughs, and the tension that was starting to build in the room dissolves. Jax cracks a smile; his favorite people are those who can dish back the same level of sarcasm he serves. Usually, Evie is pleasant and accommodating, trying to make everyone like her. But right now, she's winning over Jax by not treating him like she treats everyone else. This girl can read people like no one I've ever met.

"Since I'm already prying, why don't we make things interesting?"

Evie and Jax stare each other down. My eyes dart back and forth between them, seeing who will crack first.

"I'm listening..." Evie crosses her arms over her chest and leans forward, resting her elbows on her knees. My hands slide off her shoulders when she moves, and I don't bother to replace them. I just sit back in my chair and watch, curious where this is going.

"You're obviously attracted to him. I mean, how could you not be? Just look at that face, those freckles."

"Get to the point."

"Wanna make a bet?"

"Depends what it's about and what the consequences are."

"Naturally." Jax sets his beer down and leans forward, mirroring Evie. "How many goals do you think you'll score at the state tournament, Liam?"

His directing a question at me takes me off guard. "Uhhh, I don't know."

"Just guess!"

"I'd like to score at least one per game; there are three games in the tournament. So...three?"

Jax looks to Evie, and I can tell something is definitely brewing behind those eyes. "If Liam scores at least one goal during the tournament, you have to finally kiss him."

No one knows that we've already kissed...a lot. It's moments like this where I'm glad they don't. Daring Evie to kiss me if I score a goal is harmless. Hell, at this point, I'd be shocked if she *didn't* kiss me after the tournament.

Jax continues before Evie can agree. "And if he scores two goals, you suck his dick."

The room collectively gasps.

"What the hell, Jax!" A blonde girl next to him smacks him on the back of the head, clearly appalled by his suggestion.

Jax throws his hands up in surrender, laughing. Clearly, not all that sorry about the dare he's setting up for Evie. "I'm just having a little fun. She can always say no."

"And if he makes that third goal?" This is the first time Evie has spoken since the initial mention of the dare.

The amusement on Jax's face increases tenfold. "I think you can guess that one."

"It seems like Liam here is the only one benefiting from this arrangement. What exactly do you get out of this?"

"I get a motivated forward who's going to do everything in his power to score as many goals as he can, increasing our chances of winning."

"And me, what do I get?"

"I like to play cupid, and I'm convinced that if you give this poor fool a chance, you may actually like it. This is your chance to test out your attraction under the guise that it's all part of a dare."

Evie contemplates her position. I can't believe she's even entertaining this. Does she want this as much as I do?

She looks over her shoulder at me. "What do you think, Liam? Should we entertain this asshole's dare or tell him to stick it where the sun don't shine?"

I look down at her, completely enamored. "Are you serious?"

"Depends. How good are you?"

"At...?"

"Hockey, Liam. How good are you at hockey? What are the odds of you scoring three goals during the tournament?"

"Last year, I only scored one goal the whole tournament."

Evie shrugs. "That's not so bad. I'd reward you with a kiss for scoring a goal." She winks at me and fights back a smile.

I lean down and lower my voice to a breathy whisper. "You don't have to do this, Evie."

She looks me in the eye for a moment, a silent conversation happening between us. It's a conversation of trust. She trusts me. Turning to Jax and narrowing her eyes at him, she says, "You're on. But only because I want the team to win, and I think a little carrot at the end of a stick couldn't hurt."

I swallow, loudly, trying to choke down the whimper that was about to come out of my mouth. The reason I didn't score more than one goal last year was because our senior lineup was stacked, so I didn't get as much playing time as I do now. I've been averaging one goal a game for over half the season now. Is it cruel of me to have left out that bit of information? I mean, she should know, right? She's been to all of our home games, where I've almost always scored a goal.

Though the thought of her following through with this bet has me salivating, I can't let her do it if I score more than one goal. I'm not about to push her boundaries and scare her away just because Jax can't mind his own damn business. But damn if I don't want to.

Chapter Fifteen

EVIE

The floor of the bus rattles beneath my feet, and the familiar scent of burning diesel reminds me of when I used to ride the bus in elementary school. Around me, students are talking and cheering, the whole bus buzzing with excitement.

The school organized buses to drive students to St. Paul for the boys' state hockey tournament so that students whose parents wouldn't take them could still go cheer on the team. My parents offered to drive me and get a hotel room since they know I'm planning to go to all of Liam's games, but I told them I'd rather take the bus with my friends.

That was a lie. My only friend is already in the Twin Cities with his team, getting ready to play. I couldn't stand the thought of showing up at the game with my parents. I'd rather just blend in with the crowd of students and meet up with the public school girls who are staying at a hotel together near the rink. They mentioned their plans to me, but since no one explicitly invited me to stay with them, I didn't ask.

"Is anyone sitting here?"

I look up and see my classmate, Louisa Blake. "Ummm, no. Go for it." I gesture to the empty seat next to me, and she sits down.

Louisa and I have known each other since the first grade, but have never been super close friends. We're involved in different extracurriculars, and our friend groups are very separate–*were* very separate. We get along fine, there's no beef between us, we've just never given it an honest chance.

She's been extra nice to me in the one class we have together this semester. I think she can tell I get lonely watching all my former friends giggle together on the opposite side of the room. For the first couple of years after Liam moved here, I thought he and Louisa might have been together. But he's since told me that they mostly spend time together because their little sisters, Iris and B, are best friends and that they've never had an interest in each other.

"Were you at the game yesterday?"

I pull out my AirPods because I guess we're making small talk now. "I was. Were you?"

"No, I had some stuff to do after school, so I couldn't make it on the bus. But I heard it was a good game."

"Yeah, it was pretty exciting."

Yesterday's game was really fun to watch. I stood with all the girlfriends of the other players in the student section and cheered my heart out. Liam didn't score a goal, but he had two assists, and they still won. After the game, I waited around for as long as I could, but the bus taking students back home was leaving, so I didn't get to see him afterward.

I was bummed I didn't get to give him a hug and talk to him about the game, but after I got home, he FaceTimed me from the hotel lobby. We talked way too late. I told him he needed to rest for today, but he brushed me off and kept chatting. I'm hoping to see him after today's game, but I'm not getting my hopes up.

Lou is a lot quieter than I am, so I feel pressure to be the one keeping the conversation going. "Do you know if they're supposed to win this game?"

She raises her eyebrows at me. "I was going to ask you the same thing. Don't you have the inside source for that information?"

I rub the back of my neck, uncomfortable with the idea that Lou thinks Liam and I are that close. Even though I guess we are. "I didn't want to ask and make him nervous if the other team is supposed to be better."

"What's the deal with you and Liam anyway? Are you dating?"

"We're just friends."

"You guys just started getting close, though, right? I don't remember seeing you hang out much prior to this year."

"We've always been friendly, but we're definitely a lot closer now."

"He's a really great guy." She pauses like she wants to say something else, but she doesn't.

"Yeah, he's been a great friend." Emphasis on the word friend. I pick the chipped nail polish off my fingernails in my lap. I glance around to see if I can spot any of Lou's friends. Not seeing any of them, I dare to ask, "Where's B?" I know the two of them are close, so it's strange that they wouldn't be going to the game together.

"She drove up with Iris and Liam's parents yesterday

and is staying at their hotel with them for the whole weekend."

Of course she is. I should have thought of that. I don't know Liam's mom and stepdad very well, even though I've been over to his house several times. His stepdad is always busy with work or his hobbies, and his mom usually keeps to her room. In a drunken state, Liam once told me that his mom got really depressed after his dad passed and hasn't been the same since. He said that she doesn't come to his games all the time. If she's having a bad day, she sometimes stays home. He also told me that night that the reason he loves me is because I make him feel special and cared for, which I guess he doesn't feel an abundance of in his daily life.

Liam has told me he loves me several times, and I've said it back. But the thing is, neither of us is quite sure how the other one means it on any given day. I used to tell my friends I loved them all the time. My family is very affectionate. I didn't think much of it the first time I texted, "love ya," to Liam. Then he started saying it back. Eventually, it evolved into "love you," which then turned into "I love you." Sometimes when he says it to me, it feels friendly and comforting. Other times it holds the weight of what he truly means- that he's *in* love with me.

But I'm not in love with him.

———

"I cannot believe how close that was. God, is it worse to lose by a hair or a landslide? One way you feel like it was almost a fluke that you didn't win, which is infuriating. The other is straight up embarrassing."

Lou looks at her younger sister with narrowed eyes. "I think they'd prefer neither."

"Obviously," B says with an eye roll.

Listening to Lou and B talk has been entertaining, but all I can think about is how much I want to see Liam and give him a hug. I'm sure he's really bummed right now after the loss, and I feel this deep need to comfort him. Liam scored a goal in this game, which was incredibly exciting. The whole game was actually very exciting, until the end, when the buzzer went off, and the final score was two to three.

After the game ended, we said goodbye to the girls from the public school that we were sitting with after declining their offer to join them for dinner downtown. Instead, Lou and I head to find B and Iris before we get back on the bus to head home. Now, we're standing in the part of the concourse, chatting about the game. I was expecting the girls to be with Liam's mom and stepdad, but they're not here. It makes me wonder if they were here for the whole game or if Liam's mom had to leave early. Either way, I'm sad for him that they're not here to talk to him after such a tough loss.

But at least his sister is here. Iris has always been friendly when I go over to their house, and today is no different. She greeted me with a hug and complimented my outfit about ten times. She is such a sweetheart, and I just know that if we were closer in age, we'd be good friends.

"Alright, the bus is leaving soon, so we have to get out there." Lou hugs B, who pretends she doesn't want it, and then we make our way toward the buses.

We talked with the girls a little longer than expected, so we only have five minutes to make it to the other side of the arena. We speed walk in silence through the concourse, only talking to confirm which way we need to walk to get to the buses. This place is a maze.

Once we make it onto the bus, we settle into our seats for the long bus ride ahead of us.

The energy on the bus is somber, our dreams of being back-to-back state champions crushed less than an hour ago.

"Has he texted you yet?"

I check my phone to see if there's a text from Liam. "Not yet."

I texted Liam immediately after the game ended, letting him know that he did such an amazing job and trying my best to be consoling. I know all too well the pain of losing a game you should have won. This fall, my volleyball team was supposed to make it to the state tournament, but we choked during the last game that mattered. It was devastating, but Liam was there to support me after, so I'll try to do the same for him. At least he has one more game, one more chance to end his hockey career on a win. And one more chance to score two more goals.

There's been whispering about Jax's bet amongst those who were there that night, but otherwise, no one has bugged me about it. After Liam scored his goal tonight, a few of the girlfriends gave me a look. Little do they know, Liam and I have already kissed, so scoring his first goal didn't faze me. But I at least had to pretend like I was affected by it so they wouldn't suspect anything.

I honestly don't know what I'll do if he scores another goal tomorrow. Of course I've thought about it. I've gone through the pros and cons list in my head. The odds of him scoring two goals next game are low, so sex is more than likely off the table. Thank god. But I've felt Liam hard under his pants several times while making out with him, and I'd be lying if I said I wasn't curious.

Jax was right when he said having an excuse to go further with Liam would make it easier for me to try, but I'm afraid it will just complicate things further. I'm having a hard enough time convincing Liam that I'm serious when I tell him we're not going to date. I think in his mind, he just needs to wear me down or give me time, and then I'll eventually realize we're meant to be together. But I just don't see it like that, and I'm nervous about how disappointed he'll be when he realizes I'm not going to change my mind about this, no matter how much I feel like I need him right now. I need to go to college single. I need to explore myself and figure out what kind of person I want to be with. And I can't do that until I know myself better.

I frantically pick up my phone when I feel it vibrate on my lap.

LIAM

Thanks for coming to the game.

Sorry we lost.

EVIE

How are you doing?

Are you guys on the bus yet?

LIAM

Just packing up the locker room.

I'm bummed, but the other team played really well and earned the win.

EVIE

Wow, how are you saying nice things about them right now?

> When we lost in sectionals, I wanted to burn the other team's bus.

LIAM

That's very out of character for you.

Sports aren't everything. Obviously, I'm pissed we lost, but hockey was going to come to an end tomorrow regardless. I just want to enjoy the last 24 hours with my team and hopefully end on a win.

EVIE

> And maybe score another goal?

LIAM

Exactly ;)

When do I get to cash in my goal for a kiss?

EVIE

> Tomorrow?

> After the game?

LIAM

Won't you be heading back on the bus?

EVIE

> I convinced my parents to drive me tomorrow, so I can stay after and see you.

> If that's okay...

> I just hate not getting to see you after because of the stupid bus schedule.

LIAM

I'd love that.

A lot of the guys are out there with their families and friends now.

EVIE

Are you going to see your family?

I saw Iris briefly after the game. She gave me a hug lol.

LIAM

They left already.

EVIE

What? They didn't stay to say hi?

LIAM

I guess my mom was having lots of anxiety being in such a big crowd, so she and Frank left early.

EVIE

I'm sorry, that stinks.

Now I really wish I were there to give you a hug.

LIAM

It's really not a big deal.

I'm used to it by now.

EVIE

Well, I'll be there tomorrow with a big hug for you.

I've kinda missed you. It's strange not seeing you every day.

LIAM

I know what you mean.

I've missed you, too.

EVIE

Get some rest, I'll see you tomorrow.

Good luck!

LIAM

Thanks again for coming.

EVIE

Of course!

Goodnight. Love ya

LIAM

Love you too.

"How's the team doing?"

I put my phone in my jacket pocket and twist in my seat so I'm facing Lou. "Bummed of course. But Liam is weirdly doing okay."

"Well, duh, he finally gets to kiss you."

I stare at her, my face blank but my heart racing. "What do you mean?"

"Come on, Evie, everyone knows about the bet."

I'm sure I look like an idiot right now, unable to wipe the shock and embarrassment off my face. "Everyone?"

She shrugs. "Mostly everyone, I guess." A cheeky grin spreads across her face. "Are you really going to do more than kiss him if he scores more goals tomorrow?"

"Definitely not! That whole thing was a joke. I'm probably not even going to kiss him." Why am I lying? I don't know. It's just that the idea of our whole class knowing about the bet has my stomach in knots.

"Whatever you say." The grin on her face tells me she isn't buying my bullshit.

I try to deflect the conversation away from Liam, not wanting to answer any more questions about that stupid bet that I'm now seriously regretting. It was fine when I thought that the only people who knew were the few people in the living room at the party. But knowing that people are talking about it, knowing it's spreading like wildfire, makes me want to curl up in a ball and roll myself under this seat, never to be found.

I cannot be talking about this right now. Or ever. "Speaking of tomorrow's game, are you planning to take the bus again?"

She narrows her eyes at me, clearly disappointed that I'm changing the subject. "Yeah, that's the plan."

"Would you want to ride with me and my parents? I convinced them to drive me."

Her face lights up, and with no hesitation, she says, "I'd love to."

An anxious weight I didn't even know I was carrying lifts off my shoulders. I think I was expecting her to make some excuse as to why she couldn't ride with me, or at least say she'll think about it. It's been a while since someone other than Liam was that enthusiastic about spending time with me.

As we continue back into casual conversation, I feel a small piece of my tattered heart stitch back together. I don't expect Lou and me to become instant best friends or to even continue talking after we graduate and go to different colleges, but I'm flooded with joy knowing that someone enjoys my company and wants to spend time with me.

It makes me question if I actually like Liam or if I've just been so starved of friendship for so long that I clung to the first person who offered. Add another layer of conflicting emotions piled on top, and I feel like this thousand-layer cake that is my life is about to topple over.

I shake those feelings away. I can't think about this now. I need to be there for Liam tomorrow, regardless of how I feel. At the end of the day, he is my friend, and a damn good one at that. He deserves my full support.

————

LIAM

The arena is filled with cheering fans. Parents, friends, family. Everyone is here to support us and the opposing team. Getting to play on a rink like this last year was a dream come true. Having the opportunity to be back here is a gift that not many small teams like ours get.

At least that's what I keep telling everyone and myself, trying to sound convincing that losing yesterday wasn't one of the most devastating losses of my hockey career. And tonight, it all comes to an end, regardless of whether we win or lose. I at least want to come out of here with a third-place trophy, and if I scored another goal or two, I definitely wouldn't be mad.

During warmups, I scanned the student section for Evie and found her sitting next to Lou. I saw the same thing yesterday and had to do a double-take. Lou and Evie take up space in very different parts of my world that have never intersected before. It makes me happy to see them together. It also makes me wonder why I never thought to have them hang out before.

Knowing Evie is here makes me play better. Knowing that someone in that crowd wants nothing but the best for me and is here to support me no matter what is all I've wanted for years. My dad used to be that support for me. And my mom, too, before she changed. I tell her it's fine and that I completely understand when her mental health gets in the way of her showing up for me, which I do, but it still sucks not knowing if they're here watching me. With Evie here, some of that disappointment fades away.

————

THE GUYS ARE on fire tonight. Our shift changes have been in sync, our passes crisp and actually hitting their intended targets, unlike yesterday. It feels good, it feels right. I'm trying to stay focused and not get ahead of myself, but I can't help but feel like we're going to win this.

There are three minutes left in the third period, and we're up two to one. If they score in the final minutes, we go into overtime. But I'm going to do everything in my power to prevent that from happening. As thrilling as a win in overtime would be, I'm not willing to risk a loss. We need to control the ice. No mistakes.

I hear Coach whistling from the bench, indicating a shift change, so I wait for my teammates to secure the puck down by the other team's goal before skating over to the bench. I skate up to the boards and step off the ice.

The time spent on the bench is necessary for recovery, but agonizing knowing there's nothing I can do from here to help my team. I watch as another shift change takes place and wait until it's my turn to get back out there.

With a minute left, the right winger and I climb over the boards and skate out. This is it. I'm not letting this go into overtime. This is the final minute of my hockey career. That thought alone has me choking up. But I need a clear head, so I sweep away those emotions.

After a few passes up and down the ice, trying to stop the other team from scoring, I manage to get the puck with nothing but open ice between the other team's goalie and me. I take it up the left side, crossing over to center, carefully handling the puck. I check over my right shoulder to see if anyone is on my tail, but it's clear.

I already used my favorite move on this goalie in the first period, when I scored the first goal of the game, so I decide to switch it up. The puck goes flying off the blade of my stick and right into the upper left corner of the net. The cherry goes off, and seconds later, I feel my teammates slamming into my back, throwing me down to the ice.

All I hear is screaming and loud hype music playing. All I see is our team colors flashing in front of my helmet's cage as my teammates fall around me.

We did it. There's no way they're coming back from a two-point deficit in under 30 seconds. We won!

Even as my teammates unstack themselves and get in position for the face-off, I can't wipe the smile off my face. The music quiets and the fans settle down. For a moment before the ref drops the puck, I swear I can hear chanting coming from the other side of the plexiglass behind me. A quick recall reminds me that's where the student section is. They must be freaking out right now. At least, selfishly, I hope they are.

Usually, I tune out the crowd, but I'm too excited, so I listen to their chants and cheers. The puck drops, and I pause for a moment.

Wait.

Are they chanting...?

———

EVIE

My ears are turning red, and not from the cold temperature in the arena. One second, I'm cheering my heart out, so excited for Liam that he scored another goal. The next, I'm burying my face in my hands, praying to the universe to strike me dead, right then and there.

I try my best to block out their cheers, but it's too loud, too many people joining in.

"Evie! Evie! Evie!"

The last 30 seconds of the game feel like they last an hour. The whole time, I fight to hold down the concessions I had during the game. I just want it to be over so I can get out of this student section and go home.

———

LIAM

"Come on, Liam, the bus is leaving."

"Coming..."

I pick up the handle of my gear bag and start wheeling it toward the exit. When I checked my phone after the game, I was greeted by a singular text from Evie.

EVIE

Great game! I'm so proud of you!

I texted her back, letting her know when I was done showering and heading out to meet her. She never replied. I've been waiting here for 30 minutes, watching my team-mates talk with their families all around me. I looked everywhere for her, but she's not here.

Chapter Sixteen

LIAM

Evie's been so busy avoiding me that I don't even think she realizes I've been ignoring *her*.

I'm still hurt about her leaving after the game and not waiting around to see me like she promised. It's been three days, and she has yet to apologize. And for some reason unknown to me, she's been avoiding me. She won't answer my texts, which I stopped sending after the second day, and she hasn't been talking to me in class like she used to.

I think I know why. The first day back at school was rough for her. Everyone was talking about the game, which ended with me scoring my third goal of the tournament and everyone chanting her name. I don't know how word got out about the stupid bet, but I'm going to kill whoever spread it. She was really upset by everyone asking her for updates on the bet, even though we both knew nothing came of it.

Today, the gossip has died down a bit, given its fruitless efforts. So I'm hoping by tomorrow she'll be ready to talk.

As I watch her walk to her car after school, I feel a mix of emotions. On one hand, I'm upset that she left me all alone on what was arguably the most emotional night of my life. Something that has been a part of my life since I was five, something that I shared with my dad when he was still alive, is now over. She knew that, and she still left. On the other hand, I want to be there for her right now while she's going through a hard time. I want to shove anyone away who dares to hurt her and hold her in my arms until she stops crying.

Now that I'm thinking about her and how badly I want to comfort her, I start to wonder why she didn't feel that same way after the game. The answer is obvious now. She doesn't love me the way I love her. I'm not a priority in her life like she is in mine. She doesn't see a happy future for us together like I do. I can feel my chest tightening, squeezing my heart, making it hard to breathe. I've known these truths for a while now, but I never let myself admit it. I never entertained the negative thoughts that wracked my brain, not when I was around Evie.

After Evie drives out of the school parking lot, I get in my car and drive home, where I hope answers are waiting for me.

"So what's new?"

This weekend, Bear texted me and wished me good luck at state. He also informed me that he would be back home for his spring break this week and suggested we hang out.

Bear is my best friend. He graduated last year and went off to college, so we don't see each other much. I saw him over Thanksgiving and Christmas, but that's it. I miss him. Bear and I played hockey together, but we also hung out together outside of hockey season. He was always the one to text me and invite me to parties. When I first moved here, Bear was one of the first people to make me feel welcome. Other than Evie...

Goddamnit, why am I thinking about her? Oh yeah, because Bear asked me what's going on in my life.

"You watched the state games, so you know all about that."

"You played awesome, dude. Even in that second game that you guys lost. That goal was sick."

"Thanks, man."

"How are things going with Evie?"

When I saw Bear over the holidays, it was hard to hide my feelings for Evie. Every time her name popped up on my phone, I smiled. Of course, he gave me shit for it, but as a guy who's in a long-term relationship, he actually understands these sorts of things, so I confided in him. I told him about her rejecting me. He agreed with Evie that it was way too soon to be asking her out. And I told him about the night I took off my pants in her car. He also gave me a ton of shit for that one. Overall, his advice was to stick with it, so I'm curious what he's going to say this time.

"Not great."

"That's not what I was expecting you to say."

"I mean, they are until they aren't. Just last week, things were great. I really thought we were getting somewhere. But then this weekend, everything flipped. Again."

"What did you do?"

I huff. "Wasn't me this time."

"You sure about that? One thing Olivia's taught me is that things are usually *my* fault, even if I don't realize it. And if I don't realize it, she so kindly informs me of what my faults are."

We both chuckle, knowing there's a little bit of truth behind his sarcasm.

I fill him in on the events that played out after that final game. I also tell him about the bet and how the entire student section started chanting her name after I scored that third goal. He mostly listened, clearly brewing up some big speech for me in his head.

Or so I thought. All he says is, "It's probably for the best."

Something about his words struck a chord in me, and not in a good way. "What's that supposed to mean?"

"I'm sorry to say it like this, but she's clearly not as into you as you're into her."

"I know that."

"So, why keep wasting your time? At first, it was a fun chase, but now it's getting a bit ridiculous. She's playing you. Why do you keep going back?"

"Because I love her, Bear. I told you that." My words are sharp, and I'm starting to feel my emotions boiling up inside me.

"Why, though? What's so special about her? I promise you could easily find a better girl in college who will—"

I cut him off. "Absolutely not. I'll never find someone who makes me feel the way Evie does. The thought of going off to college and finding someone else makes me sick." I run my fingers through my hair and grab the longer parts with my fists. "Evie makes me feel seen. She makes me feel joy. Both things that I rarely felt in my life before I got to know her. Hell, if I'm really being honest with myself, she made me feel those things the moment I first met her." I release my hair and slam my fists into the couch before resting my head in my hands, staring at the carpet beneath my feet. "When that bubbly brunette popped her head into my homeroom on my first day at St. Francis and greeted me with more intention than I'd ever experienced, I felt seen.

Every time I had a class with her, I didn't even realize it, but I looked forward to those classes. I knew she was always going to be there and lift the spirit in the room, regardless of how boring the class was. She exudes warmth and kindness, and I literally can't be unhappy when I'm around her, even if I'm mad at her. She's so annoyingly optimistic. I mean, except about us. But with most things in the world, she always looks at them with such hope. I never used to be optimistic about anything. I always look for the worst possibilities and try to prepare myself for them. With her, I've learned that if I'm so focused on the potential bad in the future, then I don't enjoy the present. And god, no one makes me laugh as hard as she does since my dad.

I literally can't picture my life without her, and I just want to shake her when she says she doesn't see it like I do. She's just getting in her own way. She's so logical. I don't know how to save her from that. As much as I know how heartbroken I'll be if she doesn't give us a chance, I'll be even more devastated having to watch her experience regret when she realizes she made a mistake in giving up on us."

For the first time since starting my rant, I take a look up at Bear and take a deep breath.

"Ultimately, you need to do what you think is best. I think that if you decide to move on, you'll eventually get over it and find someone just as great, if not better. Just remember, she doesn't have to hold all the control just because you're all in and she's not. You can always choose to walk away if it means you won't have to hurt like this anymore."

The silence that follows is filled with reflection and

doubt. Where do I go from here? Do I reach out to Evie, or do I wait for her to reach out to me?

The doorbell finally breaks the silence. Bear grabs his phone off the couch and stands. "Let's go eat some pizza."

"Okay." I nod and follow him up my basement stairs and into my living room.

I go to the front door and grab the pizzas from the delivery guy. As I walk to the kitchen with the boxes stacked up, I see the girls barreling down the hallway at me. "Whoa, what's the rush, ladies?"

Iris and B lift the lids of each box, nearly knocking them out of my hands, until they find their pizza. "We're starving!" B yells as she slides the box off the top of the stack.

"No! That dessert pizza is ours!" I try to snatch it from her hand, but she pulls it away and runs down the hallway after Iris. They turn into Iris's bedroom and slam the door shut. I hear the lock click, and I know we're not getting it back. "At least leave us a few pieces!" I doubt they can hear me over their loud music, but it's worth a shot.

———

I SHUT the front door and lock it behind Bear. As much as I enjoyed catching up with my best friend, I couldn't stop thinking about Evie. All I want to do right now is go hide away in my room and pace back and forth as I contemplate my next move.

And that's exactly what I do. I've done about 1,000 laps around the dark blue shag rug at the end of my bed. It's times like these when I *really* miss having a piano in the house. If I had access to the one at the school right now, I'd be there, letting out my feelings through my fingers. That's how I process things, even since before my dad died.

I barely hear the knock on my door through the music in my headphones. I pull one out and open the door to find Iris and B standing there, looking suspicious.

"What do you two want?"

Iris smiles and holds out the dessert Bear and I ordered. The one that they stole from us. "We wanted to bring you what was left."

I reach out, grabbing it from her. I'm slow with my movements, afraid that this is some sort of prank. I wouldn't be surprised if there were bugs in this box or something that would pop out at me. Iris and I are known to pull pranks on each other. Some are harmless, and others may go a little too far at times. Iris is especially devious when B is around. So I cautiously open the lid and peek inside. Nothing but a couple of pieces of the giant cookie.

"What's the catch?"

"No catch. Just wanted to be nice since we stole it from you."

"Mhmm. Sure..." I look at the bottom of the box, the back, and open it again just to be sure it hasn't been tampered with.

"Seriously, Liam! We didn't do anything to the cookie!"

"Okay. Thanks."

I start shutting the door, but B throws her hand out to stop it. "Wait."

"What?"

"We have a favor to ask you."

I grumble and throw the door back open. "Of course you do."

"Come on, have an open mind. It's not that bad."

I gesture for B to continue, knowing damn well she's going to be speaking for her and Iris.

"Iris and I are going to audition for the end-of-the-year talent showcase with a couple of other girls."

"Good for you," I deadpan.

"We need someone to accompany us."

"And you want me to do it."

"Yes."

"No." I take out a slice of the giant cookie and take a bite.

"Come on, Liam! You can just be in the dark in the background. For all the audience knows, you're not even there, you're just a recording."

"Why can't you just use a recording?"

Iris chimes in, "Because we need to change keys, and it'll be easier to make small changes to accommodate the needs of the quartet if we have a live pianist."

I stand there, thinking about their offer. Of course, Evie pops into my head. That damn girl can't stay out of my head for one whole hour, even when I'm not talking to her. I think about all the times she's asked me to audition for the showcase, and I told her no. I think about the look she would then give me, those puppy dog eyes.

"What song?"

Iris already has her phone in her hand, as if she anticipated my question. She presses play and turns the screen toward me. I'm familiar with the song, but I listen for a few seconds to give it an honest chance. As I listen, an idea pops into my head.

"No."

"Liam, will you please do this one thing for me, and I won't ask you for anything else from now until you leave for college."

"I'll play for you guys." Her eyes light up. "Just not that song." Now she looks pissed.

"Are you serious? You want us to change our song?"

"How long ago did you decide this was going to be the song you sing?"

"Today."

"Then you'll be fine changing it." Her eyebrows scrunch together. This was not an Uno reverse card she was expecting. "I promise you'll like it."

"You already have another song in mind?"

"It just came to me, but yeah, I do. Give me your phone."

She hands it over, and I pull up the song I have in mind. As it starts playing, B blurts out, "I *love* Ben Platt!"

Iris elbows her. "Shhhh, I'm listening."

About a minute in, Iris steals the phone back and pauses the song. "Fine. I'll ask the girls and let you know if they all approve."

I wasn't expecting her to roll over that quickly. Something about her demeanor changed when she started listening to the lyrics. "Just send the sheet music to my email when you've decided."

She nods. "Thanks, Liam. You're the best." She steps into my room and goes up on her tiptoes to wrap her arms around my neck. The hug is surprising, given our family isn't a very affectionate one, but so is what she says next. "Is this about....?" She doesn't need to finish the question; we both know it is.

"Yeah," I whisper back to her, letting her go.

She backs away with a soft smile on her face. "We'll get you the sheet music by the end of the week."

Chapter Seventeen

LIAM

For spring break every year, our school offers a ski trip for seniors. This year, a decent amount of us signed up and paid to go, including Evie and me. We had signed up for this long before our fight. We were so excited to go skiing together and get away from everything. We haven't talked or even texted since the hockey game over a week ago. Now, I have no idea how she feels about being stuck on a train with me for 24 hours one way, a three-day ski trip, then another 24-hour train ride back home. But I'm guessing she's not too thrilled.

I thank my lucky stars that Alex and his friends aren't on this trip. No, they were too cool for a class ski trip. They're all in Mexico with Layne's parents, getting tan while we freeze our asses off on a mountain and sleep in bunk beds. The accommodations for this trip have been pretty vague, but I heard from Bear that they have us stay at an unused religious retreat center. Basically, it's just a bunch of cabins full of bunk beds and a main hall that has a kitchen. And of course, there's a church there too. It wouldn't be a Catholic school field trip without daily mass, of course. Yippee…

Since this trip is both a thrilling adventure and a religious exploration, we've got an odd mix of classmates here. There are even kids from a different private school a few towns over. My classmates vaguely know them from past trips they've put us on together over the years. But since I've only been going to St. Francis for four years, I don't know any of them very well. They seemed nice enough in the 30 minutes we spent together at the Amtrak station prior to boarding.

Everyone is milling about the train now, looking for their seats. As I walk down the aisle, towards my assigned seat, I discover that my fear has come true. The whole drive from St. Francis to the city where the train station is, I wondered who I'd be seated by. The thought crossed my mind that I might be seated by Evie since our names were on the sign-up sheet next to each other.

From three rows away, I can see Evie sitting in my row, head buried in a paper map. God, I can't remember the last time I saw one of those.

"Hey."

Her head pops up at the sound of my voice. She wasn't startled like she usually is, so I fear she saw me coming and was trying to ignore me as I passed by.

"This is my seat." I point to the empty seat on the other side of her. "But I can go find someone to swap with if you'd like."

She folds up her map and shakes her head. "No. It's fine." She stands up and shuffles into the aisle, leaving me an empty path to my seat. "Go ahead."

I already put my luggage in the luggage rack, so all I have with me is my backpack. I slip it off and shuffle my way into my seat. Once I'm situated, Evie slips back into hers, next to me.

"Can we—" she says at the same time I say, "Evie, I—"

Neither of us smiles, because this isn't funny. Her eyes are full of sorrow, and she looks tired. I'm certain my face is an exact reflection of hers. I haven't been sleeping well without being able to text Evie at night. Instead, I've just been scrolling on my phone till all hours of the night, trying to distract myself so I don't call her. I promised myself that I would wait for her to reach out first. I didn't want to force her to talk if she wasn't ready. But I guess the universe had other plans for us and decided we'd had enough torture for two sorry souls in love.

"Can I go first?" Her words are quiet and timid, not like the confident Evie I know and love.

"If you want to."

I don't know what they're called, but the train equivalent of a flight attendant gets our attention. "Excuse me, can you please pull out your tickets so I can check them?"

We both scramble to grab our tickets out of our bags and hand them to the worker.

"Perfect!" She punches them with some sort of fancy hole punch. I thought they only did that in The Polar Express. "Thank you. Enjoy your trip." She hands them back and moves on to the seat behind us.

Once she's out of earshot, Evie continues. "Liam, I..." She looks away from me and down at her hands, fiddling in her lap. After a deep breath, she continues, "I'm really sorry."

I can hear the pain in her whispered words. I want to comfort her, but I sense she has more to say. So I wait.

"I shouldn't have left after the game. That was so horrible of me. I should have been there for you." I can't see her face well, but I spot a tear fall from her cheek and soak into her pants.

I want to reach out and hold her, but I'm afraid to. God, I missed her so much. I feel my own eyes start to well with tears. Shit. I was not supposed to cry during this. While she's still looking down, I quickly wipe the sleeve of my sweatshirt under my eyes, pretending to be rubbing the sleep out of them.

"I was just so embarrassed. When everyone started chanting my name, I wanted to curl up in a ball and die. All I could think about was myself in that moment. Lou tried to get me to wait for you, but I just couldn't get myself to stay there a minute longer. My mind was running as fast as it could away from the situation, and my body blindly followed."

The lights in the cabin dim as the train gets ready to depart the station. The night trips are cheaper, so that's what they booked for all of us. Most of our classmates wandered off to the lounge car to chat and play games, so we're mostly surrounded by strangers and empty seats.

Sensing that she's done saying what she needs to say for now, I finally respond. "Evie." Against my better judgment, I put my hand on her thigh. "I'm so sorry they did that to you. I can't imagine how that made you feel."

To my surprise, she wraps her hands around my bicep and buries her face in my shoulder, sobbing. I cradle her head with my hand and kiss the top of her head. I whisper into her hair, "It's okay. Breathe."

Luckily, it's dark enough in here that no one who's just glancing around would notice us.

"You've just been so good to me and so patient, and I don't deserve it." Her words are muffled by the sleeve of my shirt, but that doesn't lessen their impact.

"Hey. Don't talk like that."

"But it's true."

"You deserve a lot more than you give yourself credit for, Evie."

"But I don't deserve you..."

I don't know how to respond to that, so I don't.

She sits up, pulling away from me. She drops one hand from my bicep and the other trails down my arm. When her hand reaches mine, she laces our fingers together. "Can we please be friends again?"

"Of course we can." I stare into her eyes, wanting her to say she wants more, knowing she doesn't. If she'd let me, I'd kiss that look of sadness right off her face. I'd kiss her and touch her until she forgot all about that stupid bet and the pain of the last week and a half.

"There's one more thing we need to talk about."

I know what she's about to say, but I play dumb, hoping I'm wrong. "What's that?"

"The bet."

"Evie, you—"

"I just need to clear the air. I know you never expected me to follow through with anything, but I know a part of you probably hoped I would."

I sigh, reluctantly. "Of course I did. But I wouldn't have let you do it for the sake of a bet. I only want you to do those things with me because you want to."

She nods. "Well, I wouldn't have done anything with you...because I don't want to."

I can tell she's lying. She has to be lying. I know that her pitch rises when she's hiding the truth, and I swear it just did. Didn't it? I try to replay it in my head, but now I don't know if I actually heard it or if I just wanted her to be lying.

"I want to have a great senior ski trip with you like we planned."

"Me too." I want things back to normal so badly.

She straightens in her seat, facing forward again. She leans over and rummages through her backpack. She pulls out her laptop and sets it up on the tray in front of us. "So, what movie do you want to watch?"

"Quit acting like I have a choice," I tease.

She giggles, and I see her smile for the first time in weeks. It lights up my heart to know that I can still make her smile like that.

"Well, there is this romcom that I've been dying to see..."

"I knew it." I dramatically roll my eyes, pretending to be annoyed with her. She jabs me in the side with her elbow, and I nudge her back. "Pull it up."

She claps her hands together like a little kid. "Yay!"

Someone from a few rows up shushes her. We look at each other, both our eyes as big as saucers, and giggle. And all feels right again.

———

EVIE

I wake up to the sound of people laughing. I realize I'm lying down, scrunched up in a ball, with my head on Liam's lap. I sit up and take in the sight of him, so peaceful. I like watching him sleep. It's something not many other people get to do.

He stirs, and I look down at my phone, pretending to send a text. Then I look up as he blinks a few times, letting his eyes adjust to the lights that are now on. "Good morning."

"Morning." I look around. "I'm gonna go find the bathroom."

"I'll be here." He smiles at me, and it makes me want to curl up in his lap again. But I don't. Instead, I stand up and start looking for the bathroom.

As I walk, I think about my conversation with Liam last night. Relief washes over me because the conversation I'd been dreading finally happened, and things are back to normal. I was so grateful when he forgave me for leaving the game. The past week and a half has been torture. For the first time since Alex dumped me, I felt completely alone without Liam there to comfort me. It showed me just how much I take his love for granted, and it made me feel awful for what I did to him.

I felt so awful that I couldn't even be around him without guilt overwhelming my system. I was praying that time would speed up so it would be graduation, and I could flee town and never come back. Even though I'm still very excited for graduation, there are still a couple more months left of senior year for me to enjoy. First prom and then graduation.

I've tried not to think about prom. I have a feeling Liam is going to ask me, and I don't know what I'm going to say. I kept telling myself that I would just go with my gut in the moment, depending on how things were between us. After our make-up last night, things are good, but I'm still not sure how I feel about going to prom with him.

Prior to Liam's birthday, I'd been hoping that Alex and I would reconnect and he would ask me. But that's clearly not happening at this point, and I think I can finally accept that. A small part of me still wants Alex to hurt, though, and I don't think going with Liam is going to do that.

I find the bathroom, but there's a line, so I stand

behind the last person and wait my turn. As I wait, I scroll on my phone. Most of the posts are pictures of people on beaches for spring break. Why I agreed to go to the snowy mountains is beyond me. Liam and I thought it would be a fun way to go on spring break together since our parents would never let us go somewhere like Myrtle Beach together.

All the posts are starting to blur together as I mindlessly scroll, until I scroll past a familiar face. I immediately scroll back and stare at the picture for way longer than I should. Layne posted a photo of himself with Alex and the rest of the friend group. They're sitting poolside with drinks in their hands. That should be me. I should be there with them.

"Makes you wonder why we chose such a snowy destination, doesn't it?"

The voice over my shoulder makes me jump, and I turn around to put a face to that unfamiliar voice. It's a girl I recognize from the other private school that's on this trip with us. "You're…"

"Celine. And you're Evelyn, right?"

"You can call me Evie."

"I feel like we've met before, but not officially." She extends her right hand for me to shake. "It's nice to meet you, Evie."

Celine is gorgeous. Her olive skin and almond-shaped eyes, framed by straight, black hair, would make any girl jealous. On top of that, I've heard she's really nice.

"Which hottie are you pining over?" She nods toward my phone screen, still on the picture of the guys shirtless by the pool.

Usually, I'd find her question odd or off-putting, but the way she said it tells me she gets it. Like she's had her heart broken too, and for some reason that makes me trust her. "That one's my ex." I point to Alex in the picture.

"Oh yeah, I remember him. That sucks. How long has it been?"

"Five months."

"Never really goes away, does it?" When I don't respond, she elaborates. "The longing for things to go back to how they were."

"No, it definitely does not."

"Is he on this trip?"

"No, this is what they're doing for spring break." I flash her my phone screen one more time before locking it and putting it in my pocket. The line for the bathroom is moving painfully slow, so we're going to be here for a bit. "I'm glad to just be away from St. Francis for a while."

"Me too. Well, my hometown, not yours." She giggles. "I've never actually been to St. Francis."

"You're not missing out." We both laugh at that.

I think we're going to get along just fine.

Chapter Eighteen

LIAM

"UNO!"

"Goddamnit, Liam! How do you keep doing that?"

"You can just start calling me the king of UNO if you'd like."

"Get over yourself." Evie throws an unopened bag of gummy worms at my head.

"I love it when you get violent. It's cute."

She narrows her eyes at me. "Cute?"

I also love riling her up. "Yeah, cute. Like a little princess throwing a temper tantrum."

"Oh, now you're de—"

"Hey now!" Celine throws her arms out, one toward each of us. She holds us apart, as if we were actually about to brawl. The ridiculousness of the situation makes us all crack up. "Let's keep the peace and remember that this is just a card game."

I can't help myself; I have to get one last taunt in. "Yeah, Evie, it's just a card game."

"Are you sure you two aren't siblings? Because you sure fight like it."

Hearing Celine say that Evie and I act like siblings makes me cringe. The things I want to do to Evie when we're alone are things siblings should never think about. Not even step-siblings. "Evie's an only child. And as an oldest child, I feel the need to give her the sibling experience. It'll help her become more adjusted to reality." I wink at Evie, hoping her joking temper doesn't turn into real anger.

I know I'm safe when she throws it back at me. "And Liam seems to forget that being a cocky ass when he wins is an unattractive oldest sibling move that's not going to get him laid any time soon."

"Wait. Hold up. I thought you two weren't together." Celine's eyebrows are scrunched together in confusion.

"We're not," we both say at the same time.

Lou laughs, covering her face with her fanned-out cards. I'm pretty sure she has about 20 cards in her hand.

"Got it. I was confused there for a second."

"I was just speaking hypothetically."

When Evie came back from the bathroom, she brought a new friend, Celine. Then Lou came and found us after she woke up. The four of us have been playing UNO in the lounge car for a couple of hours now. None of Celine's close friends from her school came on the trip either, so I think she'll be hanging around.

It's nice to see Evie make more girlfriends. Her old friends are really missing out. I couldn't believe it when Evie told me why they'd stopped talking to her. I mean, I know religious values are important and all, but to ostracize someone you've known since kindergarten over having sex with their long-term boyfriends is ridiculous. Especially since I've heard a few rumors about a couple of them that don't paint them in the most saintly light. Technically speaking, just because you're putting it in a different hole, it doesn't make it less of a sin. Bitches.

Evie plays her next card, then Lou, and finally Celine lays a blue number two card. All three girls look at me, likely hoping I won't be able to play. I look down at my last card and then back up at them.

"Oh, just lay it down already!" Evie is very cute when she gets impatient. And I do love to push her buttons.

"You've got me stopped." I look down at my blue four and draw a card.

———

EVIE

The 24-hour train ride went faster than I was expecting, thanks to the entertainment provided by Liam, Lou, and our new friend, Celine. We're now getting our things unpacked in our cabins. Each cabin can hold eight people. They split the cabins into boys' and girls', then left the rest of the decision-making to us. Celine, Lou, and I got bunks next to each other. Two more girls from my school and three girls from Celine's school filled in the rest.

My goal for this trip is to avoid any run-ins with my ex-best friends and not let anyone from the other school think that Liam and I are together. So far, so good. Luckily, the girls I used to call sisters have managed to claim the furthest cabin away from me and get put in a different group for activities than me. And with Lou and Celine hanging around me, Liam and I won't be able to give people the wrong impression.

Speaking of Liam, I think he accidentally took my headphones. "Did either of you see which cabin Liam went into?"

"No, I didn't. Sorry." Celine didn't see him.

"Nope." And neither did Lou.

"Is Liam the tall one with freckles, auburn hair, and the dreamiest green eyes?"

I turn around, looking at whoever just said that. It's a girl from Celine's school that I don't know. "Yeah, that's him."

"Is he dating anyone?"

"No." My response comes out so fast it almost startles her.

"He's so cute." The girl giggles with her friends and continues unpacking her bag. She points out the window by her bunk. "I think I saw him go into the cabin next to us."

I look through the window at the cabin she's pointing to, 30 feet from ours. We got in around 8:00 pm, so it's already dark outside. But the lights outside the cabins reflect off the snow, making it easy to see. I contemplate going over there, but decide to wait. I don't want to risk walking in on any of the guys changing.

The thought of Liam shirtless pops into my head. I've seen him without a shirt a few times when he's changed at my house, and that one time he got completely naked in my car. I start thinking about his smooth skin over his washboard abs. After snuggling with Liam a few times, I knew he had a nice body, but the first time I saw him shirtless this year, I ran a red light. He looked very different than when I saw him shirtless a couple of years ago at a classmate's pool party. I knew logically that he's likely gotten more fit over the years, but the idea I had of Liam in my head did not compute with the guy I saw standing in front of me.

When I realize that I've just been staring at his cabin

through the window, I play it off like I was looking at the view of the mountains that are illuminated by the moonlight. "It's so beautiful here." I break my stare and turn to Celine and Lou. "You guys want to go on a little walk before bed?"

Celine looks at me like I'm crazy. "No way in hell am I going out there in the dark."

"I just want to go check out the main cabin." I put my ski equipment in there earlier, but we entered through the back door, so I didn't get a chance to look around.

"Just wait until the morning."

"That's probably smart." I glance back through the window at the boys' cabin next to ours. "But I'm gonna run and grab my headphones from Liam quick. I'll be right back."

The girls don't bother to stop me as I slip on my snow boots and a sweatshirt. With my phone flashlight on, I walk through the snow to the cabin next to us. I knock on the door with my gloved hand. No one answers. I start to worry that the sound was too muffled and they didn't hear me, so I take off my glove and lift my hand to knock again. The door opens before my fist hits the metal, and a boy is standing in the opening, staring at me.

"Hi."

The boy continues to stare, like he's never seen a girl before.

"Is Liam in there?"

He shakes his head.

"Okay...do you know where he is? He's tall with red-ish hair."

The boy turns around and yells into the cabin, "Is there a Liam that's staying here?"

A chorus of male voices shouts, "No," back to him.

"I'm sorry. I thought he was staying here." How embarrassing. I look back at my cabin to make sure this is the one the girl had pointed to.

The boy starts to shut the door, and I walk back toward my cabin. When I get close, I look over my shoulder and spot another cabin hidden behind some trees to the left of the cabin I just went to. Maybe that's the one she was talking about? Since I have nothing better to do with my time and I really want my headphones, I walk towards the other cabin.

When I get there, I take off my glove and knock. Someone answers the door, someone who's not Liam. "Hi, is Liam in there by chance?"

"No, sorry."

"That's okay. Sorry for bothering you." I start to walk away, but stop when he continues talking to me.

"He *is* staying in this cabin, though."

"Oh...where—"

"I think he's in the main cabin, putting some stuff away."

"Okay, I'll check there. Thanks."

The trek to the main cabin isn't long, but at this point, I've been walking outside for longer than I anticipated. I would have worn warmer clothing if I had known I was going to be exposed to the elements for this long. But I've already committed to finding Liam, so I continue on.

The main cabin is warmed by a fire crackling in the large fireplace. For a moment, I wonder why they would leave the fire unattended, then I remember that the teachers and chaperones are staying in the rooms just off the common area. The lights are off except for the one in the kitchen. Some of that light spills into the main area, lighting a path toward the back half of the building.

I walk through the kitchen, expecting to find Liam in

there, but no luck. I exit out the other side and walk down a long hallway of doors, toward the equipment room where I put my skis earlier. I pause halfway down the hallway when I spot him through a cracked door. I push the door open and step in. The small room is filled with a keyboard, a drum set, a few guitar cases, and several speakers.

"Am I ever going to stop finding you like this?"

He doesn't respond, and I realize that the reason I can't hear the piano is because he's wearing a set of cheap over-the-ear headphones that are plugged into the side of the keyboard. I step forward and put my hand on his shoulder, trying not to startle him.

"Shit!" He jumps, making me jump.

I start laughing as he slips the headphones off and turns toward me. "You scared the shit out of me."

"My bad. I didn't know how else to get your attention. How is it that you always manage to find a piano wherever you go?"

"It calls to me, and I can't help but be drawn to it," he replies in an overly dramatic way.

I roll my eyes and walk over to where he's sitting on an oversized wooden piano bench.

"I recently got the sheet music for a song, and I've been dying to hear it. I figured they had to have a piano at a church camp, so I went searching for it."

"And how does it sound?"

"These old headphones are a little scratchy, so the quality of sound isn't that great."

"What song is it?"

"Now *that* I can't tell you."

I was wondering why he snatched his tablet off the piano as soon as he noticed me over his shoulder.

"What? Why?"

"Can't say or I'd have to kill you."

"Liam, come on. Just tell me."

His face softens. "It's a surprise."

"For me?"

"Mhmm. I agreed to play piano for Iris and her friends at the talent showcase concert."

"Ohmygod! Liam, that's great!" I throw my arms around his shoulders from behind and squeeze him, swaying side to side. "I'm so excited to hear it!"

He places his hands on my forearms, which are currently across his chest. He pulls up the sleeve on one of my arms and presses his warm hand to my skin. "You're so cold."

"Duh, I walked outside. If you didn't notice, we're currently in a snowy mountain range."

"Why didn't you wear a jacket?"

"I thought I was just running over to your cabin quickly, but it was actually the wrong one. Then I went to the right cabin, but they said you were in the main cabin, so I walked over here. I've been on quite the journey to find you."

"You were looking for me?" He unfolds my arms from around his chest and pats the bench next to him, inviting me to sit.

"You have my headphones."

"Oh shit, I do, don't I? I don't have my bag with me."

I step over the bench with one leg and sit so I'm straddling it, facing Liam. "That's okay. I'll just get them from you before we head up to the slopes tomorrow."

Liam carefully swings his leg over the bench so he's facing me too. We sit face to face, knee to knee. His hands find their way to my legs. Warm palms move slowly up and down my thighs, making my heart race. I can't get myself to look back at him, so I look down at the bench between us.

Is this why I came looking for him? Is this what I really wanted?

I miss his touch, the feeling of his lips on mine. No. I miss feeling desired and having my needs met by someone who cares for me. And the feel of his lips on mine...

His fingers hook under my knees and lift my legs slightly off the bench. I throw out my arms and grab his shoulders to stabilize myself. Looking at him now, I can see a fire behind his eyes. A look I know all too well. That look of longing that Liam gives me when we both know I'm about to give in to him. Not because I feel pressured to, but because I want to. Even though we both know I'd never admit that out loud. He pulls my legs closer to him, scooting my butt across the lacquered finish of the bench. He releases them, and my legs rest on top of his, our hips now closer than before.

His touch is smooth and gentle up my thighs and over the globes of my ass. They slip up my baggy sweatshirt, making me shudder when he grazes them across my bare skin. They find a resting place on the crest of my hips. When Liam first got the courage to touch me, it was so soft that his touch almost felt phantom. Now, his repeating habit of making me want him and reeling me in has given him the confidence to touch me where he wants and make his presence known.

My hands on his shoulders stay firmly planted, even after he pulls me in closer. His lips hover just in front of mine. Just close enough where all it would take is one small movement for them to touch. I know what he's doing. He wants me to make the final move. He's put us into position, but he needs to know that I want this as much as he does. He'd never force me into anything I didn't want to do. But he'll sure as hell do everything in his power to make resisting him nearly impossible.

A wave of need crashes into me from behind, pushing me into him. My hands curl around his neck to pull him in closer. When our lips touch, it's like I never left his arms. I forget about the game, the bet, the fight, my promises to never be with him. All of it is obsolete in this moment. Our mouths move against each other the way they always do, but something feels different. I've always enjoyed kissing him, but the time apart and the thought of losing him make this that much sweeter.

Liam is still wearing his sweatpants from the train ride, and I can feel him growing harder where my center meets his. He must feel it too because he tries to pull back, but since I'm practically sitting on his lap, I move with him. To show him that I don't care, I wrap my legs around him and press myself into him even further.

We stay like this for a while, embracing each other, but the bubble bursts when we hear a door close in the distance. "Fuck," Liam mumbles under his breath. "Let's go."

"Are we not supposed to be in here?"

He lifts up my legs and slides out from under me. As my heart continues racing, though for an entirely different reason now, I swing my leg over the bench and run over to the door.

"I'm not sure. But we're definitely not supposed to be feeling each other up in a secluded room."

"Right." Panic sets in even more at the thought of getting caught in here with Liam by a chaperone.

I peek my head into the hallway. Spotting no one, I signal to Liam to hurry up. "Come on."

He picks his jacket up off the floor and swipes his tablet

from the top of the piano. "Coming." He starts speedwalking toward me, but quickly gets clotheslined by the headphones still around his neck. The cord rips out of the keyboard, and Liam's head is tugged back, making him slow down. "Fuck". He pulls the headphones off from around his neck and tosses them onto the piano bench. "Let's go."

There's no time to laugh, but I definitely will be later at the memory of him almost getting taken out by a pair of headphones.

His hand on my lower back urges me forward, and we sneak out into the hallway, trying to stay light on our feet. But regardless of how careful I am, my wet boots squeak against the tile floor.

"Hello?" a voice calls from another room.

Being stealthy is clearly no longer an option, so we opt for speed. We both break out into a sprint toward the exit and bust through the back door. We run through the snow and hide amongst a nearby patch of evergreens. We sink down into the snow, holding each other and laughing.

"Ohmygod, I can't." My words come out as more of a wheezing sound. I crouch down in the snow next to Liam, holding my side, which now hurts from running and laughing too hard.

"I wonder who that was that almost caught us."

"Knowing our luck, it was probably Fr. Thomas."

"That would have been bad."

We wait for a few more minutes, just to be sure no one is standing by the back door, waiting for us to come out from behind the trees. Liam takes the opportunity to kiss me again. Both our lips and noses are now cold from being outside, but his touch still warms my insides.

When we're certain the coast is clear, we sneak back to

our cabins. Liam walks me over to mine first, before heading toward his own.

"Goodnight," I whisper into the darkness.

He glances over his shoulder, then turns, walking backwards now. "Night, Evie." And he doesn't turn back around until I'm in my cabin with the door shut behind me.

Chapter Nineteen

LIAM

"My butt hurts so bad. I swear it has to be one big bruise at this point. Evie, will you rub it for me?"

"Get your soaking wet ass away from me." She spanks me and shoves me away with a laugh.

A group of us is huddled around a table near the giant fireplace in the center of the ski lodge, trying to warm up after our morning session. Empty chip bags and dirty plates litter the tables around us. It's no shocker that when you get 50 teenagers together, there's bound to be a mess wherever they go.

I reclaim my seat between Evie and Celine, where a plate of hot fries is waiting for me. "Want some?" I tilt the plate toward Celine.

Evie, who is scrolling on her phone at the moment, replies, "No thanks."

"Funny how you thought I was offering them to you."

Evie looks up from her phone, eyebrows scrunched together until she realizes that I was offering them to Celine, not her. "Oh." Now she just looks embarrassed.

My original intention was to jokingly make her a little jealous, but now I feel bad. "I was going to offer them to you next, don't worry." I slide the plate of fries toward her.

Celine reaches across me and grabs a couple of fries off the plate that now sits in front of Evie. I catch a whiff of Celine's perfume. It smells expensive. I don't know much about Celine yet, but from the looks of her ski gear, I'm going to guess her parents are pretty wealthy. I had to rent my gear from the lodge today since I've only ever been skiing once in my life. Which explains why I keep falling and subsequently bruising my tailbone.

Evie starts scrolling on her phone again, mindlessly eating the fries she just said she didn't want. "Good girl."

She flashes me a look like I said something funny. Apparently, Celine is also in on the joke because she's giving Evie a strange look and pursing her lips together to avoid laughing.

"What?"

"Nothing," the girls say in unison.

"Did I say something?"

Both of them go about their own business, smirking. Leaving me to wonder if there's some hidden meaning behind those words. Whatever, I'll Google it later when they're not around. I don't want them to catch me looking it up and make fun of me even more.

A girl from Celine's school, sitting across the table from us, yells over the noise of the lodge, "Hey Celine, have you been asked to prom yet?"

Celine nods, not bothering to look up from her phone. "Yeah, I did."

"Mmmk, just wondering who was left."

The girl goes back to gossiping with her friends at a

more reasonable volume. Evie looks across at Celine. "When's your guys' prom?"

"The second week in April."

"That seems early. Ours is the second week of May."

"It's always early at our school for some reason."

"Do you have a dress yet?"

"I do!"

"Ooooo, let me see!"

The girls talk straight through me as if I'm not even there. Celine pulls up a picture of her dress to show Evie, and they gush over how stunning it is. They show each other their dresses from last year and talk about their prom experiences. Of course, Alex gets brought up, which usually puts Evie in a sourly depressive mood, but not today. She's either less fazed by it for some reason, or she's getting better at hiding it in front of people who aren't me.

"Who are you going with to your prom?"

Celine's question stops both Evie and me in our tracks. I continue eating my fries, pretending like I'm not on the edge of my seat, waiting for her response. I know she hasn't agreed to go with anyone else; she would have told me. And as much as I'd like to think she hasn't even been asked by anyone, I'm not entirely sure. Something could have happened over the past couple of weeks when we weren't speaking. I'm praying no one did. She has to know that it's my intention to ask her. I've just been waiting for the right time.

"Don't know yet."

She doesn't so much as glance over at me for a second. It's still as if I'm not even here. Now I'm starting to get nervous. Does she have other offers that she's considering? I make a mental note to probe her about it later, when Celine isn't around.

EVIE

My muscles are sore, and I feel like my fingers and toes are frozen, about to fall off. Nothing a warm shower can't fix. After dinner, I'm heading straight for one.

"Whatcha thinking about, Evs?" Celine started calling me Evs today, claiming that Evie was one too many syllables.

"How good a shower would feel."

"That's not at all what I was going to guess."

"What did you think I was thinking about?" I know what she's going to say. She definitely thought I was thinking about Liam.

"I thought maybe you were doing some kegels."

Okay, that is *not* what I thought she was going to say. "Some what?"

"Kegels. You know, vagina strengthening exercises."

That got the attention of the girls sitting across from us. "I've heard my mom talk about those with her girl-friends!"

Suddenly, my cheeks are turning red, and I want to be anywhere but a part of this conversation. Growing up around extremely religious friends didn't prepare me for girl talk like this. Anything related to sex or reproductive organs was wholly avoided.

Celine seems effortlessly confident about it, though. No sense of shame whatsoever. "My friend who's a freshman in college told me about them. They help strengthen your pelvic floor."

I remain silent while the other girls continue on with this ridiculous conversation.

"What exactly is it good for?"

"It makes your vagina muscles stronger, so you feel tighter."

"Aren't women naturally kind of tight?"

"When we're young, yes. But as you get older, things stretch out."

"Oh yeah, I've heard guys call girls 'loose.' Is that what they mean by that?"

"Probably."

"Why would you want to be tighter? Wouldn't that hurt more? It already hurts the way it is."

"It's not supposed to hurt."

How does she know so much? I mean, I've had sex. I know how it works. But she seems more knowledgeable than I am.

"How do you do them?" The words escape my mouth before I can stop them.

Celine looks over at me, amused by the break in my silence. "Want me to teach you?"

"No, that's okay."

"We don't have to get up and personal for me to teach you. I can just talk you through what to do."

I hold my tongue, anxious to say anything that will embarrass me further. I don't want her to know how igno-rant I am, but I'm also very curious. Lucky for me, another girl chimes in.

"Yes! Tell us!"

"So all you have to do is..." Celine continues on, giving us all a little tutorial.

It took me a while to figure out what she meant, but eventually I got the hang of it. The great part about kegels is that you can do them without anyone even knowing you're doing them. How cool is that!

All of us girls are sitting around the table, practicing our kegels, when Liam comes back. "What are you guys all staring at?" He glances around the room, trying to glean what it is we're all fixated on, despite the fact that we're all looking in different directions.

The table of girls erupts with laughter, continuing to leave Liam in the dark. I hope it stays that way. Though I'm sure Liam would be fascinated by the whole thing, I'd prefer that he wasn't thinking about me flexing my pelvic floor muscles.

Celine looks up at Liam standing behind us. "Nothing that concerns you." She pats him on the chest, like he's a child who wouldn't understand what the adults in the room are talking about. This makes me crack up even more.

Liam looks down at me. "What's so funny?"

I shake my head at him and smile. "Nothing." Somehow, I'm able to say it with a straight face while pulsing my pelvic floor muscles to the beat of Your Love is My Drug by Kesha.

LIAM

The train hums its familiar tune as we make the long trek back to Minnesota. This senior ski trip was filled with games, laughter, and new friends, so I'd say it was a success. My ass will recover just fine from the beating it took, but my ego won't mend so easily.

Once Lou, Evie, and Celine discovered the power they held in outnumbering me three to one, they were ruthless. I've never been so humbled in my life. Roasting me became their favorite pastime. But you know what, if it means I get to see that smile on Evie's face more often, I'll take it.

The four of us, along with some other friends we made, already have plans to meet up this summer. And some of them are even going to the same college as me, so I'm feeling good that I'll already have some friends when I go. It's amazing how much you can bond with people in such a short amount of time when you spend all day, every day together.

I look around the lounge car at my classmates and new friends. My gaze lingers on one person in particular, the one friend I came into this with, the one person in my world who could hold all my attention if she demanded it. My Evie. I've seen her smile and laugh more this week than I have the entire school year. I feel closer to her than I ever have.

When we were boarding the train, Evie and I talked about how grateful we are that we signed up for this trip. How a beach vacation sounds better on paper, but bonding over cold toes and sore bottoms is a better story to tell your kids one day. Of course, when talking to Evie, I said 'our kids,' and she pretended not to notice. But I caught the corner of her lips turning up before she looked the other way.

Now with my back pressed up against the cold glass window, feet up on the booth seat on either side of her, I hold Evie in my arms. She leans back into my chest with my arms draped around her. I was shocked twenty minutes ago when she laid back into me and snuggled right in. I'm not complaining, it's just confusing. I lean over her, speaking quietly enough that no one can hear me over the chatter filling the room. "Hey, can I talk to you for a sec?"

She twists back, looking at me over her shoulder. "You mean like somewhere else?"

"Is that okay?"

"Ummm, yeah, sure." She seems hesitant, but willing.

She sits up and scoots out the end of the booth, and I follow right behind her. Most people are distracted by some dude that's about to snort a line of pixie stick dust, so they don't seem to be bothered by the fact that Evie and I are slipping away. We weave through the people clogging up the central aisle and make our way over to the passenger car. Along the way, we stumble upon a mostly empty dining car.

"Should we talk here or do you wanna go back to our seats?"

"This works." With timid movements, she selects a booth and slips into it.

Like always, I follow her lead.

"What did you want to talk about?" I'm not sure if the average person could sense her subtle nerves, but I can. She has to know something's coming.

"I just wanted to get away from the crowd and chat with you. We haven't been alone since the first night of the trip when you found me in that music room."

"We haven't, have we?"

"Come on...you haven't missed me?" I stick out my lower lip and scrunch my eyebrows together.

"I've been around you all week. Pretty much non-stop, aside from when we were sleeping."

"But it's not quite the same." I stare into those blue eyes, trying to search for more clues indicating how she really feels. "You know it's not."

Her foot under the table brushes up against mine. As soon as she realizes the object she's touching is me, her face flinches, and she pulls her feet back. Does she not remember being tangled up in a booth with me no more than five minutes ago, and in front of other people, none-theless? I think she got comfortable this week. With two other girls constantly hanging around, we looked less like a couple, regardless of how touchy-feely we were. Now that it's just the two of us alone, it's as if she just remembered that she's afraid of people speculating that we're together. It's as if she's once again becoming aware of my true feelings for her, and she's scared.

"I just wanted to check in and make sure you're doing okay." That's not entirely true, but I have been wondering what she thought of Alex's post. "I really hope you're not letting Alex get in your head again."

She looks genuinely confused. "What about Alex?" Oh shit, did she not know?

"Never mind. I thought you were a little off, but you must just be tired from the week and sad that it's over."

"Liam. What did you hear about Alex?"

"I just saw his dumb story post and thought it might be bothering you." God, I feel so awful right now. I should have just let her be in ignorant bliss for a while longer and hope that she didn't go on social media before his story timed out.

Too late. She grabs her phone, likely pulling it up. Why does she torture herself like this? I mean, this one is mainly my fault, but she does this all the time. She's constantly checking his profiles and waiting for any sliver of hope that the old Alex is back.

I know immediately when she sees it because her face sinks. Her features change from worried to deep sadness, then from deep sadness to neutral. No, not neutral...numb.

"Evie?"

She looks up from her phone, blinking away tears that she usually tries to hide from me. "I'm fine."

I don't believe her for one second. "I'm sorry, I shouldn't have said anything."

"No, really, Liam. I'm fine."

She sets her phone to the side with an aggressive thud. A quick glance at her screen refreshes my memory of the image I saw this morning. Alex reposted a story made by a girl in the grade below us. It's a picture of her and Alex, arms wrapped around each other. Leaning against his legs is a big poster board sign that has 'Will you go to prom with me?' written on it with glitter.

The screen goes black, and my attention goes back to Evie. "You sure?"

Her eyes are mostly clear, and her face is back to neutral. "Liam, I'm not going to let him make me sad anymore."

I reach across the table and take one of her hands in mine. "Good."

"So what did you really want to talk to me about?"

Before I answer, I take a deep breath and try to recall everything I planned out in my head. There were several plans, actually. Seven to be exact. Seven different plans I thought of before I came to the conclusion that none of those are what Evie would want. "I have a question for you." Evie doesn't like big grand gestures from me. She said they draw too much attention to us, and although she appreciates the sentiment, she would rather I show my love for her in more subtle ways. So, although this may seem extremely underwhelming, I choose to play it simple and just ask her. "Would you want to go to prom together?"

She doesn't seem surprised by my question, yet she takes her sweet time giving a response. "I'm not so sure that's a great idea, Liam."

My heart sinks, and my leg instantly starts bouncing under the table. "Why do you say that?"

"I'm really trying not to lead you on here, and to be frank, I'm getting tired. If we really are going to be friends, like we have been trying to do, then we can't put ourselves in dumb situations that are going to complicate things."

I stare back at her, those blue eyes burrowing into my soul. "We can go as friends, Evie. It doesn't need to be more than that."

"But it will be. You know it will."

"At this point, anyone you go with is going to be a platonic date, so what's the difference? Why can't it be you and me? We both know you're not going to form a romantic connection that fast."

She pulls back like I just slapped her with my words and yanks her hand out of mine. This is not the way I planned on this conversation going. This wasn't part of any of the other six plans either. I'm letting my emotions get the best of me, and I'm saying things I don't mean to say. Neither of us has lost our cool or raised our voices yet, so things aren't hopeless. But it doesn't look good either.

"I'm sorry, that was uncalled for. What I meant to say was—"

"I don't really care what you meant to say, Liam. We aren't going to prom together, and that's it. I don't know how else to say it." Her tone is even and cool, like she truly doesn't care.

Ouch. I'd prefer she were yelling at me and telling me how stupid I'm being. At least that version of Evie is showing how much she cares about me. I can't handle this indifference. It scares me. It should be my turn to pull back, but I don't. I stand my ground, determined to make her see what I see. "I'm not going with anyone else. If you don't want to go with me, then I'm not going."

"Don't be stupid. You're not missing your senior prom."

"I won't enjoy it with anyone else, so what's the point of going?"

She taps her fingernails impatiently on the countertop. We're playing emotional chess now, and we both know it. The question remains as to how far each of us will go to prove our point.

"We can go together."

"What?" Her sudden change of heart throws me off kilter.

"We can go in a group."

With my head still spinning from the sudden whiplash, I can't make sense of what she's saying. "I don't get it."

"I don't want to make things confusing, so I won't go with you as my date. But I *will* go with you in a larger group. We can find our own dates, and the four of us can all get dinner and go to prom together."

I can't make any sense of this girl. "That still doesn't answer the question of who each of us is supposed to go with if you don't want us to go together." I put heavy air quotes around the word "together" since her definitions of the word seem to be muddled at the moment.

"You could ask Lou."

"She already agreed to go with Luke."

"Shit. I forgot about that."

I see the perfect move unfolding before me. The pieces are set up perfectly. I just have to be ballsy enough to sacrifice my queen and trust that I can get myself to the finish line without her. "I could ask Celine."

Evie's eyes get a nearly imperceivable amount wider. She sucks in her lips and bites on them before relaxing into her seat. "Great. That would be really fun. You should ask her." She plasters a smile on her face that I see right through.

"Okay. I will." I mirror her, putting on the same fake smile.

Check.

Chapter Twenty

EVIE

I anxiously tap my leg under the table, waiting for my phone to buzz.

"Honey, eat your dinner."

"I am." I shovel in another bite of mashed potatoes, still staring down at my phone.

Have you ever met an almond mom who forced copious amounts of food onto their daughter? Well, that's my mom. She's been thin as a rail my whole existence, basically a supermodel. I've even seen pictures after she had just given birth to me, and she looks exactly the same.

Growing up, my mom had a lot of insecurity when it came to her weight, causing her to form poor eating habits. She vowed that if she had a daughter, she would never let that happen to them. And she kept her promise. Food has always been framed as a necessity that fuels my body. Yet if you look at her plate, it's always ultra-healthy and extremely small portions. Although she kept me away from that mind-set, she could never beat it out of herself.

It was always confusing to me, but I know I'm very

lucky to not have body image issues like most of the women in the world. And I'm very lucky to have a mom who never made me feel the way she was made to feel as a young girl.

Unfortunately, something I did inherit from my mother is her anxiety and constant need for people to like her. I think about all of this as I wait for a text. A text that has a lot of potential to embarrass me. But one that could mean sweet revenge if it plays out the way I hope it does.

Since our senior ski trip to Montana, I've been thinking more and more about who I want to go to prom with. Liam was right when he said that my chances of going to prom with anyone as more than friends have passed. I had someone in mind prior to Liam putting me in that uncomfortable situation. I just hadn't acted on it yet.

Now that I've texted them and it's taking forever for them to respond, I'm starting to wonder if it was a huge mistake.

My phone buzzes on the table, and the screen lights up, flashing the name of the person I've been waiting for. Finally!

LAYNE

Hey Evie, what's up?

EVIE

How was your spring break?

LAYNE

Super fun. But I got a really bad sunburn.

EVIE

Ouch! Hope it heals soon.

LAYNE

Me too.

So what did ya need?

EVIE

I can't just text my friend to see how they're doing?

LAYNE

You could. But you haven't texted me in months.

EVIE

I just wasn't sure where we stood after everything with Alex.

LAYNE

You'll always be my little booger eater, Evie.

EVIE

Ohmygod! That was ONE time back in the FIRST GRADE!

You have to quit bringing that up.

LAYNE

Why? It's hilarious.

EVIE

You're a jerk.

LAYNE

But you love me.

EVIE

Unfortunately, I do.

The real reason I texted you is to see if you've asked anyone to prom yet?

LAYNE

…

THOSE THREE DOTS disappear and reappear several times, causing my anxiety to spike. Again! This was such a stupid idea. I shouldn't have brought up prom to one of Alex's best friends. But Layne and I have been neighbors since I moved onto this block in the third grade. We share a special bond that I was hoping not even Alex could break.

LAYNE

I have not.

BEFORE I CAN RESPOND, he sends a picture of himself standing shirtless in the mirror. Dear god. What the hell is he doing? Layne and I have never had romantic feelings for each other. *Ever.* Actually, the thought of it makes me a little sick. I don't have siblings, but what I feel for Layne is what I imagine a sister feels for her little brother. He drives me nuts yet somehow manages to make me laugh.

I start typing a response, about to chew his ass for sending me a thirst trap for no reason. Then I spot something off about the photo. I zoom in on his abs. It's hard to see through the smudges on his dirty bathroom mirror, but I can make out some words.

EVIE

Did you just ask me to prom by writing on your abs with a Sharpie?

LAYNE

Yes ma'am. It's the best I could do last minute.

EVIE

You are seriously such an idiot.

LAYNE

So...? Wanna go with me?

I'm pretty sure you don't have many other options.

EVIE

Wow, way to make a girl feel special.

And here I was wondering why you've never had a girlfriend.

LAYNE

Girls just can't handle me.

I'm too good in bed.

EVIE

I think I just threw up my dinner.

LAYNE

Rude.

EVIE

Okay, I'll go to prom with you.

LAYNE

Hells yeah!

We're going to be the best-looking couple there.

EVIE

I'll text you a picture of my dress when I get one so you can try to coordinate your tux with it.

I know your mom will want to.

LAYNE

Good call. She definitely will.

Wait. Aren't I not supposed to see your
dress until the day of?

EVIE

That's weddings, you nut job.

LAYNE

Ooooooooh.

Whatever.

THAT WENT BETTER than I was anticipating, given that I didn't even have to ask him first. Now that one anxiety-provoking task is over, onto the next.

Telling Liam.

———

LIAM

"Are you kidding me!"

Evie stares at me across the lunchroom table. "Shut up. Everyone is going to start looking over here if you keep being that loud."

"Well, if you're going to be ridiculous, I have no choice. You can't seriously be telling me that you think all Skittles taste the same. They have specified flavors. They all taste different!"

"I am serious. They all taste the same to me."

"You're crazy! Lou, please tell Evie she's wrong."

Lou looks over from a few seats away, pausing her conversation with her friends. "About what?"

"Nothing," Evie says to Lou. Then she directs her attention back toward me. "Liam is just having a diva moment. You can ignore him."

Lou and her friends have finished their lunch, so they get up and leave, while I'm left here with a very annoyed Evie. Though she is being ridiculous about the Skittles thing, I more so just like getting a rise out of her.

"Fine, we'll just have to agree to disagree."

She rolls those gorgeous blue eyes at me and continues eating her lunch. "So, have you talked to Celine much since the trip?"

"A little, yeah. We've mostly been talking about prom stuff. Colors, flowers, and all that other crap."

"So she said yes?"

"Yeah, I drove to her house last week and asked her."

Evie's fork stabs into her piece of lettuce a little harder than necessary. "You went to her house?"

"Yeah. After school on Friday. She only lives an hour and a half away."

"You didn't tell me you went there."

"You had that thing you went to in the city with your parents."

"We went to a traveling Broadway show."

"Yeah, that thing! I didn't mention it because you were going to be gone anyway."

"Why didn't you wait till I was back? I would have gone with you."

I shrug. "I don't know. I didn't think about it. I just finally got up the courage to ask her, so I texted her and drove out there."

I'm watching her carefully, trying to gauge her reaction. The truth is, I did think about Evie when I made the plans to go visit Celine and ask her to prom. Of course I did. The reason I did it when she couldn't be there is because I know

I would have hoped she would tell me not to do it, all the way up to the moment I asked. And if she didn't stop me, like I know she wouldn't, I would be disappointed. I would want her to come to her senses and tell me to take her instead. The decision was selfish, but I did it to spare my own feelings. I needed a break from disappointment.

"I'm glad she said yes. I'm sure the four of us will have fun together."

"Did you think she wouldn't say yes?"

She shrugs. "You never know."

"Wait. You said four. Did you find someone to go with?"

"Don't act so surprised."

"I'm not. You just didn't tell me."

She shrugs again. Goddamnit, if she shrugs so casually one more time, I'm going to lose it. "Guess we both forgot to give each other a life update."

"Who?" I heard a rumor that Evie got asked to prom, but I didn't believe it for one second. There's no way she'd go with—

"Layne."

My heart stops beating. This isn't real. "Evie..."

"Liam..." she mocks me with my same drawn-out tone.

"Why would you do that?"

"What do you mean?"

"He's Alex's friend. I'm shocked he agreed."

"Actually, he asked *me*."

None of this is adding up to me. "Evie, he's not your friend."

"He's been my friend a lot longer than you have."

"Sure, but he hasn't been nice to you since Alex ended things."

"He hasn't been mean to me. He wasn't one of the people who mocked me about your stupid bet."

"First off, that wasn't MY stupid bet. Second, he was in Alex's trunk when you tried to talk with him on my birthday."

"We don't know for sure that he was in the trunk."

"You literally saw a hand come out of the access hole."

"But we don't know it was Layne. It could have been any two idiots from their friend group."

She can't be serious. "What are the odds it wasn't him?"

"That doesn't matter."

"Yes, it does."

"It doesn't matter to me, so it shouldn't matter to you. I'm choosing to believe that he wasn't a part of that."

"It matters to me because this could all be a part of some plan to embarrass you again. And if you get hurt, I'm going to be the one whose shoulder you'll be crying on."

"Stop worrying about me. I'm not your problem."

When is she going to get it through her thick skull that she is and always will be my problem? "I will always care about your feelings. I hurt when you hurt."

She stares at me with a blank expression. "I'm sorry that you put yourself in that situation."

The bell rings, signaling us that lunch is over and we have five minutes to make it to our next class. Except today we're not going to class.

A voice comes over the intercom, "Friendly reminder that all seniors are to report to the gym for fifth period today. All seniors to the gym."

Without a word, Evie stands up and walks away. We dump our trays and silently join the crowd of seniors headed for the gym. Everyone takes a seat on the creaky wooden bleachers, waiting for an adult to come tell us what to do. Because god forbid we start being productive on our own.

As soon as I sit down next to Evie, a flamboyantly dressed woman waltzes through the double doors. "Hello everyone!" She sounds, and looks, like the theater teacher from High School Musical, but maybe a little younger. She took command of the room as soon as she entered. Now all eyes are on her. "My name is Ms. Cheryl. I have been hired by your prom committee to choreograph and teach you seniors how to ballroom dance. I have been doing this for the past 15 years. It's a special experience your school gives to you as a gift."

"I feel so special," I whisper in Evie's direction.

"Now some of you are going to grumble and whine about this, but I encourage you to fully embrace the process to reap the most fruitful benefits dance has to offer. I promise you, it will be more fun than you think it'll be.

"We have five weeks until your prom, but only a limited amount of time to learn the dance. The principal and your fifth period teachers have so graciously agreed to give you the period off once a week for rehearsals. That's a total of five rehearsals before the big day. It may not seem like much—"

"Seems like too much," a guy to my left grumbles to his friend.

"—but I promise you, you'll pick it up rather quickly. I've made things beginner-friendly so that everyone can be involved."

A guy in the back row raises his hand, and she calls on him. If she knew who he was, she would have ignored him or pretended she didn't notice his hand in the air. That's what most of the teachers do.

"Does everyone have to do the dance?"

"Everyone is encouraged—"

"Because I heard from some of the seniors last year that you don't have to participate if you don't want to."

"As I was about to say, everyone is encouraged to participate, but no one will be forced. That being said, I really want to stress that everyone who learned the dances in the past thoroughly enjoyed themselves. More than they thought they would. Now, if you'll all pair up with your dates and make your way to the center of the stage..."

"You mean the center of the basketball court?"

"Precisely."

With a chorus of grumbles and complaints, the majority of the class makes their way onto the floor.

As people pair off, one of the girls asks, "Ms. Cheryl, what about people who don't have a date in this class?"

"Great question! I did forget to touch on that. For those of you who may not have a date yet, or if you have a date from another school or another grade, you are welcome to find someone else who doesn't have a partner in this class. Or you are welcome to sit out."

As soon as she gives an excuse to sit out, several guys turn back to the bleachers and sit down.

Shit. I hadn't thought about that. Celine can't learn the dance with me. Not that I gave the senior dance that much thought, but I just assumed I'd be dancing with Evie. "Are you dancing with Layne?"

She looks around for him. "I'm not sure. Let me go ask him." She walks over to where she spots Layne sitting with his friends on the bleachers. And of course, Alex is there as well.

As soon as I see Alex's face when she walks up to Layne, everything starts to make more sense. She's not going with Layne because she wants to go with him. She's doing this to make Alex jealous. To my surprise, it looks like it's working. Or at a bare minimum, he doesn't like it. It's written all over his face. It makes me wonder if Layne didn't tell him. That group of guys isn't known for their stellar communication skills.

There's an exchange of words and nods between Layne and Evie. In the end, Evie walks back over to me alone.

"Layne's going to sit this one out. Since Celine can't be a part of this, would you—"

"Yes."

She smiles up at me. "Don't seem too eager now."

"I'll be however I want to be, thank you very much." I playfully bump into her as I make my way toward center court, where Ms. Cheryl is anxiously waiting for everyone to partner up and settle down.

"Alright, everybody, let's begin!"

Chapter Twenty-One

EVIE

The grand march is over. We've paraded across the stage, showing off our expensive dresses for the crowd. Last thing to be done before we get on a bus and go to the dance is our choreographed senior dance. We've been practicing for weeks now, and within the last couple of rehearsals, everything was finally coming together. Now I'm just praying I don't get stage fright and epically fail in front of everyone.

"You'll be fine." Liam stands behind me, squeezing his hands on my bare shoulders.

"I know."

"Then why do you feel stiff as a board?"

I twist my head around to glare at him. "I am not."

Liam, still holding my shoulders, shoves me forward and catches me all in one swift motion. A little scream escaped my mouth, and now everyone backstage is staring at us.

"What was that for?"

"I was testing to see if you trust me."

"I trusted you before you did that. Now I'm not so

sure." I step out of his grip and stand beside him instead of directly in front of him.

He slings one arm around my shoulders and pulls me in close. "Come on. This should be fun, not stressful."

"I know. I don't know why I'm so nervous."

"Have you ever performed anything in front of other people?"

"Just sports if that counts."

He tilts his head to the side and places his hand on his chin. "Mmmm, nope. Not quite the same."

"Oh, and you have?"

"Years of piano recitals, remember?"

"Right." I realize that I'm obnoxiously tapping my heel on the ground and stop. "Speaking of which, when are you going to tell me what song you're playing?"

"You'll find out at the concert."

I slip out from under his arm and turn to face him. "Seriously? Just tell me."

He reaches out and smooths down a tuft of hair that must have gone rogue when he nearly knocked me over moments ago. "You just need to have some patience. It's only a few weeks away."

"Fine, be that way." I turn my back to him, indicating that this conversation is over.

The emcee announces our dance, and we all shuffle onto the stage and get into our positions. My heart is racing, and I can feel my pulse in my toes that are shoved into the front of my heels. The lights come up, and the music starts. Ms. Cheryl made a track for this dance that's a mashup of a bunch of different songs, all with different vibes. This whole thing did turn out to be way more fun than I originally anticipated. Liam had fun with it, too. We laughed together every time one of us fell or stepped on the other's toes, which happened a lot. And it was nice being close to him in front of everyone without standing out. Plus, glancing over at Alex and seeing him annoyed fueled my ego a bit.

The first song that plays is a beautiful cover of Time After Time. Liam walks a circle around me, then takes my hand in his. I rest my arm on his strong shoulder as he leads me in a waltz. I can't help but mumble the verbal cues Ms. Cheryl shouted at us in rehearsals, trying my best not to forget what comes next.

Liam squeezes my waist to get my attention. "Just look at me. And don't forget to have fun."

I stop reciting the cues and take a deep breath. I need to trust that Liam's got me. I let go of my nerves and lean into the music, letting Liam twirl me around effortlessly. I never anticipated Liam being such an effortless dancer, but I guess his musicality from playing piano and his athleticism from hockey help.

I twirl into his arms, and with my back to his chest, he whispers in my ear, "I won't drop you."

I know he won't. I trust him.

He unwinds me and pulls me close. With his hands supporting my lower back, I lean backwards as he spins me like a ballerina in a jewelry box. The back of my dress is cut low to my waist, so I can feel his fingers on my skin. There's confidence in the way Liam holds me while maintaining a gentle touch, much like his personality.

The song transitions to something a little more upbeat, and we all scatter to our next positions. This is where things get really fun. The girls hang out in the background while the guys do their little section that's making the audience laugh. The boys who agreed to do that dance are *committed*. It makes me happy that the losers who didn't want anything to do with this are sitting in the crowd and not up here with us. Their buzzkill energy would turn this from funny to awkward so fast.

I glance into the audience and spot the section where the other prom dates that aren't in the dance are watching. I spot Celine sitting in the front. She looks absolutely stunning tonight. Throughout dinner and the time we spent getting ready together, I couldn't help but look at her. I noticed how pretty she was when we first met, but all dolled up like this, she's a sight for sore eyes. And right now she's watching Liam with a huge grin on her face. She looks enamored by him. The way she's looking at him makes something in my chest ache. I can feel a little green monster clawing its way into my brain despite my efforts to stop it.

I will not be jealous of Celine and Liam.

I repeat this over and over in my head until it's our turn to take center stage again. Were it not for Lou grabbing my wrist and pulling me, I would have missed our queue.

The rest of the dance continues without a hitch. Well, except for one girl who tripped over the train of her dress and almost fell off the stage. Luckily, her date caught her, and the crowd thought it was part of the dance. The final song ends, and we all strike a pose. The crowd erupts with applause and chatter as we stand there frozen, my cheeks sore from smiling so much.

———

LIAM

The party and dance after the grand march were a blast. They bused us out to a random building in the middle of nowhere, where they had snacks, games, a DJ, and a dance floor waiting for us. Every year, they switch the location of the dance, and they don't tell anyone where it is. Apparently, it's supposed to prevent students from stashing liquor on the property ahead of time.

Their plans failed when one of Alex's friends bribed a member of the prom committee to tell him the location of this year's dance. Their friend group snuck a few bottles of liquor out here at some point this past week and have been sharing with everyone. I guess the end of high school rapidly approaching has made them a little more generous. Or maybe they just want it to be harder for the chaperones to find out who's responsible for the booze if we all get busted.

I'm staying sober so I can drive our group from the school to Lou's house after, but Evie and Celine are living it up. As I sit at our table, eating my weight in Chex Mix, I watch the two of them dancing together. The lights are flashing blue and purple, making it feel like a rave in here. And the dance floor is packed since they picked a decent DJ who is actually playing good music. Anyone would have been better than the dud they hired last year, who played an ungodly amount of polka music and 80s rock.

Evie and Celine scream-sing into each other's faces, holding each other's hands above their heads. Celine turns around and backs her ass up into Evie's front. Evie grabs Celine's hips and the two of them dance, pressed tight together. My mind immediately jumps to the gutter, picturing the two of them doing all sorts of inappropriate things together. I shake the thoughts from my head just as the song ends and the girls stumble over to the table. They sit down and pour themselves each a cup of water from the pitcher on the table, completely unaware of the images that were just running through my mind.

"You guys look like you're having fun out there."

Evie chugs her water and slams the plastic cup down on the table, releasing a satisfied sigh. "Oh yeah, Celine's been putting me through a whole workout out there."

Celine laughs and shakes her head. "I wanted to take a break after the last song, but you insisted we stay out there for one more."

"We had to! He played my favorite song."

"I would have joined you out there had I known it was your *favorite* song." The words roll off my tongue in a mocking way. Evie is constantly saying that every song is her favorite song, when in reality, she doesn't have a favorite anything.

When we first started hanging out, I thought it would be important to learn things like her favorite color, favorite flower, etc. But she could never give me a straight answer. In the end, we came to the conclusion that she is incapable of picking favorites because she feels bad for all the other choices if she doesn't pick them. As if colors and flowers are capable of getting their feelings hurt. I chuckle at the memory and wink at Evie. She smiles back like she knows exactly what I'm thinking. When she sticks her tongue out at me, I know she remembers. She's so beautiful, even when she's being sassy with me.

When I got to Evie's place earlier this evening, she and Celine were just finishing up getting ready. Layne wasn't there yet, so I sat on her bed, and we all talked while they did their finishing touches. I swear the phrase, "Does this look okay?" was said at least 100 times in the span of ten minutes. I don't even know what they were asking about half the time because they both looked drop-dead gorgeous when I arrived. I even told them so, which resulted in me getting a pillow thrown at my face.

Even now that they're all sweaty and their hair is

starting to fall out of their updos, they both look beautiful. I don't know how Layne can act so aloof when his date looks like *that*. Every now and then, he'll dance with Evie or come sit at our table with us. But as soon as Alex calls, Layne follows. Early on in the night, Alex became aware of the power he held over Evie's night and has been abusing it ever since. I'm sure when she thought up her plan to go to prom with Layne, she didn't anticipate it playing out like this.

I did. But I'm not about to piss her off by telling her that. Instead, I'll just be the supportive friend like I always am and treat both her and Celine like my dates.

Dance lessons with Ms. Cheryl really strengthened our friendship again. Evie and I haven't kissed since the first night of the ski trip, and it seems like keeping that boundary set has been helping maintain a healthy dynamic between us. As much as I want to test those boundaries, I'm prioritizing having a healthy friendship with her. That doesn't mean I've completely given up hope; it just means that I'm a little more in touch with reality now.

Having Celine to talk to has been a helpful distraction during this transition with Evie. We get along great, and she's so easy to talk to. We're both going to the same college in the fall, so we've been talking a lot about dorms, classes, and all the other things freshman stress about leading up to their first year. Though I already know a few people there, including my best friend Bear, it'll be nice to have someone in my grade to commiserate with.

Both Celine and I tried to get Evie to change her mind and come to the same school as us, but she's very set on her decision to be three hours away from me. As the countdown to graduation begins, I continue to feel her slipping away from me. And though I'm going to be gutted when she finally leaves, at least I'll know I tried everything I could to get her.

Celine whips out her phone and takes a selfie of the three of us. "When does the bus come and pick us up?"

I check my watch to see what time it is. "In a half hour."

"Well, we'd better not waste any precious time." With that, she grabs my wrist and Evie's arm and drags us out on the dance floor.

Chapter Twenty-Two

LIAM

Lou's house is packed with both her friends *and* B's friends. Everyone has changed out of their formalwear and into comfier clothing. Mr. and Mrs. Blake greeted us when we first got here, but have disappeared into their room for the remainder of the night.

Someone managed to convince their older sibling to buy booze for them, so I've had a couple drinks. I was glad that the bus ride back into town sobered up most of the group, so I didn't have to play catch-up when we got here. It made being the sober driver on prom night a lot less sad. Though I'm always willing to do it when no one else wants to.

Layne comes into the basement from who knows where and walks over to Evie. I'm sitting on the couch next to Celine, playing a card game. Evie sits across the coffee table from us, so I can sort of make out what they're saying, but it's muffled due to the loud music and constant chatter.

I'm pretty sure I heard him say he's heading out. And by the looks on her face, this wasn't communicated to her prior to now. I can see the disappointment in her eyes behind her forced smile. She nods and stands to give him a hug before he heads back up the stairs.

"What was that about?" I'm glad Celine asked it and not me.

"He had to get going."

"Had to? I thought he was staying here with us?"

"I thought so too. Alex has a group over at his place, so Layne asked if he could go hang out with his friends. I told him I didn't care, so it's all good." Again, she forces a smile, trying to convince us that it doesn't bother her. But that smile never reaches her eyes, which are telling an entirely different story.

Everyone else around us who was listening in goes back to playing the game. Evie stands up and heads toward the bathrooms. I start to follow her, but Celine puts her hand on my knee.

"Just give her some space. If she wants to talk to you about it, she will."

Though I don't believe that's true, I remain in my seat and continue to play the game. I worry about her the entire ten minutes she's gone. When she comes back, her eyes are a little red and puffy, but those eyes still glow a breathtaking bright blue.

"You okay?" I practically mouth the words, keeping my voice quiet enough so no one else can hear me.

She nods. "I was just washing my makeup off."

I didn't even notice that her makeup was gone. Shows how much I pay attention. But I have seen her take her makeup off enough times to know that it doesn't leave her eyes looking like that. *Crying* does.

I catch Evie's eyes glancing down at my lap. I look down and realize that Celine's hand is still on my leg from before. I was too distracted, worrying about Evie, that I didn't even notice. When I look back up at her, she's looking at the table, joining in the game again.

I leave Celine's hand where it is because I don't want to be rude. And if I'm being honest, it feels kind of nice. I've been getting flirty vibes from Celine all day, and part of me wants to lean into it. But another part of me feels like it would be a betrayal to Evie.

What am I saying? Evie has made it very clear that she doesn't want me. She was the one who didn't want to go to prom with me. She was the one who encouraged me to ask someone else. Why shouldn't I enjoy my senior prom night and flirt back with the pretty girl who seems to be into me?

EVIE

I was having the best night of my life up until Layne asked me if he could go hang out with Alex and the rest of their friends. He didn't really *ask* if I was okay with it; he was more so *telling* me what he was going to do. Going to prom with Layne did not have the effect on Alex that I had hoped it would. He seemed wholly unbothered by the fact that my date was one of his best friends.

I hate to admit it, but Liam was sort of right. And I hate it. Now I'm here, alone and sad, surrounded by everyone and their dates. Some of the couples here are actually dating, but a lot of them are just friends. Still, even those friend couples are giving each other their full attention. I wish I were getting that right now.

I look over at Celine and Liam curled up together on the floor in front of the couch. An hour ago, the group decided to put on a movie. Those who didn't want to watch are hanging out upstairs while the rest of us watch a horror movie in the dark. The only reason I'm down here is because I'm not close with anyone who went upstairs. I didn't want to go up there by myself, so I chose another kind of torture instead.

I *hate* scary movies. The comedy that was offered as an option was outvoted significantly. I'm pretty sure people only voted for the scary movie as an excuse to get close to their dates. I hate that it worked. Everyone is snuggled up, and I'm here on an uncomfortable rocking chair by myself. I have no clue what's going on in the movie because I've had a blanket over my eyes for the majority of it.

A creepy violin soundtrack starts playing, indicating something bad is coming, so I cover my eyes again. It's stuffy under this blanket, filled with my hot breath and the stench of my sweat. God, I'm so miserable right now. I am grateful for the darkness, though. It hides the tears that fall when my emotions get the best of me.

Something happens on the screen, behind my blanket shield, making everyone jump, and a few people scream. I swear one of those screams came from Liam, so I lower my blanket to look. He and Celine have sunk even further into the couch, wrapped in each other's arms. They're whispering to each other and giggling. It may be mean, but I hope she's making fun of him for screaming like a girl. I know I would if that were me over there...in his arms...

But it's not me. And that was my choice. I remind myself why and repeat it in my head until I've convinced myself that them being close to each other doesn't bother me. And it *almost* works.

An hour later, the movie finally ends, and half the basement crew is already passed out. There was no set plan for where people were going to sleep; it was just a general consensus that people would crash wherever they found space.

I hear Celine's voice in the dark. "Pssst, Evie. We have some room over here." Liam and Celine are now lying on the floor beside the couch, covered in a massive blanket and using throw pillows for their heads.

"I'm fine here," I whisper back.

"Seriously? You can't sleep in a rocking chair. Liam, tell her she can't sleep in a rocking chair."

"Evie never does a damn thing I suggest."

I giggle to myself, knowing it's 100% true.

"Evie, please come over here, or Liam's going to have to drag you."

Sleep tugs at my body. Today was a long day, so I'm exhausted. And sleeping on this rocking chair was never really an option. "Okay, fine. I'm coming."

I hold the blanket I was using close to my chest as I attempt to navigate through the dark. I move carefully, not wanting to step on anyone who's sleeping on the floor. I bump into a few people, even managing to kick someone in the back of the head. Somehow, I make it to the other side of the room without any major casualties.

"You happy now?"

"Ecstatic." Liam's voice is soft and deep, with a hint of amusement.

I reach down and feel around for the empty space Liam mentioned. "I thought you said there was room over here?"

"There is. Right here." Liam pats the small sliver of floor space between him and whoever is sleeping beside him.

"I'm not squeezing in there." At this point, even a whisper seems too loud, so I make my voice as hushed as I can.

Liam follows suit, and I can barely hear him.

"What?" I kneel down into that small sliver of space so I can hear him.

"I said, I'll sleep on my side, and that should make enough room for you."

"Okay." At this point, I'll sleep on top of whoever is lying next to me. Right now, I'm dead, physically and emotionally. "Thanks."

Liam lies back down and rolls on his side so he's facing Celine. They're practically spooning. I can barely make out their outlines, but I know. I lay down next to him and scrunch up the blanket I brought to use as a pillow. That doesn't leave much fabric to use as an actual blanket, so I'm stuck being partially covered.

I'm tired. I'm cold. I'm sad. And I'm alone. This night really couldn't get much worse. And that sucks because up until Layne ditched me, I was actually having a really great night. Celine was a fun addition to our group, picking up right where we left off at the end of our ski trip. I wish I were between her and Liam right now and not blocked out, lying next to god knows who.

Oh no, here I go again... The tears start streaming down my cheeks before I can stop them. I hold my breath, trying not to make any crying noises. It's too quiet in here; everyone would know. I slowly let out my breath, doing my best not to let it come out shaky, but miserably failing.

Fuck. Why does it seem like I'm always crying?

My body shakes, and I instinctively curl forward, into Liam. My head is pressed into his back, my knees shoved into what I'm pretty sure is his butt. My fists are wrapped in the blanket, strangling themselves. I want to move, but I can't. I cannot get myself to pull away from him. I'm taken off guard when I feel a warm hand on my thigh. Liam. His thumb rubs back and forth across the fabric of my leggings. His touch is comforting, like always.

An intrusive thought pries its way into my brain. *What if he's touching Celine like this, too?*

My heart can't take any more disappointment; it can't take any more pain. I choose to push those hurtful questions out of my mind and focus on the three points of contact between Liam and me. I focus on the sound of his breathing and how it matches with the expansion of his rib cage against my head. The rhythm of his breath makes my body relax, and I finally find some peace.

Chapter Twenty-Three

LIAM

"So when do you leave?" My heart clenches in my chest, and I try to mask the fact that I'm dying inside.

"I start at the restaurant the Tuesday after graduation, so I'll probably move my stuff up to the cabin the day before."

"So basically the day after graduation."

"Mhm." She acts as if this news isn't tearing my heart out.

I thought we'd have more time. I thought we'd get the summer together before we both left for college. Instead, I'll be stuck here while she flees to her parents' cabin for god knows what reason. Well, I have a guess.

"Is this about us?" I keep my voice low so our classmates can't hear. Though I'm sure with the amount of talking and *not* studying going on, they wouldn't hear me even if I asked the question at full volume. Everyone is too excited about it being the last week of school. Especially since most of us don't have any finals left.

The sound of a beaker shattering grabs both of our attention. Evie stands up, and I reach out and grab her wrist to stop her when I finally register what's happened.

"Evie, don't." I glance over at the group that was playing water pong at the lab benches on the other side of the chemistry classroom. The front of Alex's pants is soaked with water, making it look like he pissed himself. "He's not your problem anymore."

She nods and sits down slowly, still not taking her eyes off him.

"Hey." I shake her wrist that's still loosely gripped in my palm. She peels her eyes away from him, finally looking at me. "You don't have to clean up his messes."

"I know."

"Then why did you jump up like you were going to help?"

"I don't know." Realization spreads across her face. She leans over the desk top that's positioned between us, placing her head on her arms. "Ohmygod, I'm so pathetic." The words are muffled by the sleeves of her shirt. After she takes a moment to get over her lapse in judgment, she lifts her head and looks at me, puzzled. "Sorry, what were you saying before?"

"Ummm." I debate repeating my question. Do I even want to go there? "Nothing. I was just asking how you got the job."

"Oh, some friends of my parents own the restaurant. My mom asked them if I could get a summer job there to help save up some money for college."

"I thought your parents were paying for your college."

"They are. But you know, like spending money and stuff. I gotta pay for gas to come see you." She playfully bumps her fist into my shoulder, a fake smile pinned on her face.

"Right." I lift my eyebrows and nod. She keeps saying she'll come visit me at college, but if she really cared about spending time with me, why would she be leaving me at the beginning of the summer instead of the end of it, like we planned?

―――

EVIE

Afraid he'll get the courage to repeat his question from earlier, I opt for a change of subject. "So, you ready for the concert tonight?" I don't want to explain to Liam that the reason I decided to move to the cabin for the summer is because I got jealous after prom and made an impulsive decision. Either way, it's happening, and I'm just hoping it's for the best. I could really use the summer to get in a good headspace prior to leaving for college. I really want to be my best self there.

"As ready as I'll ever be."

I'm still annoyed that he won't tell me what he's performing, but I won't have to wait much longer. The concert is tonight, and I can't wait. The end-of-the-year talent showcase is always full of entertaining acts. People who you didn't even know could sing or play an instrument come out of the woodwork to shock everyone. Liam will be one of them this year. He swore me to secrecy and hasn't told anyone else, except for Lou. I accidentally let that one slip when I was a little drunk at prom.

Lou and I already got our tickets and plan to be there early so we can get seats up front. I've heard a rumor that some of the sophomores put together a glow-in-the-dark dance, and I don't want to risk not being able to see it from all the way in the back.

"You nervous?"

Liam shrugs, acting nonchalant. "A little. The last time I played piano in front of a crowd was my 6th-grade piano recital."

Lou finally comes back from whatever errand our study hall teacher sent her on and sits down at the desk next to me. "The girls are all super nervous."

"The girls?"

Liam gives Lou a look that could kill, and she instantly starts backpedaling. "Ummm, the girls in the choir. Yeah, they're super nervous."

"I'm not buying it." I shift my skeptical gaze from Lou back to Liam. "Are you performing with other people? These girls?"

"Fine..." He rolls his eyes, and I'm not sure if it's directed at me, Lou, or both of us. "I'm playing piano for B, Iris, and a couple of their friends."

"That's awesome. Why wouldn't you tell me that?"

"Because I knew you'd corner one of them and ask what the song was."

Lou and I both laugh. "This is true. I definitely would have done that. Good call, Liam."

Lou leans in. "Did you see Liam's art final?"

"Lou!" Liam bolts forward and throws his hand over her mouth. "What the hell. Are you trying to spoil all my surprises today?"

"Surprises?" I look at Liam with big eyes and a cheesy smile on my face.

He lowers his hand from her mouth, threatening her

with a serious, but not-so-serious look. "You'll just have to wait, and Lou will have to keep her mouth shut."

"Sorry." Lou covers her own mouth now, hiding a huge grin.

I sit back in my chair and think about what Liam could possibly be surprising me with. And I smile to myself, thinking about the surprise I have for Liam.

Chapter Twenty-Four

EVIE

The auditorium is buzzing with excitement as everyone waits for the concert to begin. Lou and I got here early to claim seats at the front. What we didn't anticipate was the motivation the mothers of the performers would have. When we got here an hour early, we thought we'd be first in line, but there were at least 30 moms with their kids already waiting for the doors to open. I can't judge because I know my mother would be doing the exact same if I had a single artistic bone in my body.

The seats we ended up getting are five rows back, which is still very close. Lou said that we're better off back here. She said if anyone in the glow dance routine falls off stage in the dark, we're well out of the danger zone.

I shove a handful of popcorn in my mouth. At this rate, it's going to be gone before the show ever starts. "Do you know if anyone else from our class is performing?"

"I have no clue. People are always so secretive about the lineup. I think it's in case they chicken out at the last minute. I know two of the girls were panicking yesterday and wanted to back out. Thankfully, Liam talked them off the ledge."

"How do you know that?"

"They've been practicing at our house some of the time. We have a keyboard in the basement from B's little phase when she thought she was going to be a rockstar."

That sounds on brand. "When was that?"

"Oh, I think it's still going on. Hence the need to showboat in front of the whole school." She points at the stage where the curtains are currently drawn.

Her comment earns us a nasty look from a mom sitting next to us. I'm sure she's appalled at the thought of her child's talents being perceived as showboating. Whatever, in three days I'm getting the hell out of here, so I'll probably never see her again.

Lou smiles and waves, trying to recover from her insult. "Just kidding."

The audience starts to settle as the lights dim.

"Do you know when they go on?"

"I think B said they were one of the last ones."

"Well, here we go."

WE'RE APPROACHING the two-hour mark, so we have to be getting close to the end. There were a couple of performances that had me questioning whose dick they sucked to get selected. But overall, this year's talent showcase has been surprisingly good. No one fell off the stage during the glow-in-the-dark dance, which I would consider a win. However, one of the glow sticks strapped to a guy's leg flew off into the crowd when he was doing a cartwheel. So far, that's been my favorite act.

The curtains open again, and soft blue lights start to illuminate the stage. Four girls stand evenly spaced apart with mic stands in front of them. I spot Iris's wavy red locks and B's bright blue hair in two braids.

"This is them!" Obviously, Lou knows since she can see what I see, but I can't help but be excited.

"Here, read this." Lou hands me a folded-up piece of notebook paper with the fringe still on it.

"What's this?"

"Liam asked me to give it to you before they started."

The music starts as I take the note from Lou. I quickly unfold it and read the note written in Liam's near-perfect handwriting. I always admired the fact that he doesn't have messy boy handwriting. It shows his attention to detail. I guess that's the artist in him.

The emcee introduces the performers and announces that they'll be singing Grow As We Go by Ben Platt. Never heard of it.

I spot Liam behind them on the piano. As he starts to play, I have to pry my eyes off him to read his note.

Evie,

I picked this song when I still thought there was a chance between us. I picked it for you. Please know that, though it kills me, I respect your choice to leave. Still, this song speaks quite accurately to how I feel. Take that for what it's worth.

Love,

Liam

JUST AS I finish reading the letter, the piano intro is over, and Iris starts singing. She's actually really good, making it easy to listen to the lyrics. I've never heard this song before, but something is familiar about the tune. As I listen closely, I realize that Liam has been humming the melody for weeks. I settle into my seat and listen closely. After all, Liam said he chose this song for *me*. The least I can do is try to understand the message.

I start crying not even one minute into the song. I wasn't expecting it to hit me like a ton of bricks the way it is. At some point, I completely forget about the girls on stage. I can only stare at Liam behind the piano.

I barely notice Lou tapping me on the shoulder. "Here, I brought these for you." She holds out a pack of tissues.

She knew what song they were performing. Did she know I was going to be a sobbing mess? Is it that obvious that my feelings toward Liam are as clear as a muddy window? Does everyone know that despite my stubbornness, deep down I know I love Liam, and I crave the way he adores me?

As the song continues, the tears come harder. I work my way through the entire pack, my purse now full of crushed and sopping wet tissues. Though I'm sunk down as far into my chair as I can be, I don't dare look around me to see what kind of attention I've drawn to myself. As much as I want to run out the side door of the auditorium so no one can see me bawl my eyes out, I have to stay until the end. After all I've put Liam through, I owe it to him.

The song ends, and the auditorium erupts with applause, as expected. The girls crushed it, and I'm pretty sure I wasn't the only one in the crowd with wet eyes. I even saw Lou dab the corner of her eye with her sleeve at one point.

As the applause dies down and the lights fade, I use the cover of darkness to mask my exit. As I pass her by, I whisper to Lou, "I'll be right back." She doesn't bother to ask where I'm going. My raccoon eyes make it obvious.

I slip past the rest of the people in our row and speed walk down the aisle to the back of the auditorium. I wait until the lights come back up before opening the doors, trying not to draw too much attention to myself. Instead of going to the bathrooms close by, I jog down the hallway to the locker rooms.

As soon as I'm out of sight, I unleash everything I was holding back. It's hard to believe that there's more bottled up in here after the embarrassing water show I put on in my seat. My body goes into a full-blown meltdown. I feel like a kid who skipped their nap and just got put in timeout without any explanation as to why I'm being punished. I'm confused. I'm sad. I'm scared. The difference is, I know why. And it's all my fault.

I sit on the floor, back against my old locker, and let it all out. I don't care that my sobs are echoing off the brick walls and cheap laminate floor. No one will hear me way down here unless they're also looking for a place to escape.

Though I made it look easy, saying no to Liam those ten times was hard. Yes, ten. He kept count and continuously reminded me of his persistence. I think the hardest part about it was the fact that I know he would make a great boyfriend, and I *do* love him. But my analytical brain did the math, and the cons outweigh the pros. And yes, Liam's great, but the odds of me finding someone who makes me just as happy in college have to be high. My pool of men to choose from is going to multiply a hundred times. Why would I limit myself to the boys who go to my small, private high school? Especially when I'm so desperate to get out of here and leave this place behind me. That makes sense, right? Am I delusional?

I lift my head off my damp knees and tilt it back, trying to use gravity to stop the tears from flowing. Instead, the only thing I manage to do is smack my head against the locker behind me. "Ow."

Chapter Twenty-Five

LIAM

The last two days of school were a joke. Once we all finished our finals, there was no point in being there, except for the fact that we had to be. We had several snow days this winter, so to make up for those days, we tacked them on to the end of the year. So, where the seniors usually get a couple of days off, we had to be in school.

The teachers even understood how lame that was and practically gave us free rein of the school. We played kickball in the gym, watched *several* movies in the auditorium, and tried to stay out of trouble. Though we definitely did things that should have gotten us in trouble. We did things that I imagine wouldn't fly at a bigger school. I guess there are some perks to a small town after all.

The most entertaining part was watching several pranks play out. A group of guys in our class took it upon themselves to mess with the teachers, the underclassmen, and even the poor janitors. Though some of them went a little too far, most were harmless.

One of the teachers has a serious phobia of cheese. It makes absolutely no sense, and she won't explain it to anyone, but it's a commonly known fact at the school–Mrs. Kessel *loathes* cheese. For one of their pranks, the guys bought a case of pre-sliced cheese from Costco. You know, the kind that's sticky and contains very little real cheese. They unwrapped all of them and stuck them to her desk. I mean, completely covered it. I was at the other end of the school when she found her desk in that state, but I could still hear her scream. I'd consider that a harmless prank if she didn't pass out and have to go see the school nurse.

The last couple of days were a blast, but I'm happy to say that today is finally graduation day. Looking around at my classmates, all dressed up in our caps and gowns, has me getting a little emotional. Evie really has been rubbing off on me.

I spot her over by the gym and make my way over. She's standing with her parents and who I'm assuming are her extended family members. I approach cautiously, in case she doesn't want me over there right now. But she spots me and waves me over.

"Congrats."

"You too."

As we hug, the polyester fabric of our gowns makes a swishing noise, and the stupid squares on our hats knock into each other.

"They really didn't think through the design of these things, did they?"

Evie's mom laughs at my joke like she always does. If there's one person I can count on to always make me feel funnier than I am, it's Mrs. Bordeaux. She loves me.

"Let me get a picture of the two of you!"

"Mooooom."

"Evelyn, someday you're going to be thankful for all the pictures I've taken."

I swing my arm around Evie and hug her into my side. "Smile, Evelyn," I say through smiling teeth.

"You are not allowed to start calling me that." She pinches my side for emphasis.

"Sometimes I forget that you have a full name."

"And let's continue forgetting it, thank you."

Evie's mom holds up her phone like a mom. You know, with two hands and way too far away from her face. "Smile!"

"Okay, Mom, I'll meet you guys at home in a bit."

"Alright. I have to get back to stirring the crock pot anyway. Don't forget to take some more pictures with your friends!"

Evie is already dragging me away before her mom finishes her sentence. "I will!"

We march down the hallway, Evie leading the way. "Where are we going?"

"To my car. I have your graduation present there."

"You got me a present?"

She looks at me through the corner of her eyes. "Of course I did."

"Good, because I got you one too. And it's also in my car."

"How about we both go grab them from our cars and then meet on the steps?"

"No, it'll be too crowded there. How about by our bench?"

"Perfect."

There's a bench on the side of the school that sits beneath a big willow tree. It's where we usually ate lunch together in the warmer months. It'll be nice and private over there. Not that I'm embarrassed by my gift, but I'd like her to open it when we're alone. I taped a card on the back of it that is for her eyes only. If she decides to read it right away, she wouldn't want anyone else around.

I run to my car and rip off my cap and gown, throwing them in the back seat without a care. I giggle to myself when I hear Evie's voice in my head telling me to fold it so it won't wrinkle. I grab the canvas and head towards the bench.

I'm only waiting there a couple of minutes when she rounds the corner. God, she's beautiful. She strides over in her heels and short blue dress, taking my breath away. When she showed up at school this morning, she was already in her graduation gown, so I didn't get to see her like this.

"You look great."

She does a cute little twirl for me. "Thank you! You don't look too bad yourself."

"Iris dressed me."

"She did good."

She hands me the giant gift bag she's carrying and plops down on the bench next to me. It's too big to fit on my lap, so I set it down on the ground in front of me.

"Open it!"

I pull out the tissue paper and pin it under me so it won't fly away in the breeze. I reach in and pull out something bulky. When I saw the size of the bag, I figured it was a bunch of smaller things, but it's one big item.

"Evie..."

She's grinning from ear to ear, clearly proud of herself. "Do you like it?"

"Love it." I stare down at the massive acrylic paint set in front of me. "Thank you." I'm slightly in shock, so I don't know what else to say. This had to have cost a ton. Actually, I know it did because I've been slowly collecting colors over time, because a single tube is ridiculously expensive.

"There were several different color options, and I couldn't decide which one you'd want, so I just got the big one with the most colors."

"This is amazing, Evie. It makes my gift look super lame."

"Stop that. You're not allowed to compare. Remember how the birthday gift you got me blew the one I got for you out of the water? Consider us even."

"Alright. Well, here's mine. Lower your expectations."

She rolls her pretty blue eyes at me. She holds my gift in her lap and slowly starts tearing away the wrapping paper. "It's wrapped so nicely, I don't want to ruin it."

"Iris wrapped it for me."

"Sounds like you're gonna be a mess without Iris around next year."

"Probably. But you're not allowed to tell her that."

"Your secret's safe with me." She gives up on being gentle and tears the paper right down the middle, exposing a strip of the acrylic painting. "Ohmygod." She makes quick work of removing the rest, discarding it on the bench between us.

As she ogles over it, I crumple up the paper and place it in my gift bag along with the tissue paper I'm sitting on. When I look back at her, she has tears in her eyes. Usually, I hate seeing her cry, but I'm pretty sure these are tears of joy. Or at least I hope they are.

"Say something."

Her hand flutters over her mouth before brushing carefully over the textured plaster and acrylic paint. "It's... you're so damn talented, Liam." Her fingers curl around the edge of the 16" by 20" canvas as she takes in the painting. Her eyes are fixed, taking it all in, lips slightly parted.

"This was my art final that Lou mentioned."

She looks at me with eyes as big as saucers. "Other people saw this?"

"Just my teacher and a few classmates. I hope you don't mind that I used you as my muse..."

Her lips stretch into a smile. "Your muse, huh?"

"I'm not trying to be funny, that's what it's called."

"Makes me feel like Rose on the Titanic."

I notice her cheeks turn a little pink, and I can't help but try to make them red. "Except you're not naked in this. I tried to paint that at first, but I couldn't get the nipples quite right."

Evie's closed fist smacks into my chest faster than I can blink. "Liam! Don't you dare joke about that."

I rub my chest as I laugh. "Ouch. You brought it up."

She looks back at the painting, acting like she didn't nearly knock the wind out of me. "It really is beautiful."

"I never thought I'd hear you say that about yourself."

"I'm talking about your art. It's abstract enough where I can pretend I'm not staring at a portrait of myself. It's cool because some people might not be able to see it, but I can tell it's me."

"It's the eyes."

"It is..." She leans in to inspect it closer. "How did you do that?"

"When you spend a ton of time staring at something, it's pretty easy to replicate the little details that make it unique."

Her expression changes to something more serious. "I need you to listen to me, Liam." She points to the painting. "This is not normal. Very few people are this talented. I know I sound like a broken record, but you seriously need to consider pursuing this as a career. I know that's not your plan, but it would be a shame if you let your talents go to waste."

"I've already registered for classes."

"Change them. Or change your major after the first semester. People do that all the time."

I shrug. "We'll see."

She stares me down a moment longer. "Consider it."

"I will." I say the words, but we both know there's not much honesty behind them. We've gone around in circles about this very topic. Art is something I do as a hobby. For most people, it doesn't lead to a fruitful career, and I'm not sure I'm willing to risk my future like that.

"Regardless, I love my painting."

Hoping that she's done pestering me about this, I change the subject. "You never said what you thought of the performance."

"I texted you that I loved it."

"Yeah, but everyone says that."

"It really was great. You crushed it, Liam. And I had no idea B and Iris could sing!"

She's dodging the real question, but today is supposed to be a happy day, so I won't push it. "It was really fun playing for other people again. It's one thing to play in a room by myself, but making music with others is so much better."

"The song was beautiful. Your note said you picked it?"

"I did."

"The girls didn't want to pick their own song?"

"They had a different one picked out, but I told them the only way I'd accompany them was if I got to pick the song. They all agreed to it, and that was that."

"I loved it."

"I second-guessed it a lot, but then it was too late to change it."

"Lou gave me your note. I understood. It was really sweet of you, regardless."

"Did you cry?"

Evie scoffs. "Rude! You can't ask a lady if she cried."

"You definitely cried."

"Stop it!"

"It's not a bad thing. I love how much you feel your emotions. It's a gift."

"No, it's a curse."

"Sometimes I wish I felt a wide array of emotions as deep as you do. You feel joy and excitement more than anyone else I know. And not just your own feelings. You're a total empath, and I love that about you."

"That makes one of us."

"Well, Negative Nancy, you ready to go to the grad party?"

"I have to run home first and spend an hour or so with my family. I'll text you when I'm ready, and we can ride out together."

EVIE

I walk into my house carrying a tote bag full of stuff from the graduation ceremony. I can hear my family in the living room before I even open the door.

"There she is! Our graduation gal!" My uncle pulls me into an aggressive hug, almost crushing my bag.

When he lets go, I check my bag to make sure Liam's painting didn't get ruined.

All clear.

My mother catches me looking at it and walks over. "What's this, sweetie?" Being the nosy mother she is, she pulls it out of the bag before I even have a chance to answer.

"Liam made it for me."

"Oh my. This is beautiful. It's you, right?"

I nod. "Mhmm."

"This has to go up in your room. Do you mind if I hang it up for you?"

"Go for it."

She doesn't budge. Instead, she stands there admiring the painting as my aunties all crowd around her to look at it. I want to feel embarrassed, but my situation with Liam hasn't really been private—most of my family knows and has even met him. "It really is a shame you two didn't meet in college."

Her words aren't meant to hurt me, but I still feel a pinprick in my heart. "Yeah..."

Since I told my mother I wanted to go to college single, she has been in full support of my decision, even reminding me when I waver from that path. She's not pushy, she just gently reminds me of what *I said I wanted.*

My mom and I are close; she knows *everything* that happens in my life, for better or worse. My parents are *the* definition of helicopter parents. But that'll happen when a woman who struggles through years of infertility finally gets her baby girl, and then never has a successful pregnancy after. It used to bother me that privacy was hard to come by in my house, but after learning more about Liam's relationship with his mom, I've grown to appreciate the closeness I share with mine.

Don't get me wrong, Liam *loves* his mother. But when

you have to become the "man of the house" at the age of twelve, it changes the dynamic.

"What time is your party?"

My mother's voice gently pulls me from my thoughts, and I realize my aunts have dispersed, and it's just me and my mother standing in the entryway.

"I'll stay here for an hour or so, then text Liam to come pick me up."

"Did you text me that address yet?"

"I'll send it to you."

"Now please."

I pull out my phone and scroll through the group chat to find the address the girls sent to me.

"Come on, sis, give her a break. Let the kid live a little," my uncle shouts from the living room.

My mother ignores her brother and waits for her phone to ping with the message I just sent. "Thank you, honey. You know I just want to make sure you're safe, right?"

"I know." I nod, trying my best to reassure her.

"I still don't know why you're not just going to Layne's graduation party out at the farm? I'd feel so much better if I knew the parents who were supervising the event."

"Mom..." She knows why I'm not going to my class's grad party. There isn't anyone there, other than Lou, that I want to see me with lowered inhibitions. That's why when Liam's hockey friends invited us to their grad party, I didn't hesitate to accept their offer.

"I know, I know. But you can't keep letting Alex ruin everything for you."

"He won't after tomorrow when I get the hell out of here."

She flinches, and I realize that my wanting nothing to

do with the town she chose to settle down in might be a tad insulting.

"You know what I mean."

"I know, honey." She pulls me into a one-armed hug, still holding Liam's painting in the other, pressing a kiss to my temple. With a heavy sigh, she admits, "I've always known you were bound for bigger and better things than this place."

Chapter Twenty-Six

LIAM

My ears ring with the vibration of the speakers that I unfortunately chose to stand by. Actually, why the hell am I still standing here? I look down at the drink in my hand. Oh yeah, I was refilling this. I've had my fair share of drinks tonight, which probably means I don't need another. But tonight is a special night, and I'm mostly around people I trust. It's a huge party that the public school kids are throwing, so of course, I don't know everyone. But all the seniors on my hockey team are here as well as some of their friends I've met over the years.

I look over at Evie dancing, drink in hand, and a huge smile on her face. I can't help but feel a twinge of sadness, knowing this will be our last night in St. Francis together. But I am glad we chose to come to Jax's house instead of Layne's. This way, we don't have to worry about Alex ruining her night. We can just focus on letting loose and celebrating the end of one chapter of our lives. I hope that we have many more to celebrate in the future, but I'm not getting my hopes up anymore.

The song ends, and she walks over. I note the sweat dampening the hair along her forehead. "I need some fresh air. It's getting stuffy as hell in here."

"I'll go outside with you."

As she walks to the door, I can't help but place my hand on her back. This earns me a wink from Jax as we walk by him. He probably thinks I'm getting laid tonight, but I know that would be an insane turn of events.

Evie stops abruptly in front of me, and I catch myself before I run into her. "What's—" I cut myself off when I get my answer.

Two girls about ten feet in front of us are causing a traffic jam. They've managed to grab the attention of everyone around them by eating each other's faces like their lives depend on it. I'd be lying if I said it wasn't hot as fuck.

I put my hand on Evie's back again, trying to guide her around the crowd so we can get outside. But my gentle gesture doesn't make her budge. I step to her side and look down at her. Her eyes are fixed straight ahead. At first, the look reminds me of the time she saw Alex kissing someone for the first time after their breakup. But this is different. Instead of pain on her face, there's a slight smile. And her eyes...there's a fire there that I know all too well. My head twists to confirm that she's staring at the girls and not something else.

Her trance is broken when she finally notices me staring down at her. "Why are you staring at me like that?" A crease forms between her eyebrows, as if she wasn't just staring at two girls making out like she wanted to join them.

"Were you just...?"

"Was I just *what*?"

The wheels in my head start to turn. I can practically

hear the gears squeaking from lack of use this past week of doing nothing but fucking around in class.

"Evie, do you...?" Like women? I can't get myself to finish the sentence out loud. But the pained look on her face tells me I don't need to.

"I need some air." Her shoulder bumps me as she passes by aggressively, speedwalking toward the door.

"Wait! I'm coming." I follow after her, weaving my way through people as best I can. She's smaller than I am, so she makes it to the door before I can catch up.

She slams the patio door behind her so hard that it bounces right back open. Luckily, the music is so loud in here that only a few people notice before going back to their previous entertainment.

I throw open the door and close it behind me, more gently than Evie just did. I look left then right, spotting her walking toward a row of evergreens that extends well into the darkness of the night. Jax lives out of town on a huge lot surrounded by nothing but forest.

"Evie!" She doesn't bother turning around, just continues straight for the trees. She disappears into the branches, and I jog across the massive gravel driveway to catch up.

When I get there, I push my way through the overgrown limbs that intertwine between the individual trees. The pine branches scratch my bare arms, but I keep going.

Part of me expected her to already be halfway down the row, but to my surprise, she's standing right there. Her back is facing me, so I approach slowly.

I put my hands on her shoulders and attempt to lighten the mood. Whatever's going on is likely just a symptom of alcohol and exhaustion– it's been a long day.

"Why is it that I always find myself chasing you?" I start

to rub her shoulders, but she steps away from me, and I let my hands fall to my sides.

"I didn't ask you to."

"Fair. But I'm not just going to let you wander out into the night by yourself."

She turns on her heels, her long curls whipping over her shoulder and across her face. "Just stop."

"Stop what?" I say with my hands raised in surrender.

"Trying."

I don't know how to respond to that. I didn't think that following her out here would upset her like this. She knew I was joining her to get some air.

She's facing me, but she can't look me in the eyes. "Hey."

Her mesmerizing blue eyes reluctantly find mine.

I lower my hands, taking a risky step toward her. "What's this really about?"

She shakes her head, keeping her lips pressed tight between her teeth. But she doesn't retreat when I take yet another step closer, closing the gap between us.

I calculate the odds of this blowing up in my face and decide it's worth the risk. The three shots I took earlier are likely skewing my data, but I do it anyway. I grab her face with both my hands and pull her toward me. Just before our lips meet, hers part in a gasp that I snuff out with my own.

It's been months since we've kissed. I almost forgot how euphoric it feels to have her like this.

She relaxes into the kiss, so I take it deeper, sweeping my tongue in, against hers. Her hands slide up my chest and cling to the front of my sweatshirt. Everything is perfect for all of a minute before her hands release the fabric and flatten against my stomach, shoving me away.

Fuck.

Her palms press into her face, covering any evidence that this is just as hard for her as it is for me. "Liam, I can't do this."

I step forward and reach out for her, but pull my hands back when she takes a step away from me. "Goddamit, Evie. Come on. What are we doing here?"

"We were doing so well." Her voice is still muffled by her hands, and I want nothing more than to rip them away from her face so she has to look me in the eyes when she rejects me for the eleventh time this year.

"Why are you so against this?"

Her hands fall and cross over her chest. "I'm not explaining this to you again."

"Humor me."

"I am going to college single. That's what I want. End of story."

The door on the side of the garage that we came out of slams, grabbing my attention. A group of girls giggle as they stumble across the yard to the row of trees on the other side. When I look back at Evie, I catch her staring at the girls like I just was, and it reminds me of the look that was on her face only minutes ago when those two girls were sucking face in the garage.

Those cogs that were turning start to move again. "Ohmygod," I whisper.

That gets her attention. "What?"

"You like girls." It's not a question.

She recoils the way people do when someone really insults them. "What? No."

"It's okay. You can be honest with me." No response. "It actually makes a lot of sense."

Her face turns from hurt to sour. "You'd like that, wouldn't you?"

"I mean—"

"You think that if I say I like girls, it explains why I don't want you."

"Evie—"

"Well, it doesn't!" Her voice keeps rising in intensity, but not volume.

"I didn't say—"

"But you were thinking it, weren't you?" She cocks an eyebrow.

"It would explain—"

"It wouldn't explain *shit*, Liam! The reason I continuously reject you isn't because I'm secretly in love with women." She takes a step toward me, and for the first time tonight, I wish she wouldn't. "It's much simpler than that." Another step closer. "Have you ever thought that maybe I truly just don't want *you*?"

"I don't think you mean—"

"Oh, I mean it!"

"Will you stop cutting me off!" I don't even recognize my voice. This isn't her. This isn't me. What are we doing?

"I already know what you're going to say before you even say it. I know you, Liam. I've spent seven months getting to know you better. And you know what? I still don't want you."

Her words cut deeper and deeper. Every insult is just confirmation that there's no coming back from this.

"I can't be here anymore." She turns and pushes her way through the trees.

"Evie, wait." I follow her, desperate for any sign that she doesn't really mean what she says.

"Leave me alone."

"Where are you going?"

"Home."

"How? I drove you, remember?" She stomps toward the driveway full of vehicles, looking around for god knows what. "Just come back inside. We'll get you some water, and you can cool off. I'll even give you some space."

She turns to me, a sadness I've only ever seen once before etched on her face. "We both know you're not capable of that."

An engine purrs and headlights flood my vision. I throw up my arm to block the blinding light. Feminine voices are barely audible over the sound of the car.

I walk out of the spotlight and see Evie leaning over, talking to the driver through the window. By the time I get over there, she's standing up and walking toward the door to the back seat.

"Evie, we need to talk."

She pulls open the door, and I stand there frozen as she steps around it. She gets one foot in the car and pauses, turning to look at me. "We're done talking, Liam. Better yet, do us both a favor and don't try talking to me ever again."

The door slams shut, and it feels like my heart is wedged between the frames.

"Have a good summer!" I don't recognize the voice that yells at me as the car drives off, but I know it's not Evie.

"*Fuck!*" My voice is swallowed by the trees surrounding the house.

I turn and do the most illogical thing I've ever done. I ram my fist into the side of the truck next to me, likely shattering my knuckles and denting the door panel in the process. Pain blasts through my hand and up my arm, but it doesn't compare to the pain in my chest. I cry out, but no one is around to hear me. No one is around to care. And once again, I'm surrounded by people but completely alone.

Chapter Twenty-Seven

LIAM

Can we talk before you leave?

Hope you made it to the cabin safely.

Will you be back for Thanksgiving? I'd love to talk.

Merry Christmas.

EVIE

Merry Christmas.

LIAM

Happy Birthday, Evie.

EVIE

Thank you. Happy belated birthday.

LIAM

Do you have any fun plans?

Chapter Twenty-Eight

Four Months Later

LIAM

"What's your major?"

I bend over so the attractive brunette I'm talking to can hear me over the loud music. "I'm undecided right now."

"Me too. I don't get how they can expect us to know exactly what we want to do for the rest of our lives when we haven't even lived yet."

"That's a good point."

Someone walks behind her and pushes her into me. When they pass, she doesn't bother to take a step back. Instead, she places her free hand on my chest and looks up at me through her thick eyelashes. "Wanna get out of here?"

I swallow hard. I've had a couple of girls back to my room since college started, and every time it's like the last. We make out for a while, I lose interest, and then they get annoyed at me and leave. Who's to say this one will be any different?

"My roommate actually has a girl back there right now." I don't actually know if he does, but he's pretty popular amongst the girls in his poetry class, so I wouldn't be surprised if he did.

"We can wait our turn." She bites on her bottom lip. She's a gorgeous girl, so it should work, but all that pops into my head is Evie.

Fuck.

I've been doing so well the last few weeks without thinking about her. I've been avoiding the piano practice rooms that they let students rent out, because every time I play, I think of her. At the beginning of the semester, I tortured myself in those rooms for hours, putting all my anger and sadness into those keys. Now, I save myself the heartache and just binge-watch Netflix shows to fill my free time.

I realize that she's still staring up at me, and I wonder how long I zoned out for. "I..."

"It's all good. You can just say no."

I'm not sure if she's disappointed or annoyed, but I'm grateful for the out. "Sorry, I'm just not in a place to be doing that right now."

"Well, if you are later, come find me." Her hand slowly gazes down my chest before she walks away.

I wait until she's with her friends again and make my way toward the door. I need a minute to collect myself, to get out of my own head.

I step out into the backyard, and I'm instantly reminded how cold it is. My sweatshirt is thick, but not enough to keep me from freezing out here. I spot a light on in the garage and decide to take my chances.

I trudge through the packed snow, my feet occasionally sinking in when I put too much weight on one leg. Snow falls into the top of my shoe, freezing my ankles. This was such a dumb idea. This door better be open.

I get to the side door of the garage and twist the handle, relieved when it gives way. Thank god. I step inside and am greeted with a cloud of smoke that smells like weed. Sure enough, on the couch in the corner of the garage is a group of people, lighting up a joint.

"Hey there," the one with a hot pink bun on top of her head greets me.

"Hey. Sorry to intrude. Just needed to get out of the noise for a bit."

"No worries. Come on in and have a seat. We just rolled some new ones." She holds out a joint for me to take.

"I can't smoke a whole one of those, or I'll be stuck to this couch for the rest of the night."

"I'll share with you." A beautiful girl with perfectly done box braids, sitting at the end of the couch, scoots over and pats the newly open space next to her.

Why the hell not? I sit down next to her, trying not to crowd her space. She picks up a lighter off the coffee table in front of her, and the group goes back to chatting about whatever they were talking about before I interrupted. She starts it, taking a few puffs for herself, then hands it to me. I take a hit and pass it back. Releasing all my air, the smoke trails out from between my lips. I instantly feel calmer. My hands, which I didn't even realize were shaking, become steady.

"So, who are you hiding from?"

I cough a little before replying, "No one."

"Come on...we're all hiding from someone."

I'm not sure if she means hiding out here in this garage or just life in general. She hands back the joint, and I take another small hit, noting the faint stains on her fingertips that look like they were made by blue acrylic paint. "I wouldn't say I'm *hiding* as much as I'm trying to get out of my own head."

"Well then, you've stumbled across the right place."

"Seems so."

She smiles at me with her straight white teeth, and I feel my whole body start to relax.

"Sometimes I feel like I need to go deeper into my own head before I can get out."

I'm not sure if it's the weed or if what she's saying actually makes a lot of sense.

"Here." She scoots over a little more and pats the back cushion of the couch. "Lean back and close your eyes."

I do as I'm told, readjusting in my seat so I can rest my head back on top of the cushion behind me. Once I'm comfy, I close my eyes.

"Just like that. Now, picture your happy place."

I open one eye to look at her. "My happy place?"

"Yeah. Everyone has a happy place. Somewhere you always feel good." She uses her finger to force my open eye closed.

Until these past few months, my happy place was sitting in front of a piano. Now, it's tainted by the memories of Evie that haunt me there. "I don't think I have one."

"Yes. You do." I hear her take another hit, and then I feel her place it between my lips. I inhale again and exhale when she removes it. "If you can't think of anything current, then think of the last time you didn't feel stress or worry. Think of the last time you felt free to just exist."

The first thing that comes to mind is that I haven't felt that way since before my dad passed. That was truly the last time I didn't feel like I carried anyone else's burdens. The only thing I had to worry about back then was what color I wanted my rug to be.

I'm transported back into a memory. I'm standing in my room at my parents' house. The old one where I lived with Mom, Dad, and Iris, before Dad died and before we moved to St. Francis. I remember how that room always smelled like whatever Mom was cooking in the kitchen directly below. I look down and see that I'm standing on my circular blue rug. The one that Mom let me pick out all on my own. It's an odd shade of blue, but I love it. I still have it in my room at Mom and Frank's house. I can feel the shag of the rug on my bare feet. The way it tickles between my toes. I laugh. I look around at the hockey trophies on my dresser, my posters hanging on the wall, and my Superman bedspread. Damn, I loved this room.

I hear my dad calling my name from downstairs. Except he's calling me "dude" and it's not my dad's voice...

My eyes shoot open, and I glance around. The girl with the box braids is staring down at me with a smile on her face. I blink a few times, my eyes feeling dry. I have no idea how long I was out for, but it couldn't have been long since she's still holding the lit joint in her hand.

"Where did you go?"

I could tell her. I could explain that my childhood bedroom is the last place I truly felt at peace. But we don't even know each other's names, and I need to get home. "My happy place, I guess."

"I love that for you." Her smile is so genuine. It reminds me of Evie.

Except this time, the thought of Evie doesn't make me want to tear my heart out. I just remember how much I enjoyed her smile while I had her. And now I at least hope she's finding everything she was looking for, whatever it is she didn't see in me. I really do hope she's happy.

Chapter Twenty-Nine

One Year Later

EVIE

"That was delicious, Mom. Thank you."

It's been two years since I've had my mom's deep-fried Thanksgiving turkey. I didn't realize how much I missed this—a loud house, a home-cooked meal, and endless card games. I didn't miss my cousins flexing their perfect families in my face, though. But I guess it's not their fault that I'm unhappy.

Last year, my freshman year of college, I begged my parents to take us on a vacation instead of me coming back to St. Francis for the holiday. They heard my plea and booked flights to Jamaica the next day. Then, for Christmas, we went to Cancun. Last summer was spent like the summer prior, at the lake with my parents, working at a restaurant nearby.

I couldn't bear the thought of coming back here. I couldn't risk running into Liam, or Alex for that matter. My luck, Alex would ignore me, but with Liam... Well, I've been running from that problem for a year and a half because I don't have the strength to face him.

We haven't talked since the grad party, aside from happy birthday texts sent back and forth. But there was no catching up, no asking how we're doing, nothing. There were plenty of drunken nights when I was a split second away from calling him or replying to one of his many texts. And there were many nights spent wondering if he was doing the same. But I kept my distance, for the sake of my own sanity, and I told myself that it was better for him as well. Things will never be the same between us.

I spent months grieving the loss of his friendship, despite it being mostly my fault that we had a falling out. I shudder at the memory of my drunken rage. Truly one of my weakest moments.

After clearing my plate, I wander over to the living room and find a comfy spot on the oversized L-shaped sofa. In our family, whoever helps cook doesn't have to clean up. A tradition I will absolutely be continuing with my own family one day.

My granny wanders over, shuffling her feet across the hardwood floors. I grab her by the arm and help her onto the couch, next to me. "Hey, Gran."

"Oh, I'm so glad to see you, honey." She leans over and squishes her lips into my cheek. "We missed you last year."

"I know. I missed you guys, too."

"So what's all this nonsense about not wanting to come back home?"

I think through my answer before I say anything. I don't want my grandmother to think that seeing her isn't important to me. "I just wanted a change of scenery."

"Hmmm." She seems unconvinced, but drops it. "How's college? Your mom told me you're taking classes to be an engineer, just like her."

"It's going well. Engineering classes are hard, but from what I've learned from Mom, I think I'll like the work."

"That's good. And what have you learned?"

"Let's see," I think for a moment, "this semester I'm taking Calc 3, which sucks. And—"

"No, sweetie. I mean, what are you learning outside of school? What are you learning about *yourself*?"

I've never been asked that before, so I don't have a prepared answer. "I'm not sure."

"You can't tell me you're the exact same Evelyn that started there three semesters ago."

I think about who I was when I left St. Francis—a heartbroken girl running from her problems. "Definitely not."

"Then what's changed? I remember when your mom went to college, she came back an entirely new woman. In the best way, of course."

I can't help but laugh at her phrasing. An entirely new woman? My mother? "I'm not sure I know what that means, Gran."

"Everyone goes through growing pains and comes out the other side a little different. For some, they're wiser, freer, bolder. And some get cautious, skeptical, and more careful. You know, depending on whether good things or bad things shape you. So tell me, who is the Evelyn sitting next to me?" She pats my thigh with her frail hand.

My gran has never been a surface-level woman. She could make a grown man cry in church with her invasive questions. She always digs, trying to get as much meat out of every conversation as she can. When she passes, no one will be able to say she didn't know them better than their own mothers.

I know I've changed, but I've never sat and thought about the specifics of it. When I think of an answer, I can't help but giggle to myself. This lesson was learned the hard way and was quite a change-up for an only child. "I'm much better at sharing my space with others."

"Oooh, yes, dorms are very trying. They'll make a girl go mad, or turn her into a considerate young woman."

"It did drive me a bit crazy at first, if I'm being honest."

"Of course it did! Who wants to share a shoe box with a stranger? Go on..."

"I learned that I don't actually hate Brussels sprouts. Mom just sucks at making them. Don't get me wrong, she makes plenty of amazing foods, but her Brussels sprouts just aren't one of them."

Gran laughs at that.

"I've learned that college guys aren't all they're cracked up to be." Or girls, for that matter. But I'm not even going to go there with my grandmother. She wouldn't understand. No one in my family, or all of St. Francis for that matter, would understand.

"I didn't even go to college, and I could have told you that."

"Well, I unfortunately learned that freshman guys are just teenage boys with less supervision and easier access to alcohol. God, are they stupid."

Gran laughs so hard she starts coughing.

"You okay, Gran?"

She finally catches her breath and shoos me away. "Oh, quit fussing over me. You're starting to sound like your mother."

"Is that such a bad thing?"

Her demeanor shifts back to something soft and serious. "No, it is not. And that is something that took your mother much longer to realize."

"What's that?"

"That mothers aren't as crazy as their children think they are. Well, maybe we are a little crazy, but it's our children and our husbands that make us that way. At our core, we are very agreeable and understanding, which are wonderful things to be. Someday, when your husband tells you you're being just like your mother, you look him straight in the eyes and say *thank you*."

I forgot how much I love this woman and how damn funny she is. "I'll remember that."

"Good. Now tell me more about these boys pretending to be men. I want aaaaaall the details." She pats my leg again, and this time I reach out to take her hand in mine.

I go on to tell her about all the guys I've been on dates with, all the guys I thought I liked until I actually got to know them. I leave out the part where I tried to date a couple of girls.

After graduation night, I never talked to Liam because I wasn't ready to have an honest conversation with him about my sexuality. I wasn't even able to be honest with *myself* at that point, but of course, he saw it and called me out on it before I even had a chance to process my own realization. After all, it wasn't one grand awakening; it was a slow creep over time—little hints here and there. But growing up in a religious household and going to private school forced me to seal that closet door shut with super glue.

Being at a college far from my hometown with no one who knew the old me was the opportunity I needed to explore that side of me. But dating girls wasn't all it was cracked up to be either. Yes, I'm attracted to them and fantasize about them just as much as guys, but I found that I prefer dating men. The women I tried to date were constantly caught up in drama. And as a conflict-avoidant only child, I avoid drama like the plague.

So no, I don't tell my grandmother about that part of my college experience, but I do tell her how I haven't found a spark with *anyone* and how I'm worried I won't ever find it. These are all things I haven't openly admitted to myself yet, so it's strange pouring it all out to her, especially having to omit crucial parts of my story. She has a way of getting people to open up and share their secrets, but I haven't had *that* much wine tonight.

There's something about her that makes people trust her, and I'm currently falling victim to her charm. But am I going to start spilling my filtered thoughts? No chance.

"I think the hardest part about not being able to find my person is that I've felt those feelings before. I know what it's like to want to be near someone all the time and to get butterflies when you see them. I know how it feels to touch someone and sense the raw chemistry between you. I haven't felt that with anyone I've met at college, and I'm starting to get really discouraged. There's this guy I was recently talking to who's great on paper. I think if I didn't know what it felt like to love someone so deeply, then this guy would seem great to me. But it's the knowing that it can be so much better that made me end things... Does that make sense?"

"It makes perfect sense, my dear. Do you miss him?"

"The guy I was talking to? Not really."

"Don't play dumb, Evelyn." She lifts one wispy, silver brow. "You're not a dummy."

"Gran!"

The shock must show in my face because Gran immediately defends herself. "I said you're *not* a dummy."

"I heard you." Despite the offense I'm trying not to take, I laugh at her audacity.

"You know very well who I'm talking about."

"I don't even remember *what* we were talking about at this point."

"You were crying about how you know what it feels like to be loved and how you don't feel it with this new guy. And then I was politely trying to remind you that the person you felt those things with is still an option."

I understand now. "He's not, though."

"Bullshit."

"Gran!" Who is this woman, and what did she do with my sweet, agreeable granny?

"What? I'm a grown woman. I can cuss around you now that you're not so impressionable."

"You're *something*, that's for sure."

"All I'm saying is that if you want to feel those things again, you know where to find them."

"Thanks for the advice." I'm not exactly sure what to make of her suggestion, but I'm not going to forget what she said any time soon. She was right about the growing and changing in college thing. I have changed a lot since leaving St. Francis. Maybe she's right about this, too.

Chapter Thirty

EVIE

We walk into the bar and unzip our winter jackets. The sign by the door says 'Seat Yourself', so Lou spots an open table, and we claim it for ourselves.

"I can't believe you guys talked me into going out."

B scoffs. "Lou, quit acting like you don't love our holiday traditions."

"I'm not sure I'd call it a tradition if this is the first year we've done it."

"Well, it's going to be a tradition. Every year when we all come home for the holidays, we go to the bar and eat our weight in fries. God, I miss these fries."

"You've been at college for four months."

"Four months is a long time without my favorite fries." B pulls her hair up into a bun like she's getting ready to start a hot dog-eating contest. "They're pretty much the only thing I miss about this place."

I look around and take in my surroundings. The bar still smells exactly the same as it has since I was a kid, and even has the same decor. In our small town, the bar also doubles as a restaurant, so people under 21 are allowed in before 11:00pm; they're just not allowed to drink. We wouldn't even dream of trying to get away with using our fake IDs here since the bartender knows us all by name.

I texted Lou this morning to ask her if she wanted to hang out. I also haven't talked to her since graduation, so I was nervous she wouldn't want to talk to me. She texted back almost immediately, telling me that she had plans to go out with B tonight and invited me to join them. I went back and forth for hours, trying to decide if it was worth the risk of running into Liam. When I didn't respond, she texted me and told me that Liam wouldn't be out tonight. I guess she saw right through my vacation holiday schemes last year.

I was nervous about seeing Iris, since I know she's best friends with B, but she's not coming out till later. By that time, I plan to be plenty drunk, so it shouldn't be a problem.

Even though we can't order drinks at the bar, there are still plenty of ways to get drunk around here. We chose the safest option and put shooters in our pockets. It's simple; when it's busy, you order a Coke and take it to the bathroom with you. Boom. Rum and Coke.

We order food, and I watch Lou and B play a game of pool while we're waiting. B lost and obviously wants a rematch, but only after she eats her weight in fries.

"Lou, who are you texting so much tonight?"

B takes it upon herself to answer for her sister. "Her new boyfriend, Jay."

"You have a boyfriend?"

"I sure do." She doesn't even bother looking up from her phone, which her eyes have been glued to all evening.

It's getting to that point in the night when they open up the dance floor and turn on the karaoke machine. More and more people fill the bar with every minute that goes by. I made the mistake of picking the side of the table that faces the door, so I get to see everyone who enters.

I can't tell if the repeated chill in my spine is from the draft when the door opens or the fact that it always seems to be someone I know walking through that door. Or at least someone I *knew*. If I've changed as much as I have in the past year and a half, who's to say they're the same person they were when I left?

"Oh shit."

Lou, who's sitting across from me, looks up from her burger, concerned. "What?"

B looks over to the door and spots the problem. "Alex is here with his loser friends. I bet they all have micro penises."

As much as I want to, I can't tear my eyes away from him. "I can promise you at least one of them doesn't."

Lou turns around, discreetly. "Couldn't he have at least started balding or something?"

At the moment, all three of us are staring at him, and he happens to glance our way. Lou turns around faster than a tornado, B's eyes shoot down to her plate, my eyes go wide, and my heart starts racing. Oh fuck. We make eye contact before I'm able to avert my gaze.

Of course, I thought about this as a possibility, but fantasizing about it and living it are two very separate ordeals. As far as I can tell from his social media, he doesn't have a girlfriend. He's had a couple since we broke up two years ago, but I think he broke up with his most recent one this summer. One day his feed was all bikini pics and tan lines, the next it was gone. Like she never existed. I remember what it felt like when he deleted all of our pictures. So many memories wiped away in minutes.

Lou lowers her voice to a whisper. "Where are they sitting?"

I watch them as they find a seat. "Over in the booths by the bar."

"Are you going to say hi?"

"God no! Are you crazy? He didn't talk to me when we were in a classroom of six people, what makes you think he wants to talk to me two years later in a crowded bar?"

"We can go somewhere else if you want."

"I'm fine. I don't need to let him have that kind of control over me anymore. I already let him stop me from seeing my family for two holidays last year."

Lou's face contorts in confusion. "You didn't come back because of Alex?"

"Sort of."

"I figured it was because of—"

"No way. That bitch stole my karaoke song!" B cut Lou off before she could explain. But she doesn't need to. I know how that sentence ends.

Over at the karaoke machine, some girls from our high school are screaming I Want It That Way by the Backstreet Boys at the top of their lungs. They all graduated the year before Lou and I did. One of them in particular is Olivia, who is now dating Lou's high school ex-boyfriend, Bear Michaels. Everyone liked her in high school, but there was always something about her that gave me a bad feeling.

"They didn't even sing all the lyrics. They're right there on the screen in front of you, honey." B is sassy and sarcastic as hell tonight, and I'm here for it. "Now I feel the need to get up there and show those girls how karaoke is supposed to work."

"Do it!" Hell would freeze over before I went up there, but I'd love to see B get up there and sing her little heart out.

"Only if Lou comes with me."

"What? No. I'm not going up there."

"Oh yes, you are. You can put that damn phone away for four minutes and sing a song with your favorite sister." B wraps her hands around Lou's arm and practically drags her out of her chair.

Lou reluctantly follows B over to the table where the sign-up sheet is. I sit and wait for them to return, but the line must have been short because they immediately get called up to the stage. The song "iSpy" starts playing, and a wave of nostalgia hits me. I can't believe they're up there, about to sing this banger from our high school days. I've never sung karaoke and I never will, but damn if I don't want to sing along right now.

Out of nowhere, a cold hand lands on my shoulder, making me jump. As my butt temporarily floats off the seat, I twist to see who's behind me. By the time I land on the seat again, I have my answer. I try to utter a simple hello, but nothing comes out. The shock I'm experiencing must be written all over my face because he starts to get this cheeky grin on his face, like he's amused that his presence can leave me speechless.

"Hey, Evie."

Finally, something comes out of my mouth. "Alex. What are you doing here?" But I wish it hadn't. Such a stupid question. He's here doing what everyone else in this bar is here to do.

"Just came to get a bite to eat with some of the guys. I wanted to get out of my parents' house for a while."

I glance over his shoulder to see if I can spot any of his friends watching us. I feel relieved when I can't see any of them. The last thing I need right now is to feel like I'm about to be made the laughing stock in front of his friends again.

"Mind if I sit? Looks like you're going to be alone for a few minutes." He tips his head toward the back wall, where Lou and B are crushing it on the karaoke machine.

"Ummm, sure."

He pulls out the chair next to me and takes a seat. He's so casual. How is he this calm right now? Do I really not make him feel even a fraction of the nerves I feel when he's around me?

"How has school been going for you? Are you still planning to be an engineer like your mom?"

I swallow hard and try to put together a sentence that doesn't make me sound like a blubbering idiot. "Yeah, I am. Classes have been hard, but the social part of college has been really fun."

"That's great. You were always super social, so I'm sure you have no problem making friends."

He's being strangely nice to me right now, and I'm not sure what to think of it. The guy in front of me is acting like his old self. He's acting like *my* Alex. The Alex that loved me for three years, and the Alex I knew for nine years prior to that. I'm trying not to get swept up in it, but that's easier said than done. "How's college been for you?"

"It's been good. Same thing you said, the school part isn't any fun, but the rest makes up for it.

I can't shake the feeling that this is all a cruel prank. "Alex. What are you doing here?"

"I already answered that question."

"I mean *here*, at this table, talking to me."

He shrugs and takes a beat before he responds. "Just wanted to say hey and see how you're doing."

From the corner of my eye, I can see Layne. I can't help but watch him and a couple of the other guys as they approach my table. The moment Alex notices them coming over to us, he stands. His body language completely shifts.

"Evie!" Layne comes over and gives me an awkward, hunched-over hug since my legs didn't get the memo to stand first.

"Hey, Layne."

In the background, I hear the song end, and the crowd applauds. Thank god, Lou and B will be back soon to rescue me from this nightmare.

Layne is the only one who greets me; the rest are standing around Alex with their thumbs up their butts. Layne and I make small talk for a minute or two until the girls get back to the table. Now that everyone else is standing but me, I scoot my chair out and get on their level. I don't register what kind of exchange occurs between them because my focus is on Alex. He can't even look at me right now. What happened to the guy who was warm and welcoming to me just moments ago?

I walk around Layne, over to Alex. It takes him far too long to acknowledge my presence. He's too busy pretending to be engaged in whatever bullshit Layne and Lou are talking about. "Alex." I finally get his attention, but his eyes are blank, cold, and bored. "Do you want to finish catching up somewhere quieter?"

I said it quietly so his friends wouldn't hear, but apparently it was too loud for his liking. His eyes get big, and he quickly looks around to see if any of them heard me. One of them is looking between us, clearly confused by my invitation. Alex looks back at me with a solemn expression. "Not really."

Ouch. I take those words as a direct blow to my heart, like they were intended. Confusion, pain, and rage flood my body and take over my thoughts. I lean in close to Alex. Close enough to make him visibly uncomfortable. "Fuck you too, Alex." As empowering as those words should have felt coming out of my mouth, they didn't. Instead, they were laced with the pain I've carried for two years, the pain he caused me.

Having nothing more to say to him, or anyone for that matter, I walk around the table and grab my purse and jacket off the back of my chair.

Lou grabs my arm as I slip the other one into my jacket. "You're not leaving already, are you?"

"Yeah. I just remembered I promised my mom I'd watch a movie with her tonight."

Her eyes lock with mine, and I'm sure she can see the hurt in them. She drops her hand from my arm and subtly nods, indicating that she understands my urgency. "Okay. Have fun. It was good to see you." She pulls me in for a hug and takes the opportunity to whisper in my ear. "Please don't let him get the better of you. He's not worth it."

I pull back but don't say a word. There's nothing I feel I need to say.

With her hands on my shoulders, she forces me to make eye contact with her. "Okay?"

"Yeah, okay." Though that was not a convincing performance by any standards, she lets me go.

I don't bother saying goodbye to anyone else. I try to convince myself they're not worth my time, but as I walk out the front door, the tears start to fall. Here I am, once again, wasting tears and energy on people who clearly don't give a shit about me. Why do I do that to myself? I stomp through the parking lot and aggressively tug on the door handle, forgetting that I didn't unlock it yet. My frustration leaves my body in the form of a growl as I dig through my purse for my keys. When I finally manage to unlock the door and get in the driver's seat, I slam the door shut.

Chapter Thirty-One

EVIE

During the drive home, I have my music playing on full blast because I can't stand the sound of my own thoughts right now. I need to drown out the negativity and self-doubt before they completely take over. But it seems as though the effort was for nothing because when I get home, I feel more upset than when I left the bar. I ignore my mother's questions as I pass her in the living room and trudge down the stairs to my old bedroom. Halfway down, I decide I should at least give her the courtesy of a response, so I shout back at her, "I don't want to talk right now!" In hindsight, I probably would have been better off not responding. She's definitely going to give me an earful about my attitude later.

I remember how good it felt to slam my car door, so when I get to my room, I slam the door shut behind me, releasing some of my pent-up rage. The door slams harder than I anticipated, making the walls shudder. The trophies on my shelf clink as they tip into each other, and some land with a light thud on the carpet.

Shit.

I flick on the light, and before I pick anything up, I take a moment to rest the back of my head on the door and take a deep breath. I seriously need to calm down. I listen for my mom to see if she says anything, but she doesn't. Once my hands stop shaking, I open my eyes and assess the damage. A few trophies and ribbons litter the floor. Next to them lies a canvas painting. It takes me a moment to remember that it's the painting Liam made of me for his art final. The one he gave to me as a graduation gift a year and a half ago.

I squat down to pick it up, afraid to flip it over and find that I ruined it. But as I reach out, I notice something. It almost blends into the white fabric on the back of the painting, except for the neat handwriting that spells out my name with a heart next to it. I carefully tear off the envelope that's taped onto the back of the canvas and open it. I completely forgot that Liam told me there was a card. After opening hundreds for graduation, cards start to seem pointless. They all have the same cliché messages that congratulate you on your big accomplishment. We all know the card is just the vessel that usually houses the gift we really want—money.

As I slide out the contents of the envelope, I realize that it isn't some cheesy Hallmark card. It's a handwritten letter on thick, creamy paper that's neatly folded in three. I unfold it and find a letter that is two pages long. Holy shit, did he write me a damn book?

My hands start shaking again as I read through his words, carefully spelled out on the page. Each line is carefully crafted, each sentiment well thought out, none of it cliché or even having to do with graduation at all.

Evie,
It's hard to put in writing the way you've

changed me over the course of these last eight months. If I'm being honest, which is the whole point of this letter, you changed my life from the moment I met you on my first day at St. Francis. I remember it clear as day; this bright-eyed, bouncy girl waltzed her way into my homeroom to introduce herself. Back then, I thought your positivity and the way you carried yourself were a facade. I thought that eventually you'd show your true colors like everyone else. But I was wrong. I learned quickly that's just how you exist in the world; always making life better for whoever is lucky enough to be around you. The kind of joy you exude is not something I've had an abundance of. You brought color to my life in more ways than a painting ever could, but I had to try to capture it.

I painted this portrait of you not because of your beauty or because you consume all my thoughts, but because I wanted to show you the color and vibrance you bring to my life. Not just mine, everyone's. Anyone who doesn't see that or anyone who has taken you for granted is an idiot, and I hope one day they will feel the loss of your friendship and realize their grave mistake. I hate how much they've made you doubt your worth, so I hope when I'm not around to constantly remind you how amazing you are, that you'll look at this canvas and remember that someone out there sees you for all you're worth.

I see you, Evie, and I love you.

Every part of you.

And I always will.

Every ounce of heartbreak I felt over the past eight months, though at times it didn't feel like it, was totally worth it. Time spent with you is never wasted, and I would be a fool to look back on it with any regrets. It was torturous trying to get you to see how much better we are together, but I love you enough to respect your decisions and trust that you're doing what you think is best for you. Even if I wholeheartedly disagree. But that wouldn't be the first time, would it?

I will grieve the loss of what we had and what we could have been. I hope that letting you leave won't become my greatest regret, but in this moment, I'm worried it will. I'll always wonder what would have happened if I'd fought harder for you. I'll wonder if I could have done more to show you that everything you need is right here. Not here in St. Francis, but here with me or wherever we are together. I would give you the world if you'd let me. I'd leave this town and never look back if that's what would make you happy. But I fear even you don't know what would make you happy at this point.

I truly hope you find it. Even if it's without me. I only want what's best for you and for you to live the grandest life this world has to offer you. And if your happily ever after doesn't involve me, you'll still always have a piece of my heart. I think that I'll *always love you and that I won't ever be my best self without you.*

Who am I kidding? I WILL always love you, Evie. There's no doubt about that. The bigger question is, will I be able to live a full life despite the piece of me you still hold? One day, I may realize that this loss was just a step on my journey to finding a greater love with someone else, but in this moment, I find that incredibly hard to believe. In this moment, I know in my heart that I'll always wait for you. No matter how long it's been, if someday you realize that I'm what your heart needs, I will be there for you. I'll be there to pick up the pieces if they're broken, or if you come back to me standing taller than you do now, I'll be there to hold you up and show the rest of the world how you shine.

I love you, Evie, more than you'll ever know.
Liam

I have to take several breaks while reading to dab away my tears. One escapes and lands on the page, smudging the ink.

The pain I felt when leaving that bar doesn't compare to the pain I feel right now. I realize that Liam probably thought I had read this letter when he gave it to me. At the graduation party, he was likely hoping for any sort of sign that his words meant something to me. He left the ball in my court, and I didn't even know we were playing a game. He poured his heart out to me, and all I did was act like a total brat and abandon him there.

To be fair, I don't think this letter would have changed my mind about being with him. But having him think I acted that way after reading this makes me sick to my stomach.

How will I ever explain this to him? *Sorry, Liam, I thought it was just another graduation card, so I brushed it off. Then my mom hung it up on my wall, and I never thought of it again. Sorry, Liam, the love letter you poured your heart into didn't get read by the intended recipient until a year and a half later, but don't worry, no one else read it.*

It feels like an elephant is sitting on my chest, and I'm struggling to catch my breath. I feel the panic starting to sink in. I need to be around the one person who can make sense of this all. The one person who can calm me down and make everything okay. The one person who would jump off a cliff if it meant making me feel better. Liam. I need to see Liam.

Chapter Thirty-Two

EVIE

I jump in my car and drive to the McAllister house. I wonder if Iris has left for the bar yet. The last thing I need is to make a scene in front of his whole family. But I would if it meant getting to talk to Liam. The ache I feel in my body for him is so visceral, I fear I might implode.

I don't bother texting him because I can be at his front door in three minutes. And I don't want to give him an opportunity to reject me. If I'm standing there in front of him, pleading for his forgiveness, he'll have a harder time denying me the chance to explain myself.

I only have three minutes to come up with what I want to say to him. How am I going to convince him that I didn't know about the letter? I glance over at the paper sitting on my passenger seat. Will he believe me if I tell him that I just found it tonight? Or will he have spent the past year and a half resenting me so much that he no longer cares? That thought alone makes my body shake as a chill runs down my spine.

No. The Liam I know is patient and forgiving, a hopeless romantic. He'll have kept his promise. He'll have waited for me. Not that I deserve it.

There have been no signs on social media that there have been any girls in Liam's life since high school. Then again, the last thing he posted was of me. He stopped posting altogether after our senior ski trip. He's thrown me some likes over the last year and a halfF, so I know he's still active on his accounts, but just as an observer.

I pull into his driveway, all the memories of the last time I saw him flooding my brain. When I drove away from St. Francis the next morning, I didn't stop crying until I got to the cabin. I spent the whole drive wondering if I had made a horrible mistake. What would have happened if I had found the letter then? I can't think about the 'what ifs' right now. I'm sitting in his driveway, about to do one of the boldest things I've ever done. I've never been the one to make grand gestures or put my heart on the line. That was always Liam. I never realized just how vulnerable he must have felt. Right now, I feel like I'm about to hand Liam a sword, not knowing if he'll use it to defend me or stab me in the heart.

I finally muster up the courage to unbuckle my seat belt and get out of the car. The walk up to his front door feels like miles as my heart races a million miles an hour. Why am I nervous? I've been to Liam's house plenty of times, walked up to this very front door, and rang that doorbell without batting an eye.

I reach out and knock. The doorbell feels too aggressive, too formal. Maybe, subconsciously, I don't want them to hear me, so I still have the option to leave if I chicken out. Too late. I hear footsteps coming down the stairs. The front door opens, and it's Liam standing on the other side of the threshold.

"Evie?"

I can't get any words out, so I awkwardly wave.

"What...I mean...hi. Come in. It's freezing out there."

In my rush to get over here, I didn't put on my jacket. The weird part is that I didn't even realize how cold I was until I stepped into the warm entryway of the house. My skin tingles as it rapidly heats up, and I realize how hyper-aware I am of my body at the moment. Anything to distract me from how I'm feeling, standing here in front of Liam.

This string of complex emotions that's floating between us is palpable.

"What are you doing here? Did you text me?" He checks his phone.

"No, I didn't. I...umm...look, Liam, I really—"

"Liam?" a female voice echoes from the top of the stairs, cutting me off. "Where did you say the extra charger was?"

Both Liam and I look up the stairs to where a gorgeous woman stands in sweats and Liam's high school hockey sweatshirt.

"Oh god." I meant to say those words in my head, not out loud. I know what Liam's cousins look like. She's not one of them.

He has a girlfriend?

My stomach twists in a knot, and I feel like my throat is closing up. Somehow, I still manage to say something. "I just wanted to come say hi. But you know, I actually forgot that I left a pie in the oven." Well, that was stupid.

"Okay...?" Liam doesn't seem convinced. And why should he? It's complete bullshit. I clearly came here for something. He glances back up at the girl at the top of the stairs, who is clearly waiting for a response from him. Then he looks back at me.

I see cogs turning in his head, but I bolt before he has the chance to explain. I don't want to meet her. I don't want to know who she is or where she's from or why she's here. I don't want to know how she's better for him than I am, or be forced to accept the fact that he didn't wait for me. The once familiar feeling of jealousy comes creeping in as I turn the doorknob and show myself out. I shut the door behind me and start jogging to my car. I can't get out of here fast enough.

As I start my car and put it in reverse, I can hear him yelling my name, but the ringing in my ears and the hum of the engine drowns out his voice.

Twice. Twice tonight, I was made to look a fool. Each time by one of the only two guys I've ever loved. Could tonight get any worse? How could I have been so stupid to think that he'd wait for me? He was being blinded by love when he optimistically wrote that letter. He wrote it hoping I'd read it and change my mind, that I'd go running back to him. He probably couldn't have imagined that I'd come running back a year and a half later after accidentally finding the lost letter. For all he knows, I've moved on. Of course he would move on too. I'm sure girls were throwing themselves all over him at college. Guys like Liam, who are funny, kind, and not a total idiot, get swept up fast. To think he'd still be single shows a serious lapse in judgment on my part.

I check my rear view mirror as I pull away, only because I hate myself enough to knowingly hurt my own feelings. I see Liam barefoot in the street, staring after me. This is the part in romance movies where the guy chases the girl's car down the street, and she stops, then they make up and share a passionate kiss in the rain. Well, this isn't a movie, and Liam has a girlfriend. So in reality, if I stopped, I'm only subjecting myself to more embarrassment and pain. That's enough to convince me to keep driving.

Chapter Thirty-Three

LIAM

The girl I've loved for two years just walked back into my life, threw a hand grenade, and ran. As I watch Evie's car turn the corner and disappear from sight, I try to unscramble my thoughts. I start walking back to the house, my bare feet freezing as they step across the frozen ground.

I pick up speed, wanting to catch her before she gets back into her house. If I let her get inside, then I risk her not answering the door. And as much as Mrs. Bordeaux loved me, I doubt she's going to let me in if she thinks I've hurt Evie in some way.

When I run back into the house to grab my keys and shoes, Ali is there waiting for me.

"Who was that? Is everything okay?"

"A friend from high school, and I'm not sure."

"What did she want?"

"I don't know."

"Wait. Is she...Is that the girl you told me about? Evie?"

I pause with my hand on the doorknob. "Yeah...that's her."

EVIE

Once I reach my parents' driveway, I park in my usual spot but don't turn my car off just yet. Less than 30 minutes ago, I went into the house, made a scene, then left without explanation. Now that I'm back again, my mother is going to probe me until I tell her what's going on. I can't deal with that right now. I can't lie to her, and I can't bear to tell her the truth either. I just need a moment to collect myself before I go back in there.

Tears flow from my eyes that are now stinging. I rub my fists against my eyelids, trying to soothe them, but all I do is make my vision more blurry. A few hard blinks make things clear again. I stare at the steering wheel, trying to distract myself from the pain that radiates from my heart through my whole body. How could I be so stupid? Liam isn't mine to claim; he's not going to be waiting in my back pocket for whenever I need him. He has a whole life at college that I don't know anything about. For all I know, he's a completely different person.

I think about the girl and how beautiful she was. Tall with legs for days and thin but still curvy in the most feminine way. I think about the way her shoulder-length blonde hair complemented her face shape perfectly. She looks like she could be a damn Victoria's Secret model. The more I think about the interaction, I'm pretty sure I heard an accent, but I can't place it.

I scream into my sleeves that are bunched around my fists. The release only alleviates a fraction of my pain, but now my throat is raw.

A second later, I scream again when I hear a tap on my window. "Everything okay in there?"

Dad? "I just need a minute." I speak loudly so he can hear me through the window. I don't want to roll it down and let out all the heat.

"Okay. Your mom just wanted me to check on you."

"I'm fine." My words are clipped and laced with anger. I forgot what it's like having my parents always hovering around and worrying about me.

"Alright, but don't stay out here too long. It's freezing."

"I'll be in soon."

I don't bother watching him as he walks away. I wouldn't be able to see more than a silhouette anyway through the fresh tears that flood my eyes. I dig in the cup holder for my phone so I can turn on some music. It's far too quiet in here, giving my inner voice plenty of room to remind me how horrible this night has been.

Another knock on my window doesn't startle me as much as it enrages me. "I said I'll be right in!" I turn my head and glare at my dad through the window. Only it's not my dad, and it's not my mom, who would have been my second guess.

"Liam?"

"Can I come in?"

The click of my doors unlocking has him walking around the back of the car to the passenger side. He opens the door gently and slips inside, only letting in a little bit of frigid air.

"Brrrr. How are you not wearing a coat right now?" He rubs his arms and puts his hands over the vent to warm them.

If this is his attempt at small talk to appear casual, it's not working. I could feel his nerves as soon as he sat down, just moments ago. "I left the house in a hurry." I never did get a chance to put on my music, so the car engine is the only thing filling the silence between us. "What are you doing here, Liam?"

"Are you seriously asking me that?"

He rubs his hands together, then adjusts himself in the passenger seat so he's facing me, giving me his full attention. I wish he wouldn't. I want to find a cave to crawl into and hibernate until everyone forgets who I am. It would be even better if I could forget who everyone else is. Start fresh.

"Evie, you show up to my house unannounced after a year and a half, just to run out the door before saying anything. Of course I came over here to check on you. The better question is, what are *you* doing here?"

"I'm back for Thanksgiving."

"Obviously. Can we please cut the bullshit, Evie? Just tell me what you came over to my house to say after over a year of not having anything to say to me."

For the first time tonight, I get a good look at him. When he opened the door earlier, I was too in my head to notice how he's changed. His jaw is more angular, his hair is cut differently, he has a full beard now, and he even seems taller. Not that I would be able to tell with him sitting down, but he seems to take up more space in my passenger seat than I remember. He looks more like a man than the boy I said goodbye to. There's a confidence that wasn't there before. A sureness that only shows when someone knows who they are and what they want. This is what I pictured when I talked about waiting to meet a guy at college. I pictured someone who effortlessly looks like they have their shit together. Not these boys at my school that are masquerading as men, when in reality they still have to call their mom to ask how to do their own laundry.

I get so lost in him that I almost forget it's my turn to say something. "It doesn't matter now."

"It absolutely does. Just fucking talk to me." He's trying to hide it, but I can tell he's getting annoyed with me.

How do I even start to explain this to him? In all the chaos since finding the letter, I never did come up with a good way to say it to him. I had hoped that a good explanation would just come to me when I saw him. But clearly, I didn't even give myself a chance for that to work. "You're not going to believe me."

His eyes scrunch like he's in pain, like what I just said erased all trust he thought we had with each other. "When have I ever not trusted you?"

He's right. Not once has Liam ever questioned my words, except for when I repeatedly told him I didn't want to be with him. But looking back, I think he could sense it was a lie even though I couldn't.

Fuck it. I just need to say it, regardless of the outcome. "I came to tell you that I found your letter."

His head shakes as he processes the information. "The letter on the back of the painting?" His jaw flexes as he clenches his teeth together. "You never read it?"

"I read it for the first time tonight. I'd gotten swept up in the graduation party and packing to move to the lake that I never got around to opening it. Then my mom hung it up on my wall, and I completely forgot about it."

His lips part, and his mouth hangs slightly open, confusion written all over his face.

"Liam, I swear if I had known the nature of that letter, I wouldn't have forgotten about it so easily. I didn't know what was in it. I didn't know that you poured your heart out to me." I choke on my words as my lower jaw starts to tremble. "Goddamnit, can't I just keep it together for five minutes!" We both huff a laugh, knowing that the day I stop crying is the day hell freezes over.

Liam reaches out and wipes away a tear with his thumb. "You know I like seeing all sides of you." His hand lingers on the side of my face, and it takes every ounce of my self-control not to lean into it.

I start to give in when I remember his girlfriend waiting for him at home. I pull my face away and wipe my own tears. "Liam, stop. Like I said, it doesn't matter now. I fucked up. I got the message too late, and you moved on." I sniffle, trying to stop snot from running out my nose, like the big fucking mess I am. "She's gorgeous, by the way." My words are laced with defeat. This is my official surrender.

"Ali? Oh god, Evie, no. She's not my girlfriend. I can see how it might look like that without any context, but it's not what it looks like."

"What?"

"She's a foreign exchange student from Switzerland. I met her at the beginning of the fall semester when she started. She didn't have anywhere to go for the holidays, so I invited her here. I promise you there's nothing between us. Never has and never will be."

I rearrange my thoughts to accommodate this new information. Though my initial reaction is relief, I can't help but wonder what other invisible obstacles are in our way. "Why not? She's practically a supermodel."

"Are you serious?" He laughs even though there's nothing funny about this conversation.

I shrug, not knowing what else to say. It seems pretty self-explanatory to me. Two very attractive college students spend the holiday at a guy's house. They fall in love. The movie practically writes itself.

"I meant what I said in that letter, Evie. Every word. And if you think I don't remember what I wrote, then quiz me."

I glance over my shoulder at the crumpled-up letter in my back seat.

"Evie, I'm not into Ali because she's not *you*. I know that sounds cheesy and dumb, but I'm not joking. Trust me, I wish I were." Any trace of humor is now completely gone from his voice. "I wish I wasn't still hung up on you. I wish my therapist didn't know you as well as she does. I wish I didn't compare every girl I meet to you, just to write them off almost immediately when they don't even come close. It's exhausting being in love with you. I would stop myself if I could."

I can't decide whether his words are meant as a compliment or an insult. But I guess it doesn't matter, because they're honest. "Liam, I'm so sorry. I'm sorry I left last summer and that I never texted you. I thought I was doing what was best for both of us. Instead, I just ended up hurting you and myself." I bury my face in my hands again. "I screwed everything up."

"You didn't."

"Yes, I did."

"No. You didn't. Evie, look at me." He pulls my hands away from my face and locks eyes with me. "Let's think about this for a second. If you'd have opened my letter that day, hell, even that month, do you honestly think it would have changed anything? Because I don't."

"Then why even write it?"

He shrugs. "I had to say what was on my mind. Evie, we both know that you would have read that letter and rejected me a twelfth time. You were so dead set on going off to college single. My letter wasn't going to change that. But you finding it now...maybe it was meant to happen like that?"

I scoff. "You know I don't believe in fate."

"I know. But I'm still a hopeless romantic, so just let me have this one, okay?"

The corner of my mouth involuntarily lifts. God, I hate how he has the power to make me smile even when I'm this upset. "Fine. I can admit that I'm more open-minded now that I've experienced some life outside of St. Francis. But that doesn't make the pain we both felt any less awful. Not having my best friend this past year and a half was miserable." And here come the tears again...

As I try to hide my face, he lifts my chin with his knuckle, not allowing me to pull away from this conversation. "I'm still your best friend, Evie. We just took a little time away from each other. Did it hurt like hell? Yeah. But I'm here now. *You're* here now." He stares so deeply into my eyes, he caresses my soul. "God, I've missed you so damn much."

"I've missed you, too." My voice is nothing more than a whisper.

"Regardless of the backwards steps we took since graduation, I still want to be your friend if you want to be mine."

I choose my next words carefully. "What if I want more?"

He lowers his hand from my chin. His face looks pained, his jaw muscles flutter as he once again clenches his teeth together. "Do you want that? Is that what you came to tell me?"

I nod. "Yes." I bite my lower lip so hard I nearly draw blood.

"Okay." The pain on his face eases, relaxing into something similar to a smile. "How about we start by getting each other caught up on the last year and a half of our lives?"

"I'd like that." It takes everything in me not to reach across and pull his face closer to mine. "But can we go inside? My mom's gonna come banging on my door if I let this car run idle in the driveway any longer."

"Let me just text Iris and Ali quick. They were trying to talk me into going out with them tonight. I'm going to tell them to go without me."

He sends a text, then we're opening the car doors, ready to brace the cold. I start jogging toward the front door since I'm freezing out here without a jacket. I hear Liam's footsteps following me, his strides much longer than mine. I'm stopped suddenly by a set of hands holding my shoulders and pulling me back. Next thing I know, I'm being turned and pressed up against the side of the house. Liam hovers over me, pressing his warm body into mine. Though his body heat takes some of the chill away, I can still feel my nose and cheeks stinging from the cold, crisp air.

His hands wrap around the back of my neck as he dives in. A spark ignites in my stomach when his lips meet mine. He kisses me the way he always used to, like he'll starve without me. I soak him in, and it feels so right. He sweeps his tongue in, and I feel a fluttering between my legs. I've forgotten all about the cold or the fact that we're outside where any of the neighbors can see us. All I care about is having my Liam back.

I feel something cold and wet hit my cheek. At first, I think I'm crying again, but quickly realize it isn't me. I regretfully pull back to see if it's Liam, but it's not him either. Then I feel another. I look around and see a sky full of snow flurries dancing in the air, reflecting the light from the street lamps. It's not a dramatic kissing in the rain scene, but it's honestly better. It's peaceful, and it's perfect.

Chapter Thirty-Four

LIAM

A couple of years ago, if you had told me that I'd be lying next to Evie Bordeaux on her bed, I would have said, "Duh." But if you had told me that two months ago, I would have known a miracle had happened. My biggest fear was never talking to Evie again, never being as close as we once were. When I lost her, I lost a part of me. And I didn't think I'd ever get that back.

"When did you get this?" She holds my hand close to her face and points out a scar. "I swear you didn't have this before."

"Because I didn't. I got it this past spring."

"What object assaulted you?"

"It was an X-Acto knife."

"Isn't the point of those that they're supposed to be precise?"

"Precisely."

She rolls her eyes at me. I missed that.

"I was cutting into acrylic on a canvas, the blade was dull, and it slipped."

"Canvas? Did you take an art class?" Evie's face lights up. "Oh, that makes my heart so happy! You should take one every year if you can. Don't leave those skills locked up in a closet." She kisses the scar on the base of my thumb and lays my hand back down on my chest.

"Actually, I'll be taking several every semester since it's sort of my major."

The spot where her head once lay on my shoulder is now vacant as she sits up to look at me. "What? Liam, that's amazing! What made you decide to change it?" Her hovering over me like this is tempting beyond belief. We've only cuddled and talked since coming down to her room.

"I didn't want to let you down."

She squints her eyes, like she's trying to see if she can detect a lie.

"It's the truth. But it's also because I wanted to do it; it felt right. Like this." I palm the side of her face, pull her down to me, and kiss her softly. God, I missed this.

When I finally release her, she smiles at me before settling her head on my chest. I spread my legs so she can fit between them. Even with her full weight on me, I still need her closer. I want to squeeze her so hard that our bodies morph together. That way, she can never leave me again.

She rests her chin on her hands and sighs. "Speaking of closets..."

I lift one eyebrow, questioning where she's going with this, but waiting for her to steer the conversation in case I'm wrong.

"You were right." She clears her throat and glances away for a second, something she does when she's nervous, before continuing. "I do like women. I also like men. Obviously." She pats my chest.

I chuckle a little, mostly to myself, and watch the tension leave her shoulders. "What made you finally realize it?"

"I think a small part of me always knew, but it didn't really matter because I was always in relationships. With guys."

She lifts herself up to a sitting position, and I do the same, wanting to give her my full attention. As if she ever has anything less.

We sit across from each other on the bed, and I can't help but wonder if this space between us is intentional. Is she pulling away from me again?

"I actually dated a few girls in college."

"You did?"

"Mhm." She scoots a little closer and rests her hand, casually, on my leg. "At some point during senior year, I had my heart set on trying it in college to test out if I actually was bi or not."

"And?"

"*Definitely bi.*" The corner of her lip quirks up, and I can't help but smile.

"So what does this mean? For us," I clarify.

She shrugs. Not really the reassurance I was looking for.

"It doesn't have to mean anything. I just wanted to tell you that you were right and say I'm sorry. I shouldn't have gotten so upset with you that night. I just got scared."

"It's okay. I mean, it would have been a helpful thing to know, but I get why you did it. I'm sure that had to be really scary and confusing."

"It was. But I should have confided in you about it."

I reach out and take her hand in mine, lacing our fingers together. "Do I dare ask...?"

"If it was the reason I wouldn't be with you?"

I nod, scared of the answer but dying for it all the same.

"Partially, yes. Overall, I just felt like I needed to explore being single outside of St. Francis. With both guys and girls. I wanted to know that I chose my person, not for lack of options."

"That makes sense. I knew that back then, too. I was just too stubborn to admit that it was probably what you needed."

"I think we were both a little too stubborn for our own good."

I pull her forward, between my legs, and she turns so her back is pressed to my chest. I lean back against the head-board and wrap my arms around her. I press a kiss to her temple, and my heart sighs when she leans into it.

"How's Celine?"

Her question takes me by surprise. "I'm not sure. We don't really talk."

She turns her head to look at me over her shoulder. "What? But you guys were so close. I thought you'd made plans to hang out in college?"

"We did. We hung out a few times, but then she stopped messaging me back."

"That's weird."

"Not really." When Evie's eyebrows scrunch together, I know I'm not going to get away with leaving it at that. Evie's the queen of details. I should have known she'd ask about this and that I'd have to explain it thoroughly. "The few times we hung out were all initiated by her. We had fun, and it was nice having someone there that I knew. But eventually she wanted more. And I didn't."

"How do you know?"

"Because she told me. We got into a little fight about it, actually."

"Wait, I'm confused. She told you she liked you and wanted to be more than friends, and you turned her down? Oh, how the tables have turned."

Even though the reality of that situation isn't funny, I have to laugh a little. "The irony's not lost on me." I sweep a lock of hair off her cheek and try to tuck it behind her ear, but there's too much of it. I glance down at her wrist and notice two hair ties. I slip one off her wrist, earning me a skeptical look. I drag my fingers through her hair like I've seen her do a million times and give my best attempt at a ponytail. The whole time she's cracking up. She likely thinks I'm an idiot, but I don't care. "Much better."

She pats her hand around her head, trying to tactilely assess the situation. "Not bad. Not great, but not bad." She turns again and kisses me. "I'm guessing the reason you didn't want to be with Celine was also because of me?"

I nod to confirm, even though she already knows the answer. "Unfortunately, it's always going to be Evie or bust for me."

She gets this devilish look on her face, and I piece together the double entendre. "How about Evie *and* bust?"

"You're such a dork. You really think that corny line is gonna work on me?"

"I think my sitting between your legs already did that."

She's right. I've been growing hard ever since she laid on top of me. "Perhaps." But I'm going to at least try to play it cool.

She turns around so she's facing me once again and kisses me, with more intention. This time, I don't let her pull away. I wrap my arms around her and roll us over so

I'm on top now. I run my hand up the outside of her thigh and up her side, slipping under her shirt. Her skin is so soft, I need to know what it feels like with my lips. I crawl backwards, kissing down her neck and her chest until her shirt blocks my progress. I lift it up slightly, exposing her naval. Then I kiss the soft skin of her stomach.

Her stomach shakes when I get to the sides, and she grabs my head to stop me. "That tickles."

"Sorry," I mumble into her skin. I continue down toward the waistband of her jeans, avoiding her ticklish sides. "May I?" My hands are on the button of her jeans, indicating what I want.

She nods aggressively. "Mmhmm."

I undo the button and slide down the zipper, exposing her black lacy underwear. She lifts her hips to help me as I pull her jeans all the way down her legs. I run my hands up them, squeezing as I go. "Tell me if you want me to stop."

"Liam, you better not fucking stop. Ever."

I would take more time to argue with her, but I know Evie; if she wants me to stop, she'll have no problem making it clear. She's always been afraid to tell people what's on her mind, but never with me. It's been a blessing and a curse as long as she's been in my life. I get the best of her and the worst of her, and I'd take it all to get moments like this.

I spread her legs and situate myself between them. I pepper kisses up the inside of her thigh. I've kissed Evie in lots of places before, but never here, never like this. When my lips finally touch her center, over the fabric, she shudders. She drags her hands through my hair and grabs at it.

"Don't stop."

I'm not even close to being done with her.

I slide her panties to the side and take in the beautiful sight before me. I take my time kissing around her bundle of nerves, not giving her what she wants quite yet. I make sure my hands aren't idle, that they're constantly touching her somewhere.

When I finally give her what she wants, her thighs crash into the sides of my head, pinning me to that spot. The way she moans makes me feral. After a minute of me playing with her, she lets out a dramatic moan. I lift my head up and stare at her. "Uh ah. Don't do that."

"Don't do what?" She looks down at me, pretending not to know what I mean.

"You're not gonna fake shit with me, Evie. I've known you long enough to know when you're putting on a show. I'm gonna earn every single noise that comes out of you, and I'm not stopping until you come. So cut the bullshit. And feel free to tell me if there's anything you want that I'm not doing."

"What you were doing felt great. Just keep doing that. I can't promise it'll happen, though."

"You let me worry about that."

I play around with her until I find what she likes, and I don't deviate until she comes. Her thighs squeeze my ears, blocking out the noises she's making as she shakes beneath me, but I can feel it. She's still coming for me. I don't know how long it took her to get here, nor do I give a shit. She's mine, and I did that for her.

———

EVIE

You've got to be fucking kidding me. That's what I've been missing out on?

I've come with people I've been with in college, but it was rare, and it was never like that. I guess I can thank the years of pent-up sexual tension between us. It's like extreme edging. My whole body tingles with pleasure.

In the past, having orgasms was like doing one of those stupid stereogram things. You know, the thing where you stare at a picture with a pixilated repeating pattern, and apparently, a 3D image is supposed to pop out at you. You either see it, or you don't. No matter how hard I stare, as soon as I start to think I see the hidden image, it falls out of focus, and I lose it. At first, I thought this was going to be the same, but the way he called me out made me feel desired. He made me feel like my pleasure was his priority.

I release his head from my thighs' death grip, and he sits himself up. I can see my come glistening around his mouth. He wipes his hand down his face before leaning forward on his elbows to kiss me.

I reach for his belt and start to undo it. I feel him smile against my lips. "What's so funny?"

"Not funny. I just can't believe this is happening after all this time."

He trails his lips down my neck and sucks on the sensitive skin above my collarbone. "I know, it's crazy. Who would have thought it would feel this right?"

He pulls back. "*Me. I did.*"

"Oh shut up and kiss me."

I continue undoing his pants and pull them down as far as my arms will let me. Liam pulls them down the rest of the way and kicks them off the bed. His shirt is the next thing to go, and to even the score, I slip out of mine as well. He settles down between my spread legs, and I can feel his hard length press against my clit. I wrap my legs around him, pulling him tighter to me for more friction. He gets the hint and starts moving his hips.

My breathing is heavy, but I'm surprisingly not nervous.

This is usually the part with other guys where I realize what I'm doing and panic. "I need you inside me," I mumble against his soft lips.

Without hesitation, he reaches down and pulls off his underwear, releasing his cock. I run my hand up and down the soft skin of his shaft. Fuck me, I want him so bad. I slip out of my panties. Liam shifts to accommodate my movements before settling back on top of me.

"I didn't bring a—"

"I don't care." I wrap my legs around him and lift my hips up so his tip is seated at my entrance. "I'm clean. I want this if you do."

"I'm clean too. And you're all I've ever wanted, Evie." Without another word, he tips his hips forward, pushing himself into me. He winces. "Jesus Christ."

"What?" I panic, thinking I somehow hurt him.

"You feel so fucking good, Evie." He rests his forehead on mine as he pauses to collect himself.

"You scared me for a second."

"Sorry. I just..." he takes a deep breath, "need to calm down."

I tug at his hair so he's looking at me again. "Keep going."

He listens to my command and pushes himself deeper inside me until he's seated all the way. I tip my head back into my pillow with my mouth hanging open. As he thrusts in me, I make all sorts of noises, every single one of them well deserved. At some point, he shuts me up by putting his lips over mine and sliding his tongue into my open mouth.

His thumb plays with my wet clit, a deep pressure building in my core. "Liam, I'm gonna come again. Come with me."

"I'm not coming inside."

"Then come on my stomach. I don't care. Just don't stop!"

He thrusts harder and faster, but his thumb keeps the same lazy pace on my clit while he devours my mouth. The multitude of different things going on at once has me shaking. This man is great at multitasking. Must be all those years of piano lessons.

I wrap my arms around his back, then slide them down to his bare shoulders and dig my nails in. Electricity cascades down my legs, and I fight the urge to use them to hold him in me. I bite on his shoulder to stifle my moan while my whole body shakes. As soon as my orgasm starts to settle, Liam pulls out of me and comes on my stomach with a few strokes of his cock.

Instead of just flopping down next to me, he takes his time kissing all over my sweaty body. In this moment, all I feel is bliss, euphoria.

Eventually, the kisses end, and he walks naked into my attached bathroom. I hear the sink run, and he returns with a damp washcloth. He lovingly cleans me up and hands me my clothes. I watch him the whole time, and at some point, tears fill my eyes, but I wipe them away when he's not looking. I don't want him to think I regret anything, because I don't. I'm just so overwhelmed with emotions.

"Come here." I pat the bed next to me. "I want to cuddle."

"Thought you'd never ask." He pulls the comforter and sheet out from under me and climbs in next to me. He drapes the covers over both of us, turning me on my side so he can be the big spoon.

All of his bare skin pressed against mine still isn't close enough. His arm is wrapped around me, holding me tight. "I love you."

He kisses my shoulder, then my cheek. "I love you too, Evie."

I spin around so we're face-to-face. "How are we going to make this work?"

"You mean the distance?"

"Yeah..." The fact that we go to college in separate states has not escaped me. I've just been shoving it down, trying to ignore it because the idea of leaving him makes my heart ache all over again.

"It's only a three-hour drive between us."

"Three hours is a lot."

"Not for you, it's not." He kisses my forehead and starts running his fingertips up and down my spine. "If I leave after my classes on Friday, I can get there by 7:00, and I don't have class on Mondays until noon, so I could take off early in the morning."

"I have a pretty packed schedule, so we won't get as much time when I come visit you, but we'll make it work. I want to make this work, Liam. I can't lose you again."

"You won't."

As the tears start streaming down my face, he pulls me into his chest. He's my comfort, my safe place. He's everything I ever needed; I was just too stubborn to see it. But maybe Liam's right. Maybe I *did* need that time to get to know myself over the last year and a half. There's no knowing how things would have turned out if I had said yes earlier. I know it would have saved the man I love a lot of heartache. But one of the things I love most about him is that he constantly reassures me that I *was* and that I *am* worth it.

After losing friends and losing the guy I thought was the love of my life, I didn't think anyone would ever want to spend their life with me. Then Liam came along and changed it all. He first took the time to show me that I am a good friend and that I can have disagreements with people without the fear of them leaving me, if they're a true friend. Then he showed me that I can be loved, even if I try my hardest to shove that love away.

Chapter Thirty-Five

Present Day

LIAM

We've talked at length about the events that played out over that Thanksgiving break. But no matter how many times I talk about it with Evie or tell the story to others, I still get teary-eyed. I just can't believe that my persistence paid off and landed me the girl of my dreams. It took a year of therapy to get over losing her, but it only took a moment to accept her back into my life. And I've had no regrets over the past five years. Not a single one.

As Evie wraps up the details of the painful two and a half years we spent long-distance, all I can do is stare at her and think about how lucky I am. I'm married to the woman I love. She's growing our child inside her, who we'll get to meet in a few short months. As much as I love having Evie all to myself, I can't wait to start a family with her. I know she's going to be an amazing mom.

I'm interested to see if she'll be just as stubborn with our kids as she is with me. Or maybe they'll be so damn cute she won't be able to say no to them. Either way, I'll be right by her side, being a stay-at-home dad while I work as much as I can from my art studio at home. I can't wait.

I'm pulled from my daydream when Sam tries to get my attention. "What's that?"

Sam repeats himself. "While you were making googly eyes at your wife, the rest of us were talking about wedding videos and if they're worth the money. What's your opinion?"

"Totally worth it." I look at Evie with a smile. "We re-watch our wedding video every year on our anniversary. It's so much better than just scrolling through photos."

"Which we also do every year on our anniversary," Evie adds.

"Yes, we do."

Lou, who is newly engaged to Sam, seems very fired up about this topic. "Evie, can you show Sam your guys' wedding video? I don't think he fully understands what we're talking about."

"I know what a wedding video is."

"Not like this. It's not just straight footage from the day. There's music and candid shots; usually, they play a little voice-over from the speeches or vows. They're so cute."

"And very expensive."

I lock eyes with Sam, a man who knows he's about to get outvoted. "Welcome to marriage."

Everyone at the table laughs as Evie queues up our wedding video and hands her phone over to Lou and Sam. The music playing at the reception isn't too loud, so they have no trouble hearing the audio. However, all my attention is on the songs playing over the main speakers. Earlier, when I went to get another round of drinks for everyone, I snuck over to the DJ booth and requested a song.

Just as I start to worry that he forgot, it starts to play, and I can't help but get a little giddy. Now I just have to wait for Evie to hear it too. It takes her all of two seconds to notice, and then she's jumping up on her feet. "Liam! It's our first dance song!"

"Oh my goodness, no way." My tone is flat, letting her know that I saw this coming.

She picks up on my hint and leans over to kiss my cheek. "You're so sweet. Let's go dance."

We make our way out to the dance floor and sway back and forth as our song plays.

"Looks like our song's a pretty popular one." I glance around and see several guests getting up and dragging their loved ones out here to dance alongside us.

A sour taste enters my mouth when I spot Alex, his butt firmly planted in a chair and looking bored out of his mind. His girlfriend seems to be trying to coax him into dancing, but he doesn't budge.

"You okay?"

I look down at my wife and pull my brows together in question. "Of course. I'm dancing with my beautiful wife. Why would I be anything other than blissful?"

One side of her lips quirks up in a smile. "Well, you had this face that looked like you were smelling dirty gym socks."

I laugh, knowing exactly why my face looked like that. "I think that should be his new nickname."

"Whose?"

"Alex." I subtly tilt my head toward where Alex was sitting, trying not to be too obvious in case he's looking over here. "He's being a sourpuss over there, per usual, and I guess my face gave away my inner thoughts."

I turn us so she can glance at him without having to turn her head and be too obvious.

"Ahh, the face makes sense now. Poor girl."

"She seems smart enough. She'll figure it out eventually."

Evie sighs and looks up at me with blue eyes that still captivate me to this day. "Rehashing that whole story in detail didn't bring up any bad memories for you, did it?"

"A little. But the good ones definitely outweigh the bad. Plus, it's my favorite story of all the ones you tell."

"I love you." She presses in a little closer, resting her head on my chest, her bump squishing against me.

I lay my cheek against her head and run my hand up and down the small of her back. "I love you too."

As the song comes to an end, I dip my wife and kiss her.

"Probably not going to be able to do that for much longer." She rubs her hand on her bump and giggles. "God, I'm getting huge."

"You're beautiful."

Instead of taking our seats, Evie guides me over to where Lou and Sam sit, still watching our twelve-minute-long wedding video. We hover over their shoulders and watch with them. I've watched this video a thousand times, so I know it's coming to an end. And the end is my favorite part. I put my arm around Evie's waist and pull her into my side.

A beautiful song plays as the video shows a little montage of Evie and me laughing and holding each other throughout various parts of that day. Then there's a voice-over of Evie reading her vows. I clench my teeth together and breathe through my nose, trying not to cry yet again.

Evie's sweet voice shakes with emotion as she speaks

into the mic. "Liam, I promise to love you forever. And if someday you cross over into your next life before I do, I promise to come find you. And just like the promise you made to me all those years ago in a misplaced love letter, I hope that you'll wait for me."

Epilogue

LIAM

Tears fill my eyes as they place our daughter on Evie's chest. "You did so good, babe." I kiss her sweaty brow as she sobs and holds our baby girl.

"Ohmygod she has red hair." I can barely make out what she's saying through her sobs, but I piece it together when I notice a little tuft of orange hair on the top of our little girl's head.

"Is that a good thing or a bad thing?"

"Good. Definitely good."

"Alright, Dad, it's your time to shine." The nurse holds up a pair of sterile scissors.

"Will it hurt them?"

"No, sweetie. Neither of them will feel a thing."

"Okay." I take the scissors in my shaky hands. The nurse indicates where I should make the cut. It's over in a second, and I hand the scissors back to the nurse as another one clamps the half still attached to our baby.

I feel like I'm going to pass out, so I take a lap around

the room, grab some water off the table by the window, and grab Evie's water bottle for her.

When I look back at Evie, the baby is gone. Panic sets in, and my heart starts to race. "Where did she go?"

Evie laughs at me, still breathing heavily with exhaustion. "They took her to do some measurements and tests. She's right over there." I follow where her finger points and find my sweet baby girl naked on a tiny scale with a hospital band now around her ankle.

I walk over to Evie and hand her the giant water bottle. "Can she have this?"

The nearest nurse looks over and nods. "As long as you're not feeling nauseous."

Evie takes it from me and takes a big gulp. I grab the rag out of the little bucket of ice water and start dabbing it on her forehead. "How are you feeling?"

"I mean, I'm not on a boat with a margarita in my hand, but I'll manage."

Evie, always the jokester. "I'm serious. Can I get you anything?"

"I'm really okay, babe. But thank you for worrying about me." She reaches up and strokes her thumb over my cheek, like I'm the one who needs to be comforted right now.

A nurse comes over and gently inserts herself in our conversation. "Did you guys decide on a name yet? No rush, just wanted to get you thinking about it before they come in with the paperwork."

Evie and I look at each other. Without words, we nod in agreement that the name we chose is perfect and that we're not changing it.

"We have one picked out."

"Perfect. I'll let them know, and someone will bring in the paperwork for you later on."

"Thank you."

———

As Evie finally gets some rest, I pace back and forth across the room holding Briar. She's getting a little fussy, but I don't want to wake Evie just yet. I bounce on the balls of my feet as I walk, trying to soothe her.

Am I doing this right?

When she finally settles, I take the risk and carefully sit down in the rocking chair in the corner of the room. When I've successfully sat down without waking her, I have a mini celebration in my head.

Her cheeks are full and pink; it's so hard not to pinch them. Instead, I settle for running my knuckles across the smooth surface. "Hey, baby girl. Do you know how special you are? You are already so loved. Your auntie Iris won't stop blowing up my phone with questions about you. And your grandparents are mad at me right now because we won't let them come to the hospital to see you. But Mommy needs her rest, and I selfishly want some alone time with you."

She hiccups, and I stop rocking, waiting for the crying to start. When I'm convinced she's still sleeping, I start rocking her again.

"I hope you like your name. Do you know who you're named after?" My vision blurs and my eyes well with tears. "You're named after your grandpa, Brian. My dad."

My heart seizes up in my chest with the painful reminder that my dad will never get to meet his grand-daughter. That she'll never get to meet him. I would give anything to see him one more time and tell him I love him. Tell him about my life, introduce him to the woman I love more than anything in this world. Well, I guess now she's got this little bundle tied with her for that title.

"He would have loved to meet you and your mom." A tear falls down and nearly misses her face, soaking into her little pink hat instead. "Ope, sorry about that. Looks like your mom's crying habits are rubbing off on me. I don't mind, though. It feels good to cry sometimes. I'll try to remember that when your crying keeps me up at night, and I can't remember what day it is because I'm so sleep deprived." I bring her up close to my face and kiss her squishy cheek. "We waited a long nine months for you to be here, so I'm not going to take any time with you for granted, no matter how hard it gets. You're so worth it, Briar. You're so worth the wait. Just like your mom."

Acknowledgments

If you made it to the end, THANK YOU. It has truly been a joy sharing my story with you.

My husband - This story wouldn't exist without your persistence and unconditional love for me. Even when you were at your wit's end with me, you showed me what it meant to be loved. I didn't make it easy on you, by any stretch of the imagination, and most people would have quit after the first couple rejections. You saw what I couldn't see —that we were exactly what each other needed. I am so grateful to have grown up together, into the adults we are today.

Ben Platt - Thank you for writing incredibly emotional music that tugs at my heartstrings and fuels my creativity. Your song, Grow As We Go, was me and my husband's first dance song at our wedding. It was a bit unconventional, but so was our origin story, so it fit perfectly.

My readers - Thank you for taking a chance on an indie author publishing her debut romance series. I have no idea where this journey will lead, but I am so grateful to each of you for being a part of it. I have had so much fun sharing my stories with you all, and I hope that at least one of my characters resonates with you. If not, maybe you just haven't met them yet.

About the Author

Emma is a contemporary romance author based in Minneapolis, MN, where she lives with her husband and their two dogs. A newcomer to the world of writing, Emma has always had a deep connection to love stories. After devouring dozens of romance novels in just a few months, she discovered her passion for creating her own heartfelt and emotionally rich tales.

For Emma, writing isn't just about crafting fiction, it's about giving life to the characters who already feel real in her head. With each book, she brings her readers on a roller-coaster ride of emotions—blending spice, laughter, and deeply relatable situations that tackle heavy topics with care and sensitivity.

Her stories offer not only escapism, but a raw reflection of the highs and lows of love, creating an experience that readers won't soon forget. Emma's warmth, empathy, and infectious optimism shine through both in her books and in her life.

When she's not writing, you can find Emma sharing her journey on social media (@emma.pathy.author). She'd love to hear from you, so don't hesitate to say hello and share in the joy of her characters' love stories.

Also by Emma Pathy

1. Please Don't Leave Me

2. Please Stay With Me

Coming Soon...

4. Please Think Of Me